ONE

LAST

TIME

By James Hampson

ONE LAST TIME 9781087047577

Acknowledgements

I would like to thank my family for all of their support during the process of writing this novel.
To Ashley my fiancé, thank you for all your support and contributions.
To my Mum and Dad, thank you for believing in me when others didn't.
And finally, to my son Lucas for constantly bringing a smile to my face during moments of writer's block. And a new addition to the family, Orlah. Thank you all.

For all of my family and friends

To Joe

Hope you enjoy it!

Best wishes

[signature]

ONE

Basra, Iraq. May 2005

It was a hot and humid night in southern Iraq; the sky was orange as flames raged across the city of Basra. Basra Airfield was under attack from Iraqi insurgents, who were using RPG'S, mortars and small arms fire to attack the British held air base. Heavy artillery returned fire from within the base to try and suppress the insurgents, and RAF Tornado GR4s' dropped ordnance on various targets across the city.

Nineteen miles away along the banks of the Shatt-Al-Arab River, Royal Air Force Intelligence Officer Flight Lieutenant James Shaw squeezed the trigger of his Sig Sauer P226 9mm into the side of Saudi Born Terrorist Ali Bin Rashid's Head, spraying blood and brain matter into the air, followed by a pink mist. Shaw grabbed the manila envelope he had given Rashid moments earlier out of his limp hand, and tucked it inside his Osprey Body armour, along with the envelope Bin Rashid had given him in the earlier exchange. Shaw kicked the body down the river bank into the smooth flowing river, he holstered his weapon and climbed back into his idling Land Rover.

Ibrahim Kasim witnessed the exchange from across the river, he pulled his Mobile phone out of his pocket to make a call.

Flight Lieutenant James Shaw sat in his Land Rover in a state of shock, Ali bin Rashid was the first person he had ever killed, but it was a job that had to be done, to potentially save the lives of millions of people. He fumbled through his pockets for his cigarettes, put one in his mouth, lit it, inhaled, and then exhaled before throwing it out of the window, he lit another one, and started the big diesel V8 of his Land Rover.

He drove in the direction of Saddam Hussein's presidential palace, eleven miles away from his current location, where the British Army were based, as the airbase was on lockdown due to the insurgent attacks. Twenty minutes later he arrived at the gates and showed the guard on the gate his ID card, which had him down as 183cm tall, born in 1980, along with his photograph. The guard directed him to the main car park and told him where he could go for some rest.

Shaw stepped out of the Land Rover and walked towards the palace. James Shaw was six-foot-tall with broad shoulders, not slim, not fat somewhere in between with natural muscle, he had icy blue eyes, was naturally good looking, some would say very handsome, his light brown hair was cut short, and it had started to go blonde in the sun. An Army Captain came out to greet Shaw and he showed him to the officer's mess. Shaw thanked him for his hospitality.

They sat down and drank some tea, discussed the current situation in Iraq, and the events of the last few nights. Shaw once again thanked the captain for his hospitality before retiring for the evening.

As he lay in bed wide awake playing over and over again in his head what had happened that night, his thoughts drifted to six weeks previously; when he had first stepped off the plane in Iraq.

He walked down the cargo ramp of the RAF Hercules, he was greeted by his predecessor and friend Flight Lieutenant William Ramsey. Shaw and Ramsey had gone through officer training at RAF Cranwell, followed by Intelligence training, and had remained friends ever since.

Flight Lieutenant Ramsey handed command over to him, explaining the current situation in the Middle East, what the job entailed and introduced him to the staff that would be working under his command. Once the handover had been completed a few days later and Flight Lieutenant Ramsey had boarded his flight back to the UK, there was a knock on the door of the intelligence office, which was a portacabin turned in to an office. It was located to the north of the runway at Basra Air Base. Corporal Brown, a short skinny man from Yorkshire answered the door to a man who looked to be about five feet eight inches tall, brown hair, brown eyes, Arabic looking, dressed in scruffy clothes and carrying a briefcase. Lawrence Sharif of MI6 asked to speak to the new commanding officer. Corporal Brown invited him in, and knocked on Flight Lieutenant Shaw's inner office door, and introduced the two men to each other.

'Thank you, Corporal,' Shaw said.

He shut the door before offering Lawrence a seat, and a cup of tea which he accepted. The two men exchanged pleasantries and commented on the heat, before Shaw asked.

'What can I help you with? I presume you knew my predecessor Flight Lieutenant Ramsey?'

'Yes, we had weekly briefings, amongst other things, good man and a very good officer.'

Lawrence Sharif opened the clasps on his briefcase and took out a buff-coloured case file and handed it to Shaw.

'Have a read through this. I am going to get something to eat and I will be back in 30 minutes to discuss it with you.'

'Right ok, see you soon,' Shaw said.

He was not really sure what else to say back to Sharif.

Shaw got up from his chair and left his side office. He asked Corporal Brown what he knew about this Lawrence Sharif chap and did he pay regular visits to the intelligence office. The Corporal replied that he dropped in once a week, normally with the same briefcase, and two weeks ago had assigned him to monitor a known terrorist named Ali Bin Rashid's communications, which he had done.

Shaw thanked him and asked 'Can you make sure that all of the staff are here at 1900hrs tonight, I want to meet you all together and get to know you a bit better, and to see how you do things out here. Also, to address any concerns anybody may have.'

'Yes Sir,' Corporal Brown replied.

Flight Lieutenant Shaw stepped back in to his office, sitting down he picked up the folder left by Lawrence and opened it up. It contained information about the same Ali Bin Rashid that Corporal Brown had mentioned, and more interestingly, information about a United Nations Convoy moving Weapons of Mass destruction from Baghdad to Basra. They were due to be shipped off shore and destroyed in around six weeks' time at an undisclosed location.

Lawrence Sharif returned to the office forty minutes after he had left.

'Did you read the file?'

'Yes, what is it that you want me to help with?' Shaw asked.

'Well as you can imagine, Mr Rashid would like to get hold of weapons that are able to inflict the most damage, which he believes the UN have,' Sharif answered.

'And do they?'

Sharif didn't answer James's question directly.

He explained how he had infiltrated this certain extremist group two years ago, and that he was highly respected by all of its members. He added that he had informed Ali Bin Rashid he had managed to get a British officer to co-operate with him, by handing over information relating to the weapons of mass destruction after threatening his family.

'Who is the officer?' Shaw asked.

'You are.'

'Have you threatened my family?'

'Of course, I haven't, but Rashid doesn't know that. All he knows is, that in six weeks a convoy is transporting these weapons from one part of the country to another, and that you are the one who will be providing him with the plans of the convoy route. He believes you are doing this to protect your family.'

Shaw let out an exasperated sigh and stood up from his chair picking up his Sun hat along with his sunglasses off the office desk.

'I need a smoke; shall we continue this outside?'

'Yes, there are some fold out chairs behind this block, we should have some privacy there,' Sharif said.

They left the office and walked around the back of the building where they found two camping style chairs, and sat themselves down. Shaw opened the pocket on the left-hand side of his desert pattern shirt and pulled out his cigarettes and lighter, offering one to Lawrence who accepted.

They sat there smoking and Shaw asked.

'So, what do I have to do, meet this Rashid chap, give him the plans and just walk away? And why didn't you ask Will Ramsey to do this?'

Lawrence ignored the latter and replied to the former.

'More or less.'

'I see, it sounds straightforward, are you sure that's all it is?' asked Shaw.

'In response to your earlier question, as to why didn't we ask Flight Lieutenant Ramsey to do this. I have

studied your file from when you first arrived at RAF
Cranwell five years ago as a fresh faced Twenty-year-
old, right up until you left RAF Waddington a few days
ago, and it appears that you have an aptitude for small
arms weaponry along with hand-to-hand combat,
amongst other things, it also says that you are a natural
leader and judging from your annual assessments you
will be promoted to Squadron Leader before long.'
  'Someone has done their homework, now stop beating
around the bush and tell me what it is that you want.'
Lawrence exhaled on his cigarette.
  'This has come from the top and you have been selected
for it due to your skills, and obviously the job you are
doing out here, after the exchange with Ali Bin Rashid
you need to terminate him,' Sharif said.
In his soft Liverpudlian accent James Shaw retorted.
  'Terminate, you mean to say you want me to KILL this
man?'
  'Yes, that is exactly what you need to do, this man is
dangerous, not just to Iraq and Iraqis but the world as a
whole, this is the only way to get to him, he is always on
the move so he cannot be taken out by air, if I took him
out his body guards would kill me in seconds, thus
blowing mine and other operative's cover. It took a lot of
persuasion from me to get him to meet with you alone,
you have to do this James and only you have the skills
and access to do it.'
  'I am an intelligence officer I never expected this, I have
never fired a shot in anger, only ever on the range and
during exercises,' Shaw said.
  'Well, it is time to put all that practice to use, don't

worry it will be fine, I will talk you through it all before hand, every last detail from you taking the documents off your desk to you coming back here after it is done.'

James Shaw was in a state of shock, wondering what on earth he had gotten himself involved in.

He said to Lawrence about a minute later.

'I will do it, just as long as you promise to go through it all with me.'

Lawrence Sharif held his hand out.

'You will get all the help you need,' he said.

Shaw shook his hand, he took out another cigarette from his packet and crumpled the empty packet in his hand and placed it in the cup holder of his chair, he reached into another pocket bringing out a new packet of cigarettes, and offered one to Lawrence.

'Is Lawrence your real name or is that a cover?' James asked.

'Yes, it is my real name, my great great-grandfather was from Hejaz, which is now part of Saudi Arabia, he worked with Prince Faisal as an advisor of sorts, and he fought alongside a certain man named T.E Lawrence against the Ottoman Turks during the First World War, perhaps you have heard of him?'

'Of course, I have,' James replied.

'Well, he was a very good friend of my great great-Grandfather, together they destroyed the Hejaz railway and rode into Damascus at the end of the war. Then after the war he moved to England with my great great-Grandmother, and they had a son and named him Lawrence after the great man, and since then all the males in my family have been named Lawrence as a tribute for all the things he did to help, not just my family but the entire region during the war.'

'I have seen the film *Lawrence of Arabia* it's a great film, and of course I have read *Seven Pillars of Wisdom*. And here you are sat with me in Iraq, named after the great man, you must have some stories to tell that have been passed down, shame how he died. What a bizarre day this has been. What is it that you do here anyway and what if this Ali Bin Rashid or his men spot you coming into our base? Sorry for rambling on,' Shaw said.

Lawrence pulled a lanyard from around his neck, with his photo on, it had the name Ibrahim Kasim and the job title domestic services.

'So, they think you are a cleaner?' Shaw asked.

'That's right, so I am a double agent if you like. So, James what's your story and background obviously I have read your file but I would like to get to know you better,' Lawrence said.

'Well as you know I joined the RAF five years ago, before that I had a gap year backpacking around Spain and Italy after finishing my A levels at Merchant Taylors School, just outside of Liverpool. My Father was a Captain in the Royal Navy, he left the Navy when I was ten years old, and went to work for a merchant shipping company in Liverpool. Quite a chilled-out guy the old man, he encouraged me to join the Military. I always thought the RAF seemed the most attractive compared to the Army and Navy, hence why I am here today. My Mother is a trained nurse. I still don't know how she managed to work and still have my brother and I ready for school with packed lunches and all, she was always there to pick us up from school too, she is the head nurse now at a local hospital. My brother as you probably know is five years younger than me and is currently at Lympstone, training to be a Royal Marines Commando officer.'

Sharif said nothing and just nodded.

'I am not married, no current girlfriend and I enjoy my sports and holidays, that's pretty much it really.'

'It sounds like you have had a good life so far, your career is going well. I heard that you were going out with a girl named Claire, and just to reassure you nobody has threatened your family. I just had to say that for this plan to fall into place,' Lawrence said with a smile.

Shaw stood up from is chair.

'That is good to hear. Claire and I have been out on occasions, nothing serious though. I am meeting all of my staff at 1900 so I best go and get prepared for that, after which I will go have a beer and try to make sense of all of this madness.'

Sharif agreed with him, and said he would see him tomorrow and walked off towards his car. Shaw waved him off, shook his head in bewilderment and walked back to his office for the meeting with his staff.

At the presidential palace; Flight Lieutenant James Shaw was awoken by the sound of people talking and walking outside of his room ready for the day ahead. He stretched and yawned, and leant across to grab his watch off the nightstand, he looked at it and it read 0730.

'Shit,' he said out loud.

He was supposed to be in work for 0800hrs but the previous night's events had taken its toll on him. Quickly; he got dressed and made sure that he had all of his equipment, he left the room and walked along the corridor, down the stairs where he spotted the Captain who had looked after him the night before. He thanked him again for all of his help, they saluted each other and Shaw walked out to his Land Rover so that he could drive back to Basra Airbase, and to his office to meet with Lawrence Sharif. The sun, even at such an early hour was scorching hot and the inside of Shaw's Land Rover was like a furnace, he put his gloves on so as not to burn his hands on the steering wheel, wound down both windows, started the engine and set off for the airfield.

Thirty minutes later he had parked up, and went straight into the air-conditioned office, saying good morning to Corporal Brown and the two SAC's (Senior Aircraftsmen) before he went in to his inner office. He put his helmet on top of the four-drawer filing cabinet and started his computer up, and walked back in to the main office, taking a bottle of water out of the fridge. He was having a chat and a laugh with his staff, then there was a knock at the door. The staff switched all the screens off for security reasons, and Corporal Brown opened the door to the cleaner with his cleaning cart, which he wheeled into the office, he took his cap off, it was Lawrence Sharif. He said good morning to everybody, and he followed James into the inner office. They sat there in the cool office with Shaw at his desk and Lawrence on the visitors chair next to the filing cabinet.

'How do you think last night went then?' Lawrence asked.

'I honestly don't know how I did it, it just seemed natural, weird really.'

'A job well done I would say; the exchange went well, and then in an instant he was in a heap on the floor. I watched you from the other side of the river just to make sure that you went through with it, and to let my superiors know when it was done,' Lawrence said.

'So, this has come from the top then?'

'Yes, the very top, you did a good thing.'

Shaw picked the two manila envelopes up off his desk and handed them over to Lawrence.

'These are for you,' he said.

Lawrence opened one of the envelopes, pulling the plans for the convoy half way out, he flicked through them and placed them back inside, and closed the envelope. He handed the other envelope to James.

'You can keep that, and I will destroy this one,' he said.

James opened his manila envelope from Sharif and emptied two bricks of US One Hundred dollar bills onto his desk, each brick contained Ten-Thousand dollars.

Shaw exhaled and shook his head in disbelief.

Surely all of this is a dream he said in his head.

Lawrence sensed what he was thinking and said to him.

'It's all yours, do with it what you wish, there is plenty more where that came from, if you would like to continue working with us.'

James stepped over to the filing cabinet, and opened the

second draw down, he placed the two bricks of cash in to the open drawer, he closed it again with a thud and sat back down at his desk and looked at Lawrence inquisitively.

'You want me to kill people for you on a regular basis?'

'No not always, sometimes when necessary, we will ask you to terminate targets, and you will be compensated each time you help us out.'

James looked into Lawrence's eyes.

'OK, I will help you out. I suppose it will be easier to do what I did last night again after the first time,' he said.

Lawrence didn't answer.

Shaw added jokingly.

'When do I get my Aston Martin and watch?'

Lawrence scowled, not seeing the funny side and said to James.

'It's ninety per cent watching people and sitting around, and ten percent action, last night you were thrown in at the deep end and performed well.'

The two men sat looking at each other, then Shaw held out his hand.

'I look forward to working with you and I won't let you down but I will need guidance along the way.'

Lawrence shook his hand and smiled.

'I look forward to it also, you're a good man James. I will help you whenever you need it and I will never be too far away from you.'

'Thanks,' James Shaw said.

Lawrence got up from his seat ready to leave.

'I have to leave now but I will be back tomorrow for our daily briefing.'

Lawrence Sharif left the inner office and picked up his cleaning cart, with Shaw following out of the door behind him, both men stepped out into the searing heat and blinding sun with the sound of helicopters overhead and on the ground. The two men shook hands, and Lawrence walked away with his cleaning cart towards another portacabin. James turned back into the air conditioned cool of the office.

TWO

Liverpool, UK. May (Twelve years later)

Lyndon John Powell stood with his arms behind his back, looking out of the floor to ceiling window of his apartment at the grey sky outside, deep in thought. Lyndon Powell stood at six feet four inches tall, forty years of age and the years had been kind to him, he was dressed in a tailored navy-blue suit with grey pinstripes, a perfectly pressed white shirt with a pink tie and a pair of black brogues, being well dressed and presented was to him, half of the battle.

If you look professional, people will think you are professional was a phrase he often used. Lyndon Powell was a charming man, he had an aura about him that made people trust him, and be totally convinced by whatever it was they were being told, this is what made him so successful in his line of business.

The apartment was in a high rise that had been purpose built a few years earlier, it overlooked the River Mersey in Liverpool, and came with a concierge service. Some of the city's elite were resident in the building, and Lyndon classed himself as part of that elite group. To his neighbours, Lyndon Powell was a successful property investor.

The reality is, that Lyndon Powell is a very sophisticated conman. Who sells land and properties for development in Britain and Asia that do not exist, or are not his to sell, and then disappearing before the victim could do anything about it, once they realised that they had been duped.

The victims could not go to the police either, because in the process they were led to believe that certain palms had been greased to make the deals happen, and nobody would want a bribery charge on their record, which could result in a stint behind bars in a Chinese or Thai prison.

He grew up in a wealthy suburb of Liverpool to wealthy parents, he had been a good student in school, especially at maths. During his time in high school, he sold confectionary and cigarettes to the other pupils at over inflated prices, the proceeds from which he had never spent and over the years had amassed just under five thousand pounds.

His parents believed that he would go onto university and possibly into a career to do with maths, such as accountancy or even teaching. Instead, Lyndon decided to invest his money on the stock market and more specifically into commodities such as oil and gold. He was making a small fortune by the age of Twenty.

Lyndon had wanted to work in the City in London from

the age of sixteen, after he was told in school that it would be a good career for him, as he was so good at numbers and he had the ability to convince anybody that he was in the right, as he had on more than one occasion when he found himself in trouble at school.

Two years after finishing high school, he had completed his A-levels and had met with various representatives from different universities, and due to the prestige of his School this included Oxford and Cambridge Universities. Lyndon had been impressed by what they had to say and what they had to offer. He may well have chosen to go to Cambridge, he had always preferred Cambridge. As it was, he could not be persuaded to change his mind, which was to make it alone without spending a number of years studying, and then trying to find employment, competing with people who all had the same qualifications and skills that would gain.

After getting his A-level results, he decided to take the train to London and get himself a job in the City. He had worked on a pitch for himself to present to potential employers, and he had made a PowerPoint presentation which he had stored on a floppy disc to show them.

The evening before leaving Liverpool; at the dinner table he had announced to his parents what his intentions were. His father Richard, who is originally from South Africa and moved to Britain two years before Lyndon was born, was impressed by his son's attitude and determination. He agreed with his son but his mother was a little apprehensive at first, before agreeing that it would be good for her son to try and make his own way in life, and she believed he would succeed. His father previously owned half of a large and lucrative diamond mine in the old Transvaal Province now known as Gauteng, it was where he had met Lyndon's mother Anne, who at the time was working as a sales assistant in a jewellery store and was training to become a jeweller herself.

Anne had been sent to South Africa by her boss as part of her training, and more importantly to save the business money, the owner wanted to source diamonds direct from the mine, instead of paying higher prices for cut and polished diamonds from Antwerp or Amsterdam. During her time in South Africa, she had met Richard and they had fallen in love after spending time together. Richard made the decision to sell his share in the diamond mine and move to Liverpool to be with Anne. He opened a jewellery shop, and ran it with Anne, who was now a fully qualified jeweller. A year later they were married and a year after that their only child was born and they named him Lyndon. Richard's connections in the mining industry helped the shop to flourish and after a few years he had three stores. Today he has sixty-seven shops across the UK and South Africa, and has recently opened a shop on the Champs Elysees in Paris.

After packing a suitcase with suits that he had recently purchased, a map of London and the name of the hotel he had booked over the telephone on a slip of paper in his pocket, Lyndon Powell boarded a train at Liverpool Lime Street and set off for London.

When he arrived at the hotel after a short tube journey

from Euston station, he had not expected the hotel to be as bad as it was. It had been listed as four stars in the Yellow Pages, and he had paid a four-star price for a room that was so cramped he had to put his suitcase in the bathroom, which was bigger than the bedroom. The room had a queen bed which was springy, a wardrobe and a desk all squeezed in to such a small space, he looked at the brown curtains and wondered if they had ever been cleaned in the thirty years that he assumed they had been hanging there. There was no such thing as *Booking.com* or *TripAdvisor* twenty-one years ago. This did not discourage him, as the next morning he woke up early and got dressed in to a light grey suit with a white shirt and a patterned tie, he had some breakfast, and walked to the underground station around the corner from the hotel, and got himself on to the tube which took him into the City of London.

After emerging from the underground station, he walked into the foyer of a multi-national bank and asked at the reception desk if he could speak to whoever was in charge of the trading department, he was asked if he had an appointment, he said no, and he was told that the person in charge was too busy, the next two places he tried, told him the same thing.

Undeterred, he decided the next place he went to he would change his approach. The next building that he decided to try was an all-glass affair as far as he could see from the ground, and the inside was the same, all glass partitions, a very sterile place, it was home to a well-known Merchant Bank. Lyndon John Powell walked in to the glass building, and across the large glass foyer as if he belonged there, his highly polished shoes made a tapping noise on the highly polished tile floor, he smiled as he walked past people, it was a busy place even though it was only eight thirty. He walked towards the lifts and looked at the floor directory for the trading department and found it listed on the twenty-eighth floor, he got in to the lift followed by a few others who he smiled at. After stopping four times the lift arrived on the twenty-eighth floor, a man stepped out first and Lyndon followed. He stepped into a corridor just a little bit wider than the space the three lifts took up, it was painted white with a set of double doors on the left wall and two sets of double doors on the right, and up ahead was the end of the corridor which was floor to ceiling glass, the ground floor was the only one that was all glass, cheaper that way.

Lyndon opted for the double doors on the left, he pushed one of the doors open and stepped into a room he assumed was taking up half of the floor he was on, it was huge, on three sides it was all glass and the wall behind him was the same white as the corridor but had black screens on with letters and numbers going along like a ticker tape, some were green and some were red, the stock ticker he assumed, he noticed that there were stock tickers hanging from the ceiling at various places around the office, *so everybody can see them* he thought to himself, the back wall also had three clocks on, which had London, New York and Tokyo on signs underneath, the London clock was in the middle of them and read eight forty-three. The office was full of desks with computers and phones on them, and each desk was separated by sound proof partitions.

There was already a handful of people in the office, he noticed two of them having a chat together so he decided to go and ask who he should speak to about a job. They directed him to the head of trading who had his own corner office.

Lyndon spoke to the head of trading and after convincing him to give him a chance he was offered a month's trial which he gladly accepted and began work that day, the boss was impressed by the way he had just walked in, and thought he was worth giving a chance to. Lyndon quickly found his feet, and after a few days was outperforming people that had years of experience in trading. It was also where he started trading with his own money, using the knowledge that he had learnt on the trading floor, but using different merchant banks to buy his stocks and shares. He would meet and become friends with Mike Williams, Chris Hampshire and IT engineer Jack Reuben, who he met in the office where he was given his big break.

During the Asian financial crisis of 1997, Lyndon had read in the business pages about an upcoming property boom once the crisis had subsided, which gave him the idea of selling plots of land and potential developments, whilst prices were at rock bottom to wealthy investors both in Asia and the West. What the investors didn't know was that Lyndon Johnson, as he called himself to investors, never owned any of the land or developments, and that they had been sold multiple times to other people and groups looking to make a fast buck in a region that was ripe for investment, hoping to maximise returns on moderate sized investments ranging from twenty-five thousand pounds to half a million pounds. This was when the group started to make big money, and they quickly realised how good they were, and it continued for years, they were always one step ahead of the next boom or crash to make sure they made as much money as possible. The group had one rule, which was only con people that could afford to lose the money. They never cheated anybody out of life savings, only people that were already rich and wanted to get richer at somebody else's expense. After about a year of pulling off these scams the four of them decided to leave the merchant bank and would go it alone as people in the bank had started to become suspicious of them. After completing their working notice of a month, they took numerous business cards with them when they left, and they still had many contacts in the city which they would use down the years, making sure that they were compensated for their time. The four men had been investigated many times by the City of London Police but nothing had ever come of it, as there was a lack of evidence and very rarely was the crime committed in the UK. This was one of many reasons why they were so successful, and had made so much money, yet they always paid income tax on their earnings because the last thing they wanted was to get caught and jailed by the taxman for tax evasion.

As Lyndon Powell looked out of the window of his apartment, he was playing over and over in his head how his latest planned scheme would pan out, for this was the biggest job he had ever planned, and the rewards would be so great, that it would be his last job before he retired. Even though he hadn't yet informed his crew members of his retirement plans. Everything had been planned to the last detail for this job to work. He could afford no mistakes. There were three other members of his crew; Chris Hampshire a tall and wiry man, he was six-foot-tall with brown hair, brown eyes and he was permanently tanned, he thought it made him look Spanish much to the ridicule of the others in the group, Jack Reuben five foot eight inches tall and very overweight, he had grey eyes and grey skin from years of being indoors in front of a computer screen, he very rarely ventured outside into the sun and Mike Williams six feet two inches tall, in good shape he worked out a lot, he had dyed blonde hair, hazel eyes and was naturally tanned, he also ate whenever he could, yet didn't ever seem to gain any weight. The four of them had worked with each other for over 20 years, all of them were involved from the beginning of the Asia property scams. Lyndon sent a group text from his mobile phone saying *Meet in an hour, in the Hilton lobby, try and see if we can get in to the room early.* They had hired a conference room to go over the plans for the next job again.

Less than an hour later, the four of them arrived at the hotel lobby.
'Go and check us in,' Lyndon said to Chris.
Which he did, a concierge led them to the conference room that was set up with a projector and refreshments, a

long, dark wood table filled the centre of the room, faux leather chairs were placed all around the table, six on each side and one at each end. The four men filed into the room, and Jack who was the tech wizard pulled a laptop out of his bag and began to connect it up to the projector. Mike set about pouring some coffee for everybody and helping himself to the pastries that had been provided by the hotel.

Lyndon Powell took a sip of coffee, and placed his cup on the table in front of him, he stood up and walked towards the front of the room.
'Right gentlemen let's get started,' he said.
On the projector screen at the front of the room was the logo of Spanish Oil Company ESPoil, the logo was a droplet of oil with a flame above in red and yellow just like the Spanish flag and underneath in navy blue writing were the words ESPoil.
'This is our next target and our biggest, this will make us, but be warned we cannot afford any mistakes,' Lyndon said.
'What happens if we do make a mistake? Not that we will, this plan has been perfected to the last detail. I have been over and over it many times, I just ask out of curiosity,' Jack asked.
'We go to prison for the rest of our days, or end up dead,' laughed Mike.
'No seriously what will happen?' added Chris.
'Mike is most likely right; however, we won't make any mistakes, as we all know what we are doing and have never messed up before, and we are not going to this

time. Now can I please get on with this presentation we haven't got all day, feel free to ask any relevant questions as we go along though. ESPoil is Spain's biggest oil and petroleum company with revenues of around thirty billion euros a year.'

'With profits of around seven billion euros a year,' added Chris.

Lyndon clicked his handheld remote to move the slideshow along. A well-dressed man with jet black styled hair, olive skin and a look of someone who was used to the finer things in life appeared on screen.

'This is Javier Ramos, the head of oil and gas exploration for ESPoil, and who Chris and Mike have been in contact with to get us started on this, what can you tell us about him, Chris?'

'Javier Ramos, 52 years old, Argentinian, born in Buenos Aires to rich parents, his father used to own and run a meat processing company. When Javier was twenty, he moved to Saudi Arabia to study Petro-chemistry for five years. After that he went to work for ESPoil, working in the field, and labs before he was made head of exploration fifteen years ago. We believe he is looking to be in charge of the whole company and will do anything to achieve it, he was arrested for murdering the previous incumbent of his current job, whose name was Vicente Garcia, this was never proven and the authorities and ESPoil put it down as an accident.'

'So, he could potentially be dangerous,' Mike added.

'When we presented our plans to him his eyes lit up because he knew this would be the biggest coup for the company, and would see him rewarded by the board of ESPoil with them making him chairman,' said Chris.

'Most importantly... he sees this as an opportunity to get one over on the British, who he detests due to the Falklands war, during which his eldest cousin was killed aboard the Belgrano when it was sunk, that's why it was so difficult to get him to speak to us,' added Mike.

Lyndon and Jack Reuben raised their eyebrows and Lyndon asked.

'I can see why he hates the British after what happened to his cousin. What was the reason for him not being charged with murder?'

'Lack of evidence the official report says, personally I think he has some influence over the authorities,' Mike answered.

'Well, I for one am looking forward to taking him down and I am sure you three are too, we will have to stay on guard though! Now for the technical stuff, which Jack will take us through.'

Lyndon grabbed his cup off the table and walked to the refreshment table to pour some more coffee before taking a seat at the long table, with his chair facing the screen at the front of the room.

Lyndon Powell, Chris Hampshire and Mike Williams were seated around the long table in the room facing the projector screen where Jack Reuben was waiting to give his presentation. Jack Reuben was the technical brains of the crew that Lyndon Powell had assembled twenty years ago, always keeping pace with the changing technologies, and staying one step ahead of the people whose money they were trying to take. Jack worked behind the scenes, rarely coming face to face with the mark, when he did it was for technical reasons that were all part of the long con.

Jack looked at the screen and turned to the others in the room.

'Now it is time for the boring but important stuff, as Chris told us Mr Ramos is Argentinian and hates the British, which helps us, by playing on that hatred.'

Jack pressed a button on the remote to change the slide on the screen, an atlas style map of the world appeared. The others sat there looking bored already, then Mike spoke out.

'Every time we plan a job and have the brief do you have to show a map of the world, just put the part that we need up,' he let out a quiet chuckle to himself.

Jack frowned at Mike.

'Would you like to do the presentation?'

Lyndon interjected 'Can you two give it a rest and let's get through this so we can go and get our stuff together and get set to go on this.'

Jack clicked the remote again and the screen changed to a close up of the Falkland Islands, with the two-hundred-mile exclusion zone shown as a lighter shade of blue compared to the dark blue of ocean on the map, within the exclusion zone four red dots had been marked in a horizontal line a hundred miles north of the islands.

'As I am sure you are all aware that over the last few years it has been confirmed that there is oil in the South Atlantic, more specifically in the exclusion zone which was set up during the conflict with Argentina.'

The others nodded in acknowledgement. Jack continued. 'The company I have created for this task is called South Atlantic Oil and Gas, which is what Chris and Mike have been using for their meetings with Mr Ramos. I have secured drilling permits from the government for the four sites that I have marked out on the map, we paid twenty thousand pounds for the drilling permits. How does that make us fifty million pounds I hear you ask?' The others in the room stayed silent and shuffled in their chairs, they were used to this every time Jack discussed his plans.

'Our government has legislated that only British companies can drill for oil within the exclusion zone, South Atlantic Oil and Gas has been registered at companies house in Cardiff, with Lyndon as Chairman, Mike as Chief executive and Chris as the Managing director, websites have been made and accounts filed so any checking by Mr Ramos or his associates will bring back a company that is new on the scene but ultimately doing quite well and turning a profit, however it needs investment to develop the company further, which is the point where Mr Ramos comes in. He is willing to take control of our company for the price of fifty million pounds, which would put it under the control of ESPoil, yet remaining a British company just under a Spanish parent company. Most importantly what he wants are the drilling permits, that we have secured, allowing him to drill for oil in British waters.'

Lyndon stood up and walked towards the screen at the front of the room next to Jack, and looked at Chris and Mike.

'So where are we up to with Mr Ramos?'

'He is very much on board with this but he needs to meet with you Lyndon to seal the deal, shake hands, sign papers and all that stuff, what I don't understand is how is this a con when we actually have a company along with the drilling permits to sell?' Mike said.

'Well to put it simply it isn't a traditional con, oil exists in the South Atlantic but nobody knows for sure where it is exactly, it is all guesswork at the minute, so basically Mr Ramos and Espoil are buying our company so they have the right to drill under a British name, but the chances of them finding oil in those locations are slim.'

Lyndon walked back to where he was sat earlier, he took a sip of his coffee whilst still standing, he smiled and looked at the others in the room, he leant on the table with his palms spread flat.

'Right fellas, I am sure we have got all of the information we need for this.'

The other three nodded in unison, agreeing with Lyndon.

'We are good to go on this then?' Lyndon asked.

'Jack has prepared all of the paperwork to take with us, I will call Mr Ramos now and arrange the meeting then we can get ready to go,' Mike replied.

Mike pulled his smartphone from his pocket and dialled Mr Ramos's number which after four rings was answered.

'Hello Mr Ramos, it is Mike Williams calling from South Atlantic Oil, how are you?'

Mike waited a few seconds for Javier Ramos to finish speaking then continued.

'Very well thank you, as promised I have spoken with

our Chairman Mr Lyndon Johnson and he is very much looking forward to meeting with you and getting this deal completed.'
Another pause.
'Ok, I have got that yeah ok we will see you on Tuesday, thank you good bye.'
Mike ended the call and put his phone back away into his pocket and said nothing.
Lyndon looked at Mike and said to him.
'Well... what did he say and where are we meeting him?'
'Next Tuesday, in Seville, Spain he has his summer residence there, he will tell us where exactly we will meet when we arrive.'
'Right OK, it sounds like he wants to keep the upper hand all the way through this but let him have it his way, and let him think he is getting the better of us, we will have the last laugh on this one. Jack as you are typing away am I right to assume that you are already looking at how to get us there?'
Jack continued typing away and looked up at the others.
'No direct flight from Liverpool, we either go over to Dublin or fly to Malaga from Liverpool, and take a train from there, which takes about two hours. I have booked us rooms at a place called Hotel Ayre in the new town, which has a pool and is opposite Santa Justa Railway Station, and has a bus stop outside to get us into the old town, where I assume Mr Ramos will want to meet with us.'
'Good work we will take the Malaga route, no point in taking two flights. We will leave Sunday, that then gives us two days to get a feel for the place and find our way

around, we will call Ramos on the Monday and let him know we are there.'

'Flights are booked, we leave Liverpool at seven Sunday morning, due to arrive around eleven local time, we will take a local train from the airport to the main station, where we will get on the train to Seville.'

'Good work Jack, right then we best get packing, linen shirts and suits for me. I suggest the same for you guys I heard it is very hot this time of year but we still need to look the part.'

Mike, Chris and Jack nodded in agreement with Lyndon. Jack closed his laptop and put it in his carry bag, and the other three got ready to leave the conference room. Lyndon straightened his tie and said to the other three.

'We have a few days to relax, get ready and go over everything again before we set off.'

The four men left the conference room into the noisy and busy foyer and bar area, Chris went to the reception desk to let them know that they had finished with the room, and walked back to the other three who had not moved.

'Let's have a drink first before we go back home,' Lyndon said.

The four men walked into the bar area and took a seat at a high table with four high bar stools, a waitress came over to take their order and they ordered four Belgian lagers. The waitress brought the beers over a few minutes later, Lyndon gave the waitress a fifty-pound note, and said to keep the change, the waitress thanked him profusely and smiled as she walked away from their table. Lyndon took a sip of his beer then asked.

'How do you feel about this one then?'
Chris answered first.
'Pretty good, everything is good to go and this is the biggest job we have ever done so a bit nervous too.'
'It feels like our first job together twenty years ago, all nerves and a lot at stake, obviously this is the most we have ever tried to take and I will be very happy once we are back here with the money in our bank account,' Mike said.
'I agree with these two,' Jack said.
'I know that this will work out because we have the best team to pull something as big as this off, you really are the best and it's been a great twenty years, we have a great opportunity here and we just have to do what we do best and nothing will go wrong,' Lyndon added.
They continued chatting and when they had finished their drinks, they left the Hilton hotel and got into a taxi that the concierge had called for them. They set off for their homes to get ready to leave for Spain in a few days, and hopefully pull off the biggest shakedown they had ever attempted.

THREE

Two hundred and twenty miles away at MI6 headquarters in London; the phone on Lawrence Sharif's desk was ringing, he picked the receiver up after the second ring and pressed the little button on the console to open the line.

'Sharif,' he answered.

He listened and moved the mouse on his computer with his free hand, and clicked on his e-mails, he then replied to the caller.

'OK, copied thank you.'

He clicked off the call, keeping the receiver in his hand, he opened a new line and dialled four numbers which meant an internal extension number. Whilst waiting for the call to be answered he typed a letter in the address box on his emails, and an address came up straight away as he had e-mailed it a number of times so the system recognised it, he was typing his message when his call was answered.

'Hello Sir, I have just taken a call and we have a location for our target. I have read the briefing and I am ready to go,' he said.

He listened again.

'Yes sir, I will get my man on it and I will leave in the next thirty minutes,' he said. 'Yes Sir, I understand, I will sort it all when I arrive thank you.'

Lawrence hung up the phone and continued to type, he pressed send and logged off his computer, he picked up his sports bag which was already packed, from under his desk and left his office for Stansted Airport in Essex.

At RAF Akrotiri in Cyprus; Wing Commander James Shaw, dressed in the multi-terrain combat uniform was sat with his chair laid back resting his feet on his grey wood military issue desk with his eyes shut. He was hungover, and he had hung a sign on the outside of his office door saying *meeting in progress,* he was in no mood for visitors in his current state. His head was throbbing and his right hand had bruised knuckles. Even though his window was closed he could hear the *whap-whap-whap* of helicopters taking off and landing, along with the roar of jet engines which caused the filing cabinets in his office to vibrate and rattle, which shook him awake every ten minutes or so.

 The sound of a Eurofighter Typhoon taking off shook him awake once more, he moved his right hand to his computer mouse and noticed that he had a bunch of un-read e-mails, which he ignored and closed his eyes again. Just as he started to drift off, the phone on his desk rang, the screen showed that it was the station commander's office.

 'I am not in the mood for this today,' he said aloud. Putting his feet on to the floor he grabbed the receiver and answered the call.

'Yes, I will be there in twenty minutes thanks.'
It was the Station commander's assistant calling to notify
Shaw that Group Captain Bartlett wanted to speak to him
in his office in thirty minutes.

He stood up and walked towards the mini fridge in his
office, taking out a bottle of water, he unscrewed the cap
and downed the bottle. Shaw wiped his mouth with his
sleeve. He walked back to his desk and put the empty
bottle in the bin before grabbing his beret off the desk,
he put it on his head as he walked out of his office and
headed towards station headquarters to meet with the
station commander.

I wonder what this is all about then. He said as he
walked across the base. He met with the station
commander on a weekly basis as part of the station brief,
along with the other commanding officers for various
departments, and he spoke to him in the officers mess
some nights. The station commander had never asked for
him to meet in his office alone, except for the time when
he had first arrived in Cyprus. That was a part of his job,
to personally meet with all the new officers when they
arrived at RAF Akrotiri.

Wing Commander James Shaw arrived at station
headquarters seven minutes after he had left his own
office, he stepped into the air conditioned cool of the
building. The building was built in a T shape and the
station commander's office was along the left-hand side
of the top of the T shape. Sat behind a desk in an open
office was a corporal, who was also dressed in multi-
terrain combats, he was the station commanders P.A, the
one who had called earlier. Shaw said good morning to

him and the P.A returned the compliment, and said to go straight in. Wing Commander Shaw knocked on the door and heard a voice say 'Come in.'

He opened the door and stepped in to the office saluting Group Captain Bartlett, who was sat behind the military standard wooden grey desk in a high back leather chair. The office had a book case next to a filing cabinet, a plant in one corner, a fridge and drinks tray, which had a decanter with an amber liquid in, and glasses in another corner of the office.

Scotch Shaw thought to himself, his hangover seemed to get worse as he thought about it. Group Captain Bartlett pointed to the visitor's chair opposite his desk, which was also a leather chair but with a low back instead of the high back the station commander had, he asked James Shaw to take his beret off.

At least this is informal he thought to himself, as he was in no mood for a formal chat, he just wanted a nice easy day to get over his raging hangover.

The Group Captain was dressed in a pink flying suit, they were the standard issue in hot and sandy places, he stood up and walked around his desk to the drinks tray, and poured two drinks handing one to James Shaw.

He must be flying this afternoon Shaw thought to himself.

'There are a couple of reasons I called you here James,' he said as he walked back behind his desk and sat back down.

'I see Sir,' Shaw said before taking a sip of the drink, which he figured to be some kind of bourbon, *Makers*

Mark he thought to himself as the warm liquid worked its way down his throat and into his stomach.

'Firstly, I took a phone call from a Cypriot Detective in Limassol this morning, asking if this man was one of mine, stationed here,' he said.

He rotated the screen of his computer around so that Shaw could see the image, which was a still taken from a CCTV camera, it was him outside of a bar in Limassol with two bodies on the floor next to him.

'Is he one of ours Sir, I have never seen him before,' Shaw said with a smile.

'That's what I said to the Police five minutes before you walked in here, I said "I have gone through the systems and found no match with the man on the picture to any of our personnel." Now you are lucky that OC (Office Commanding) Police is on leave, and that he had his out of office on his e-mail because the Cypriot police called the RAF Police, and they put the call through to me, would you like to explain what happened last night or rather at three o'clock this morning.'

Shaw took another sip of his bourbon and thought back to the night before, when he had gone out with some of his staff from the Intelligence office.

'Well Sir, we went for some food in the village, and after we had finished, a few of us took taxis into Limassol, we had some drinks and then we got separated.' He took another sip of bourbon.

'I was walking along the road looking for a taxi, when a woman started talking to me, and asked if I would like to go with her for a drink, so we went to a bar nearby. I got a beer for me and a Malibu for the woman, I can't even remember what her name was, anyway after a few more drinks I decided to pay the bill and the barman showed me a bill for two thousand euros, naturally I laughed at him and said "You have made a mistake on this pal", he didn't laugh or even crack a smile.

Then two bouncers came over and started demanding that I pay up, I obviously refused, saying I didn't have that kind of cash on me. Or words to that effect. I remember looking around and I noticed that the woman had done a disappearing act. Even though I had had a fair bit to drink, I realised it was a clip-joint scam.'

Group Captain Bartlett was sat back in his chair intrigued by what James Shaw had just told him.

'What is a clip joint?' he asked.

'It is a scam, whereby an attractive woman approaches a tourist, usually a male, she asks them for a drink whilst flirting with them and when the bill comes the woman is nowhere to be seen, the bill is extortionate and you are strong-armed into paying it by intimidating doorman,' Shaw replied.

'Interesting scam, I could see how men would fall for it. So, what happened after you refused to pay?'

'The bouncers said "We will take you to a cash machine so you can pay", they were Russian I think, definitely Eastern European, we stepped outside with one behind me and one in front of me. We took about five steps forward before I launched my right elbow back smashing it back into the guys face behind me, I felt his face crush into my elbow, then as the front guy was turning around to see what was happening, I brought my arm into a forward motion, made a fist and followed through into the side of his head, they both went down like empty suits and didn't get up so I left and went to find a taxi,' Shaw said before finishing his drink.

The station commander leant forward and spoke.

'Well, the good news is they are in the hospital and will be awake soon, so I don't see the need to pursue this any further, just be careful when you are out. I will send an e-mail to all personnel about this clip-joint scam as well so as to warn them about it, not everybody is as handy as you are.'

'Thank you, Sir, hopefully they will learn the error of their ways after last night. What else was it you wanted to see me about Sir?'

Group Captain Bartlett opened the top drawer on the left-hand side of his desk and pulled out two manila envelopes, one was bigger than the other, he took a stack of paper out of the first envelope and placed the envelope on to his desk and lay the papers down next to it. James Shaw wondered what they were and shuffled in his chair to try and catch a glimpse of what was on them.

'I have here some good news. Wing Commander James Shaw as of the 20th of July you will be known as Group Captain James Shaw, and will be the Station commander for RAF Waddington, congratulations,' he said and stood up and held his hand out.

Shaw also stood and shook the Station Commanders hand.

'Thank you, Sir, I did not expect this to happen,'

They sat back down and Shaw asked.

'Sir, is the Station Commander at Waddington not usually a pilots post?'

'Normally yes, however Air Command have decided in a change of direction, primarily because Waddington is a flying base but the flying is for Intelligence and reconnaissance. They decided, starting with you they would rotate Station Commanders between pilots and intelligence, you will be the first intelligence one then when you move on a pilot, and when they move on another intelligence officer so on and so forth. Somebody obviously thinks highly of you because it is a big station to be in charge of for your first post but I am sure you will manage just fine.'

Shaw nodded in agreement and shuffled in his chair, his legs were starting to cramp up, part of the after effects from the alcohol.

'I will miss it out here. I have had a great three years. I will miss the sun most of all, I need to arrange getting my car back to the UK sooner rather than later, I don't want to get back home and be waiting for my car to be shipped, I will do that later.'

Shaw's car was a Dodge Challenger muscle car in burnt orange with a big black stripe down the centre of the car, he had gotten it imported from the USA two years ago with the money he had received from helping Lawrence Sharif on a job in Nicosia. Where between the two of them they shot dead six terrorists who were planning to detonate simultaneous car bombs outside the US Embassy and the British and Australian High Commissions.

Group Captain Bartlett picked the other thinner envelope up off his desk.

'I will make sure your car gets back to Britain, first we

need to discuss what is in this envelope but before that lets have another drink.'

Shaw stood up and walked over to the drinks tray and picked up the decanter, he poured more bourbon into the glasses on the desk, he poured himself a smaller measure than the Station Commander, he replaced the decanter on the tray and sat back down in the visitor's chair. He looked at the envelope, waiting impatiently for the Station Commander to take out the contents.

In Liverpool, Lyndon Powell had finished packing his cabin bag, which contained three suits, three shirts, ties and two pairs of shoes for the trip to Spain, then the buzzer to his apartment rang. He stepped out of his bedroom door, and walked across his hallway to the buzzer receiver and picked it up. It was Chris Hampshire and Mike Williams asking to come in, Lyndon pressed the button on the console and he heard the two of them push the door open at the base of his apartment building. Lyndon went to the front door of his apartment and opened it so that Mike and Chris could walk straight in. After a couple of minutes Mike and Chris walked into Lyndon's apartment and met him in the kitchen, where Lyndon had opened three bottles of beer for them, even though it was still morning. The apartment was a large square with the living room being the biggest room, it had a three-seat sofa and two chairs arranged in a triangle with a large television looking out at them, the two En-suite bedrooms where in a hallway off the left side of the living room where the floor to ceiling windows were and the opposite side had a hallway where the main bathroom was located and the kitchen was attached to the living room but separated by a partition, which was home to his drinks decanters and glasses. The three of them walked over to the seating area and sat down on the large sofas. Lyndon wondered why Mike and Chris had come over.

'What brings you here then? Have you begun packing yet?' he asked them.

'We just decided to check in see how you are?' said Mike.

'You don't seem as excited about this job as you normally would be at this stage,' Chris added.

Lyndon Powell took a big gulp of his beer and shuffled in his seat, exhaling deeply he leant forward holding his bottle in two hands and looked at both Mike and Chris.

'It's just that we have never tried anything like this before and with so much at stake, sure we have had trickier ones, remember that one in Shanghai when Mr Chen nearly caught us out because we had no permits to build in China, and Jack e-mailed them to us as Mr Chen was on the phone to the police or at least he said he was, Jack to the rescue on that one, where is he anyway?'

'Taking care of some loose ends before we set off on Sunday, he said he doesn't want anything left to chance whilst we are there, especially after you just mentioned the Mr Chen deal. Shanghai was great wasn't it, we made some money there and Bangkok was a good one,' Mike said.

The three of them nodded in acknowledgment. They had indeed been hugely successful over the last twenty years, and in that time, they had had some near misses in terms of being exposed as fraudsters.

One time, when they had just completed the supposed sale of part of a new development in Bangkok city centre to an American man for a quarter of a million pounds. Quickly realising that he had been conned the American hired some local help to track down Lyndon and his crew through the hot sticky streets of Bangkok. Luckily in Thailand money talks, Lyndon, Mike, Chris and Jack had been sat in a bar when two local men aged around twenty-five pulled up outside the bar on a moped. They walked over to the men and said they had been paid to find them and to call the American when they had. Lyndon offered the men double what the American was paying them to report back to him and say that nobody had seen them and that they would keep looking which enabled the crew to leave Bangkok and lay low for a few weeks before returning to snare their next victim.

'How much do we know about this Mr Ramos; from what you have told me he seems like a man not to be messed with and does he have any minders that you noticed when you met him?' Lyndon asked.

Mike sat there trying to remember the first time he met Mr Javier Ramos.

'He had two men with him, one had a silver briefcase, he was his lawyer and the other guy I think he said he was a lawyer for ESPoil, he had a black leather briefcase, that was it, I don't remember seeing any minders or anybody else that was interested in us.'

The first meeting they arranged was at a hotel in Paris at the time of an energy convention which was why Mike and Chris were there, their cover was that they were looking for investors in South Atlantic Oil and Gas, and Mr Ramos and ESPoil were what they were looking for, to get drilling started in the South Atlantic Ocean.

'You're probably right it's just me being a bit over cautious, there is fifty million pounds riding on us getting this right,' Lyndon replied.

Mike held his empty beer bottle out in front of him.

'Would you like another?' he asked.

Lyndon and Chris both answered yes and Mike walked into the kitchen to get three more beers, on his way back out he asked Lyndon.

'Do you honestly think we can pull this one off without any problems?'

Lyndon stepped over to Mike and took a beer from him.

'Of course, I do, we wouldn't be doing it if I didn't think we could do this, this is what we have been waiting for, ever since the four of us starting doing this, waiting for that one huge payday and they do not come much bigger than this, why don't both of you go back home get packed and ready to go to Spain, then come back here tonight with Jack and the four of us will go out and have some dinner, and a few drinks to unwind.'

Mike and Chris agreed and they finished their drinks.

They bid farewell to Lyndon and left his apartment to go back to their own houses and get ready for the upcoming trip.

Five minutes after Mike and Chris had left his apartment, Lyndon decided to go and see his parents at one of their jewellery shops in the City Centre, and have lunch with them. He picked up his keys from the coffee table and put his phone in his pocket and walked out of his apartment towards the lift. He rode the lift down to the ground floor and straightened his hair in the mirror at the back of the lift before he stepped out in to the lobby. He nodded to the guard who was sat behind a desk looking at security monitors, one of the inclusive features of his apartment building. As he stepped outside, the sun had finally broken through the clouds and it was now a warm day, so Lyndon decided he would walk to his parents' shop.

As he walked along the old cobbles on the riverside and looked ahead at the Royal Liver Building, he thought to himself what a good decision it had been to move back to Liverpool five years ago.

The internet had changed the game massively over the years, even more so over the last ten years with the advent of smartphones and tablets enabling anybody anywhere to access the internet for whatever reason they wished at the touch of a screen, wired internet became a thing of the past for the average person. No longer did they have to be in Dubai, Bangkok or Shanghai looking for investors, with a good webpage that showed at the top of a search engine list, the investors started coming to them, the only time face to face meetings happened was to complete the formalities. Lyndon crossed the busy six lane road on the waterfront and headed towards the main shopping area. As he walked along the pavement past people hurrying about their day, he smiled to himself as he thought about Javier Ramos, and the way he had wanted face to face meetings, he was obviously a traditionalist and liked things to be done properly. This is why Jack had produced a presentation to show Ramos in Seville, and had a prospectus made for when Mike and Chris first met him in Paris. To Lyndon Powell, Javier Ramos was the type of person he disliked, somebody that climbs to the top and throws people off along the way, not caring about anybody but himself, it was always the little people who suffered when people like him where in a position of power. Lyndon had read about ESPoil and how Javier Ramos had decided to save money, even though profits were at a record high, Ramos was cutting jobs from petrol stations and packers at drilling sites, yet increasing his own wages. This made Lyndon glad that he was meeting him face to face so he could look him in the eye when he took his money. *Arsehole* he thought of Ramos.

As taxis, buses and cars crept slowly along the busy city streets, Lyndon's phone beeped in his pocket, it was a text message and it read *I have booked train tickets for when we arrive in Spain. Shall I book a hire car?* Lyndon typed on his smartphone and replied with.

Good job on the train tickets, not sure about a car, best to get one when we are there if we do need one. Thanks Jack see you tonight for drinks. Lyndon put his phone back in his pocket and walked into the Liverpool ONE area of the city centre, then into his parents shop which, they had moved into not long after Liverpool ONE opened in 2008.

'Morning Son,' his father Richard said to Lyndon. Even though he had lived in England for over forty years he still had a strong South African accent.

51

Hello Dad, how do you and Mum fancy a spot of lunch?'

'Let me just go and get your Mum, then we will head out, how about we try that clubhouse just upstairs on the park?'

'Yes, we shall try it. I have read good things about it.'

Richard came back with Lyndon's mother Anne, the three of them walked along the shopping centre towards the lift to take them to the next level, which was the park where the clubhouse was located. It was a recent addition to Liverpool ONE, it was designed to look like a New England beach house and served classic American food such as ribs, steaks and various fried things. The three of them took a seat outside, and when the waitress came over, they ordered a bottle of South African red wine and three steaks cooked medium. Richard and Anne only drank South African wines, they considered others to be inferior, Lyndon thought the French could give them a run for their money but who was he to argue with his father.

It was his father who spoke first after they had ordered.

'So, son, as you can see my hair is getting greyer by the day, when are you going to stop arsing about in properties and whatever else you do and take over the business?'

Lyndon smiled.

'As it happens Dad that is why I asked you and Mum for lunch. On Sunday I am flying out to Spain to complete a deal, then I will be free to take over the business and put all my effort into it. You can both retire and get the pipe and slippers out as people say.'

Anne smiled. 'Thank you, son, we are so happy this day has come its hard work being a jeweller.'

The waitress brought the wine out with three glasses and filled them up before Lyndon made a toast to his parents' retirement.

'Your Mum and I have decided to retire by the beach, so when you are up and running, we are moving to Cape Town. I will notify my Gold and Diamond contacts in South Africa that you will be taking over so you won't have to worry about that, remember to visit all the stores as often as you can and keep your staff happy.'

'I will take good care of the business don't worry. I will bring Mike, Chris and Jack on board too, they can help me take the business forward and open more stores, I want a R&A Powell Diamond Specialists in every major city in Europe, and eventually the USA and China. But first I am going to open a shop on the Ponte Vecchio in Florence. Even though competition will be fierce our quality will make us stand out from all of the other jewellery shops on the bridge.'

Richard smiled at Anne and looked at Lyndon and said to him.

'I like your ambition Lyndon, and Florence is a great idea. Just remember to hire local staff and pay them a wage they can live on comfortably and not the minimum wage like most jewellers do.'

Lyndon took a sip of his wine and smiled at his mother before answering his father.

'Always Dad, I am a firm believer of look after your staff and your staff will look after you, the minimum wage is a great thing because it stopped people being exploited but it doesn't mean that's what you have to pay people, everybody should be paid properly in my opinion, as you both taught me from a young age, always look after the little people.'

After they had finished their lunch Richard and Anne returned back to the jewellery shop and Lyndon headed back to his apartment, where he decided he would watch some television before getting ready to go out that night.

Wing Commander James Shaw sat staring at Group Captain Bartlett across the desk as if to say *Get on with it*. Eventually the Group Captain emptied the contents of the final envelope.

'Right short and sweet. I will give you this to read yourself, but basically at fourteen hundred hours today, so in just over an hour you will board a Sentinel R1 to Brize Norton where you will then fly to the Falkland Islands. So, finish your drink, go back to the mess and pack a bag of clothes, you will be kitted out in cold weather kit down there, I will personally make sure your car is waiting for you when you get back to the UK, I will also send everything from your room.'

Shaw sat looking at the Station Commander like he had two heads.

'So, what are you saying Sir?' he asked.

'I am saying get your arse out of here and get packed and be on that plane.'

He handed over the papers. Shaw took the papers off him, and read under his breath.

Group Captain Bartlett
Station Commander, RAF Akrotiri

Notice to Move for Wing Commander James Shaw
Officer Commanding Intelligence Wing

Due to recent intelligence received from Argentinian
Forces regarding the Falkland Islands and other
British Territories in the South Atlantic. I hereby
authorise the immediate posting of Wing Commander
James Shaw to Mount Pleasant Airfield, Falkland
Islands. At 1200 Zulu (1400 hours local). He will
depart RAF Akrotiri aboard a Sentinel R1 to RAF
Brize Norton, where he will depart for the Falkland
Islands via Ascension Island. Upon arrival he will
assume command of the Intelligence unit for both the
Royal Air Force Intelligence Wing and the Army
Intelligence Corps.

Yours Faithfully

BT Darwin-Wedgwood
Air Vice Marshal (AVM)
Air Command
RAF High Wycombe

Shaw looked up from the letter.
'Well, I suppose I better go and throw some stuff
together and get on that plane, nothing like last minute.

This is goodbye then Sir. I have enjoyed my time here and thank you.'
Group Captain Bartlett smiled and stood up and held his hand out, James shook it, and Bartlett said.
'It has been a pleasure having you here, you are a damn good officer and best of luck when you get to Waddington for your first Station Commander Post, I am sure you will do well.'
'Thank you, sir.'
Shaw put his beret on his head and saluted the Station Commander, before turning around, leaving the office and heading back towards his own office, after stepping outside of station HQ, he changed his mind and headed towards the officer's mess instead. First, he stopped at a smoking area which was populated by junior ranks laughing and joking whilst enjoying their cigarettes, they looked up and seen Shaw coming towards them, they acted like school children who had just spotted the headmaster, they stopped laughing and joking.
'Hello Sir', they said to Shaw.
'Hello,' he said 'Please carry on, don't stop on my account, you lot look as rough as me, late night, was it?'
'Not really sir,' they replied in unison.
Shaw laughed, and said 'Of course not I am sure you were all home by midnight,' with a smile.
'Yes Sir' they replied laughing; Shaw laughed with them.
I am going to miss it here, why the hell are they sending me to the Falkland Islands at an hour's notice he thought to himself. After he had finished his smoke, he continued walking towards the officer's mess.

Upon arriving at the Officers mess, James Shaw calmly walked past the palm trees outside and strolled in through the main door, he set off at full sprint up the wide staircase taking two steps at a time, when he reached the top, he grabbed the banister and used it to swing himself round and propel himself down the corridor towards his room.

Shaw Fumbled around in his pockets for his keys, he eventually found them, on the third attempt he got the key into the lock and turned it, releasing the tumblers, he pulled the handle down and pushed the door open, he walked through the living area and in to the bedroom. In the way people hurried but didn't do things any quicker, Shaw pulled a Military issue black holdall from under his bed, flung open all the cupboard doors and pulled open the drawers on his chest of drawers without actually putting anything into the bag. Once he composed himself, he stuffed clothes in to the holdall which consisted mostly of chinos, polo shirts and lightweight shirts, his wardrobe suited to the warmer climes of Cyprus more than the winter of the Falkland Islands. After packing his clothes and underwear he reached into the bottom of his wardrobe and pulled out both of the pairs of Clarks desert boots he owned and put them in the bag.

'These will never date, best shoes ever made,' he said out loud.

He was just talking to himself as he was packing, next in was his iPad, charger and his Bluetooth headphones which he placed on the top of his bag as he would be using them for the flight. Shaw stepped into the bathroom and picked up his toothbrush and toothpaste, and put them in his soap bag along with a razor, a pack of blades and some deodorant, he used the soap bag as a divider in the holdall as he picked out two sets of multi terrain camouflage uniforms, his helmet and haversack which contained his respirator. Shaw jumped up and reached his hand to the back of the top shelf of his wardrobe and pulled down two Norwegian fleeces, which fell onto his head. They smelt musty because they had been at the back of the wardrobe since Shaw had first arrived in Cyprus and the need to wear one had never arisen. He pulled them off his head sniffed them in disgust.

'Fuck it I will wash them when I get there,' he said. Throwing them in the bag along with his field jacket, he threw his Apple watch in along with the charger and zipped the bag up, he scanned the room to make sure he had everything he needed, everything else would be packed for him and sent to RAF Waddington waiting for him in the Station Commanders house, which he would be occupying when he got there.

Shit, Mum and Dad Shaw said to himself, as he picked his car keys up from his desk, and grabbed his holdall on the way out of his room locking the door behind him. Putting the car keys and room keys in his top trouser pocket, he pulled his phone out to check the time, it was 1335, he had twenty-five minutes before the plane left. Shaw ran out of the officer's mess doors into the car park, opened his car with the remote fob and threw his bag into the boot, he walked around to the driver's side which was on the right-hand side of the car, he had paid extra for this but didn't mind as it made life a lot easier. The day before he had forgotten to put his screen up in the windscreen as he was in too much of a rush to go out, and now he was paying for it, as soon as he opened the door and leant in to sit down the heat hit him like a blast from a furnace, he put the key in the ignition and the big V8 engine growled to life. Shaw put the A/C on full power and shut the door. As the big American Muscle car rumbled, Shaw was leaning with his back on the glass of the driver's door, he pulled out his phone to call home. After six rings the answer machine kicked in asking the caller to leave a message.

Give yourselves a chance to reach the phone he said in his head.

When the machine beeped Shaw said.

'Hi mum, its James, I have just been told I have to go the Falklands today so I won't be able to holiday with you and Dad, I will try to call you when I arrive.'

The machine cut him off, he put his phone away and got into his car and headed for the terminal at the airfield.

Shaw's Dodge screeched to a halt a few minutes later as he pulled up outside the terminal building, putting the keys in the visor, as was customary in Cyprus, car theft was virtually none existent, especially on a Military base. Shaw stepped out of his car and grabbed his holdall out of the boot, a young enthusiastic SAC came running up to him.

'Sir, I have been instructed to take your car and pack it up to send back to Britain,' he said.

Shaw replied with 'Thank you, be careful with her, the keys are under the visor.'

The SAC climbed into the Dodge.
'Will do Sir.' He started the engine and drove away.
Shaw watched it until he could no longer see the orange
of his car, as it disappeared into the distance, he turned
and headed into for the terminal.
'Wing Commander James Shaw?' A voice called out
from behind a check in desk. Shaw walked over and seen
a Corporal sat behind the desk.
'Yes, that's me.'
The Corporal stood up from his chair and stepped from
behind his desk and asked to check his passport, Shaw
handed it over, and took it back a few seconds later after
the Corporal had checked it.
'Follow me please Sir,' he said.
Shaw followed him out of the building and on to the
Aircraft Servicing Platform, where there was a yellow
Toyota Hilux parked up. They got into the pickup with
Shaw putting his bag in to the cargo area. They set off
and were heading towards the grey Sentinel R1 in the
distance.
The Sentinel R1 is a Bombardier Global express
redesigned for the military, the engines are at the rear of
the plane and the elevators sit atop of the tailfin. Were on
the Global express there would be luxury seats, on the
Sentinel they had been replaced by surveillance
equipment and the windows had been taken out. As they
approached, Shaw could see the door was open and the
steps were down, the Corporal pulled up alongside the
aircraft. Shaw got out and walked to the back of the
pickup, he grabbed his bag and thanked the Corporal for
the lift. He drove off back towards the terminal.

Shaw walked towards the steps, he could hear the humming of the planes APU (Auxiliary Power Unit) above the sound of his boots clanging on the metal steps, when he reached the top and stepped in to the fuselage, he turned left towards the flight deck and pulled the curtain to the side, he could see two men sat at the controls, they were both Flight Lieutenants which he could tell from the rank slides on the shoulders of their flying suits, which were green. *They must have come from Britain this morning* Shaw assumed.

'Afternoon Chaps, James Shaw,' he said holding his right hand out.

Both the pilots turned in their seats and shook his hand.

'Welcome aboard Sir, safety brief is this, in the event of an emergency landing exit through the door you boarded through, toilet is just behind you, number one only please, take a seat at one of the consoles in the back, normal seat belts on here, for take-off and landing you need to face the front, pull the lever at the side of the seat, this will unlock it, and move it to face the front and make sure it is locked into place, when you are all strapped in shout ready and we will set off, other than that sit back relax, sleep if you want, flight time is just over four hours.'

Shaw thanked them both, closed the curtain and grabbed his headphones out of his bag before moving the seat to take off position, he put his headphones on.

'READY,' he shouted to the pilots.

'Roger,' came the reply.

The engines started with a whine before they kicked into life, howling and the vibrations could be felt through the plane as they taxied to the runway. As the Sentinel made the turn on to the runway, the engines made an almighty roar as they had been pushed up to full power, the plane shook and bumped as it sped down the runway, Shaw felt every bump in his seat, the aircraft lifted and a few seconds later left the runway and climbed up to cruising altitude and away from the Island of Cyprus.

FOUR

In Sevilla Este, an eastern suburb of Seville, Spain, Javier Ramos sat on a sun lounger at the side of his figure of eight shaped swimming pool, which gleamed in the sunlight, it was located at the back of his white washed villa, and was surrounded by eight-foot fences topped with barbed wire. Ramos was waiting for a very important phone call; he was extremely tense.

'They should have called thirty minutes ago,' he shouted whilst slamming his fist into the little side table next to him, causing his phone to bounce up off the table and on to the floor. As he reached down to pick it up it suddenly burst into life vibrating and ringing.

Swiping across the screen to answer it, he said.

'Yes, the deal will be completed next week, the steel for the rigs has been ordered and is on the way, for our plan we are going to build low level platforms, which will be ready in about eight months then we will continue and raise the platforms for drilling.'

He listened and replied.

'Yes, the Englishmen have all the permits in place and the permits are connected to the company so when ESPoil buy them out we will keep the company name, as not to attract the attention of the British government, which we cannot allow, not yet anyway.'

He listened again for a minute and replied with.

'I shall contact you when the deal is completed then you can start planning.'

He ended the call and put his phone back onto the table next to his sun lounger, he lay back down and closed his eyes to get some well-earned rest.

FIVE

The Sentinel R1 carrying Wing Commander James Shaw levelled out over the Mediterranean Sea at forty thousand feet. Shaw took off his seat belt, walked to the flight deck and asked for a bottle of water, he was told they were in the fridge just outside the curtain.

'Thanks guys and if you don't mind, I am going to get some sleep in the back.'

The pilot focused on the console in front of him and replied.

'No problem Sir, we will wake you just before we land.'

Shaw walked back to his seat and began adjusting the seat in front of his so that it rotated one hundred and eighty degrees to face him, he sat down in his own chair, pulled his phone out of his pocket and turned it back on. When his phone came on, he connected his Bluetooth headphones to it and put his feet on the seat he had turned around, he slouched down and pressed shuffle music on his phone. The first song that came on was *Losing my religion* by a band called REM.

Losing my marbles, Shaw said to himself.

He still could not comprehend what was happening, just a few hours ago he was sat in his office trying to shake off another hangover, and now he was on a plane heading for the Falkland Islands, where it as winter with a bag full of summer clothes.

Trying to put it all out of his mind, he closed his eyes and started to drift off to sleep. His mind traced back to the beginning of his RAF career seventeen years ago, when he first arrived at RAF Cranwell to begin his RAF Officer training as a fresh-faced Officer Cadet. In his seventeen years of service, he had completed two tours of Iraq, three in Afghanistan, a four-month assignment aboard a Submarine, which after initial reservations he greatly enjoyed and now has the upmost respect for Submariners, and of course his various assignments with Lawrence Sharif of MI6, which had taken them all over the world, and they had been paid well for the work that they did.

The reason they were paid so well for their work was mainly due to their targets being too dangerous to be arrested and potentially released without sufficient evidence, so they needed to be taken out of the equation. These orders usually came from the security services chiefs of staff, and even on occasion the Prime Minister. Shaw's military bosses didn't even know what he was involved with, all they got told was that he had to be in a certain place at a certain time and to leave as soon as possible. Even though he had to terminate people, sometimes with his bare hands (such as happened five years ago in Florence, Italy) he was a relaxed and easy-going man. Shaw's mind drifted to the events in Florence five years earlier, and he recounted what happened in his head.

The civil war in Syria was in full swing, and the refugee crisis was really starting to become a problem, and many of them had made their way to Italy. Among them were terrorists looking to inflict damage in Western Europe. A group of five men who were part of a Middle Eastern terror network had arrived in Italy to seek asylum, this was not granted to them. They had fled a detention centre before they could be deported. They paid cash for an apartment in Florence, and had gotten cash in hand jobs, such as working in the nearby vineyards picking grapes. They caught the attention of MI6 after they communicated with other members of the group in the Middle East using an internet-based messenger service. The plan was for the five of them to cause simultaneous explosions in Milan, Frankfurt, Paris, Brussels and Amsterdam, hitting the main financial centres of central Europe, causing death, disruption and financial meltdown, and bringing the continent to its knees. Shaw and Sharif had been tasked two weeks before they planned to carry out the attacks. On their second day in Florence; Shaw and Sharif were on their way back to the hotel they were staying at, after they had been scouting out the terrorist's safe house, when one of the terrorists spotted Shaw and immediately ran off in the opposite direction. Shaw gave chase through the Palazzo Vecchio, past the replica of Michelangelo's David and past the Uffizi gallery knocking over tourists as they sped through the city on foot. Shaw caught up to him on the packed Ponte Vecchio bridge, he kicked at the back of his legs, sending the terrorist crashing to the ground, the crowd of onlookers gasped in horror. Shaw landed a blow to the back of the head with his elbow, causing the terrorist's head to smash into the floor with such force it killed him instantly. Shaw quickly checked for a pulse, which was not there. He got back onto his feet and pointed at the body on the floor and shouted.

'Pickpocket.'

The crowd clapped and cheered Shaw as he swiftly made his exit back in to the city from the bridge.

 Later that day Shaw and Sharif let themselves into the safe house, and waited for the other four to return home, when they did, they shot all four of them with silenced weapons so as not to attract attention. Job done. They headed to the airport and returned home after another successful mission, and Europe could sleep safely for another night.

The Sentinel R1 hit turbulence and jolted Shaw awake, he took a sip of his water and closed his eyes again. This time his thoughts turned to his love life or the lack of one. Shaw had had relationships over the years, none of which lasted longer than a few months, however he had enjoyed plenty of encounters with the opposite sex. The truth was, he had never had the time for a full relationship and all the energy that went in to them, due to the nature of his job, not to mention his second job which meant he could be called away at a moment's notice, not knowing when he would be back, or if he would come back. At the age of thirty-six he was beginning to actually want a relationship. *Maybe this is something that I will think about when I get back* from *the Falklands, I can look then,* he said to himself.

Shaw still had his looks and had not aged much, a few lines around his eyes mainly from squinting with all the time he had spent in hot and sandy places, his eyes were still icy blue and after spending the last few years in Cyprus his hair was now blonde, but would go back to light brown when he returned to England. As he sat there slouched in his chair, he continued to think about settling down and how he would like to have children. He would have to stop his side line work if he did.

His thoughts then moved on to leaving the RAF in five years, once he hit the twenty-two years' service mark, making him eligible for his pension, which leaving as a Group Captain would be very handsome, and he could get a job in the private sector but didn't have a clue what he would do or even how to write a curriculum vitae.

Shaw was awoken again, this time by his stomach lurching as the plane began its descent, the call came from the cockpit that they were fifteen minutes away from landing. Shaw sat himself up and fastened his seat belt, he then turned his phone off.

Exactly fifteen minutes later the undercarriage came down and Shaw could hear the flaps being adjusted on the wings even though he could not see them, he put his arms on the armrests and held the end of them with his fingers and sat upright preparing for touchdown. A few moments later the Sentinels main wheels touched the runway before the nose wheel touched, causing James to jolt forward in his seat but the seatbelt restrained him. The pilot reversed the thrust and pressed down on the brakes, slowing the aircraft down with shakes and shudders as the earth regained the aircraft. After taxiing off the runway, it came to a complete stop and the engines began to shut down. Shaw released his seatbelt, and stretched before standing up and grabbing his bag. He headed towards the door, which one of the pilots had just opened.

'Nice sunny day,' Shaw said not expecting the sun at Brize Norton, even though it was spring.

Shaw thanked both pilots before stepping out into the sun and surprising heat. As he stepped down the steps and his eyes adjusted to the light, it became clear that this was not RAF Brize Norton.

In the near distance Shaw could see a Mcdonalds sign high up on a pole, and the sea to his left, this was a place he had never been before but he knew exactly where he was, even before he turned around. As he took a step forward Shaw turned around to see the Rock of Gibraltar protruding from the ground of the British Overseas Territory.

Walking toward him was Squadron Leader Will Ramsey, Shaws friend from the start of their careers seventeen year ago. In his hand he had a memo envelope, he reached Shaw and they both exchanged pleasantries.

'Will, what is going on?'

'I honestly don't know, about twenty minutes ago my corporal brought this into my office and said "I have been told to give these to you Sir and that a Sentinel will be landing in twenty minutes, and you are to go and meet the passenger" oh and get changed out of uniform.'

'Did the corporal say that to you or are you saying it to

me?'

'To you, hurry, no time for joking around.'

Shaw walked back up the steps, and stepped out five minutes later in a navy-blue Lacoste polo- shirt, beige chinos and a pair of Clarks desert boots.

'You couldn't look more English if you tried,' Will said with a hint of sarcasm in his tone.

Shaw scowled at Will and took the envelope off him, he reached inside, and pulled out a slip of paper along with a set of car keys. The slip of paper read *Silver SEAT Leon in the McDonald's car park in La Linea, walk straight ahead after the border.*

'What is it?' Will Ramsey asked.

Shaw smiled, shook his head and said.

'Sharif, it has to be, well I suppose I better go find out. I will call you soon and we will go for a drink, you can show me the delights of Gibraltar.'

'No problem see you soon.'

They shook hands and Shaw set off on foot for the border with his holdall slung over his left shoulder.

After passing through passport control without delay, Shaw headed for the Mcdonalds car park where he found the silver SEAT Leon reverse parked in a parking bay, he got the keys out of the envelope and used the remote fob to unlock the car. He walked over to the vehicle, looked through the front passenger window, and after seeing nothing of interest, he opened the boot and put his holdall in and closed it again.

Having not eaten all day he decided to get some food, he hustled in to the air conditioned cool of the Mcdonalds.

After getting his order of two double cheeseburgers and two large Fanta's he spotted Lawrence Sharif, who was sitting at the rear of the restaurant. Shaw sauntered over to him.

'I knew you would come in here, especially after a night on the booze,' Lawrence said.

'Funny looking Falkland Islands this, as soon as I walked down those steps and realised where I was, I knew you had to be involved somehow, you're a menace, what is all this about anyway?' Shaw replied as he took a seat at Lawrence's table.

'Not here and don't sit down, we need to get going, you can eat that on the way, oh congratulations on your promotion, well done.'

'Thank you, how do you know about that, in fact don't answer. Am I right in assuming it was you or your people at least that arranged my detachment to the Falklands?' Shaw and Sharif got up from the table and headed outside, towards the SEAT.

Lawrence got in to the driver's side and James got in the front passenger side, he put his seatbelt on and tucked in to one of his burgers.

'We needed it to look as though you are as far away from this as possible, this is top secret, what I am about to tell you is for your ears only, but first check your bank account,' Lawrence said.

Shaw pulled out his phone and logged onto his online banking, his balance showed *£364,000,* whilst he had been in the air an unknown account had deposited *£100,000* into his account.

'Very nice, who is it off, and why now, we normally get

paid at the end of our jobs not before?'

'That's right we do, and normally we pay for our hotels, cars and whatever else we need on a government credit card, not this time though, we are on our own, no clean up squads, no assistance on call if we need it, it is just me and you. You owe me two hundred euros for the car as well, I hired it for the week,' Sharif said.

'I will pay for the hotel then we are all square, what about weapons, assuming we need them?'

'In the spare wheel compartment are two Beretta 9MM's with spare magazines, suppressors and enough rounds to last a month, they let me bring those in a diplomatic bag but that's it, we are on our own.'

'Okay that's good hopefully we won't need to use them, but what is the job where is it and why all the secrecy?'

'Ever been to Seville or Sevilla as they call it here?' Sharif asked.

'Yes, twice, the last time was about ten years ago, a nice place from what I can remember, what I can also remember is this car will be no good there we will have to park outside the old town,' Shaw replied.

Lawrence Sharif started the car, pulled out of the Mcdonalds car park and headed to the main road, which would take them to the motorway towards Seville.

'Right, I will drive to Jerez where we will stop for a break, then you can take us to Seville,' Lawrence said.

'Okay sounds good to me. I will find us a hotel whilst you drive and finally get around to telling me what this is about.'

Lawrence was checking his mirrors every few seconds like a new driver, even though he had driven abroad many times, driving on the wrong side of the road still made him nervous.

'I will get to that in a minute, I have also been promoted, so it seems that this will be our last job together,' Lawrence said whilst keeping his eyes on the road and checking his mirrors.

'Congratulations, promoted to what?'

'Deputy Director of Operations.'

'Well done, have you skipped a few rungs on the ladder there, and does it mean you will be flying a desk like me when I get back to Britain?'

'Pretty much. I will be in charge of the new us, whoever that will be, the Director wanted me in there due to my "expertise in the field" he said. So, he decides to put me behind a desk, where is the logic in that,' Sharif said.

'Crazy if you ask me, like myself with the Station commander in Akrotiri, he said they want an Intelligence officer as Station Commander at RAF Waddington, I don't know why but who am I to complain.'

Lawrence and James made it on to the motorway and the Spanish countryside sped past them in a blur.

'Have a drink, you should present one of those talent shows they keep churning out on a Saturday night,' Shaw said handing one of his drinks to Lawrence.

'What do you mean?'

'The way you are keeping me in suspense about what we are doing here, I have been waiting about twenty minutes, now just tell me you tool,' Shaw said in jest.

'I will go through the details when we arrive but a brief overview should keep you happy for now, have you heard of

ESPoil?'

'Yeah, I seen one their stations by that Mcdonalds in La Linea and we passed one about two minutes ago. What about them?'

'Well do you know where their CEO is from?' Lawrence asked.

'Spain by any chance, just get on with it, you talk I will listen.'

'He is Argentinian, and we have as I am sure you are aware been monitoring the Argentinians communications.'

'Really, that's outrageous,' Shaw interjected.

'As I was saying, he has links to the government and they are working together on a plan to invade the Falklands again. A group of conmen who are based in Liverpool have become involved, however they don't know what they are getting into, they just think they are conning some person who in their eyes deserves it. after some of the things this Javier Ramos has done, that's the CEO of ESPoil in case you are wondering who it is.'

'Basically, a group of conmen are going to cause another conflict between ourselves and Argentina, and they don't have a clue about any of it, what is it they are selling anyway?' Shaw asked.

He finished his second burger and balled the wrapper up, he put it in the glove box, where he found a map which he pulled out and opened up to look at, it was a road map of Andalucia.

'They have created an oil company and are selling it to Javier Ramos and ESPoil, we only became aware of this a few weeks ago after MI5 had notified us that the conmen had made contact with Mr Ramos, they then informed me that they were heading to Seville to finalise the deal, and here we are on our way to Seville.'

'I am assuming we are to stop this deal happening by erasing this Mr Ramos before they meet.'

Lawrence focused on the road ahead as the Spanish countryside raced by, he turned and looked at James.

'Not necessarily, I was thinking let the deal happen, the Englishmen get the money, pay their taxes, and we take Ramos out before he can cause any damage.'

The car rocked and bumped with the road and passed a sign which indicated Jerez de la Frontera was fifty kilometres away. Shaw stayed quiet and scrolled through his phone.

'I have found us a place to stay, it is in the old town, a hostel with a pool on the roof, shall I book it?'

Lawrence turned and looked at James again.

'Aren't we a bit old for a hostel, wont it be full of backpacking types, we won't get much privacy to work, will we?'

'Sometimes the best place for privacy is when you don't have any, think about it, it will be full of backpackers partying and making noise, we can sit amongst them plan and discuss, and nobody will pay any attention to us, were as in hotels everybody wants to know everybody else's business, this place looks good, I will book us four beds in a four-bed room so we will be able to work in private when we need to.'

James reached into his pocket and pulled his debit card from his wallet and entered the long number into his phone.

'All booked,' he said before pulling two fifty Euro notes from his wallet and saying to Lawrence.

'Here is your car money since I didn't book a hotel, you can get the drinks tonight, how far now to Jerez I need a smoke?'

'About twenty minutes, then you are driving, see if you can put the hostel address in the Sat-Nav, we will check in, then take the car to Hertz at the railway station, then we are on foot or public transport.'

'Put your foot down then, yes we will do that, when I was last there, they had started rolling out a city bike scheme we could use those or hire a scooter each.'

Lawrence laughed and said 'You won't catch me on one of those death traps, they have a good bus network along with a tram and a metro system if we need to move around quickly.'

Lawrence moved across to the outside lane and followed the slip road off the motorway, he slowed the car down and turned in to a service station, he slowly drove through the car park before finding a space and parking the car.

Both men got out of the car and stretched out after being sat down for so long. Shaw lit a cigarette and took a long drag. Lawrence Sharif asked Shaw if he wanted anything from the shop, he asked for a bottle of water and a couple of packets of cigarettes.

Lawrence returned a few minutes later with four bottles of water and a carton of two hundred cigarettes. Shaw lit another cigarette and offered one to Lawrence which he accepted.

'Good thinking on getting a carton, one less thing to do for a few days, when are the guys from Liverpool arriving or don't you know yet?'

'Sunday, we think, they are booked on a flight from Liverpool to Malaga and I wouldn't think they would hang around down there, they will come in by bus or train.'

'Why not by car like us?'

'They haven't booked one and they have no known associates to get one, so we can assume bus or train but most likely the train, what we will do is, one of us go to the bus station and one to the railway station to await their arrival,' Lawrence replied.

Both men got in to the car, this time with Shaw in the driving seat. Shaw started the engine and adjusted the seat as he was taller than Sharif. He put the car in gear and pulled off, as he shifted in to second gear, the car made a grinding noise as Shaw tried to find the right balance with the clutch. Sharif laughed out loud.

'You need to drive proper cars instead of that American monstrosity you drive now.'

'Oh, sorry Mr Ford Mondeo, my name is Lawrence and I drive the most boring car in Britain,' Shaw sniggered.

'Shut up and get back on the motorway.'

Shaw drove up the slip road and past a sign which told him Sevilla was ninety kilometres away, he put his foot down and climbed the cars speed up to eighty miles per hour.

'Shall we start work tomorrow, there is not much point in starting today?'

'I was thinking the same, let's get checked in, get rid of the car and have some drinks, we will stop by Ramos's house tomorrow and we can see what is what, maybe see if we can find out where the deal is going to take place, he hasn't even told the con artists yet,' Sharif replied.

'Keeping his cards close to his chest I see; I am sure we will find out one way or another,' James Shaw said.

SIX

In the South Atlantic; work had already begun on the building of oil platforms at the sites that Jack Reuben had marked as being the best places to start drilling. Floating platforms had been installed, whilst teams worked on constructing permanent structures.

 The British monitored the activity on the platforms and sent out reconnaissance flights twice a day. Even though the sites had permits for drilling, they were concerned with the shipping traffic from Argentina to the drilling sites. However, they had no reason for concern as the workforce was apparently made up of Bolivians and Ecuadorians who made the journey to Argentina, to then be shipped to the drilling sites for work. The workers had even started to wave at the RAF Typhoons that flew past twice daily. The threat of an Argentine invasion, it appeared was once again just talk, as happened at least twice a year.

SEVEN

Javier Ramos had not moved from the sun lounger next to his swimming pool, he was talking excitedly on his mobile phone. His wife appeared in a long black dress, she asked Javier.

'Te gusta mi nuevo vestido' (do you like my new dress?).

Javier Ramos ended his phone call and got up from his sun lounger.

'You do not interrupt me women.'

He struck his wife with the back of his free hand, and pushed her into the pool. As his wife struggled in the water, Javier Ramos walked away, towards the house and out of the side gate, where his Ferrari California was parked. He got into the Italian supercar, turned out of his drive and headed for the city centre.

A little over ten minutes after he had left his house, he arrived outside the Alfonso XIII hotel. After parking his car, he stepped into the hotel lobby and approached the reception desk, where a man and women were sat like they had been waiting all of their lives to help. Javier Ramos asked them if he could book a conference room for the next week, the man said he could and it would cost him one hundred euros, Ramos paid and returned to his car and set off back to his house.

EIGHT

Whilst Javier Ramos was parking his Ferrari back on his driveway, James Shaw and Lawrence Sharif were sat in traffic in the old town on a single lane street. As they inched through the traffic looking for their accommodation, they argued about what to do when they arrived. Shaw wanted to get a shower and have some drinks, whilst Lawrence wanted to plan their strategy and get a feel for the city.

'We have until Tuesday, tonight we unwind, have a few drinks and act like tourists,' Shaw said.

Eventually, Lawrence agreed with James. A few minutes later they arrived at their accommodation, which was on a single lane one-way street. James Shaw put the hazard lights on and they climbed out of the car.

'We will check in, then I will take the car to the train station and head back here.'

'Yes, okay.'

They grabbed their bags and hardware out of the boot of the car.

The reason Shaw had booked a four-bed dorm for the two of them, was to ensure privacy, he knew the idea of a hostel was a good place to hide in plain sight. Where nobody would ask questions of what they were doing, if anybody did ask then they would just say that they are tourists on holiday.

After checking in and putting their bags in the room which had two sets of bunk beds along the walls and a window at the opposite end to the door, Shaw ran back down the stairs to the car and set off for Santa Justa railway station.

Once he had returned the car to the right lot and handed the keys back to the clerk in the office, he went to check out the station in preparation for the arrival of Lyndon Powell and his crew on Sunday. The station's concourse had seating areas, shops, bars, restaurants and a ticket booking hall. The concourse had two front entrances and two from the sides, and a further two sets of doors leading to the platforms, which were on the lower level, accessible by stairs or flat escalators to make it easier for carrying luggage up and down. Shaw thought of three ways to keep eyes on Powell and his people, he assumed that Ramos would also have people in the station. The first place would be old school, he would sit in one of the bars, waiting for them to come up from the platforms. The second would be to sit or stand near the notification boards like a normal passenger keeping watch on his train's status. Third would be a more direct approach, he would accost them on the platform, hopefully before anybody else could.

Shaw didn't hang around for long, he left the station and jumped in to a cab outside the main entrance and asked the driver to take him back to the hostel. He would work his approach out in more detail with Sharif.

Shaw arrived back at the hostel to find his clothes had been folded and put away in a drawer, with his bag placed on the top bunk, but Sharif was not in the room. James left the room and checked the door was locked by jiggling the handle before walking away, he said *hello* to people in the hallway and on the staircase, which wound its way to the top floor, he reached the top of the stairs and stepped out onto the roof terrace, which had seating areas, a gazebo and swimming pool. Located inside and to the right of the staircase was a bar, where Lawrence had come from with a plastic glass of lager in each hand, he handed one to James, and they sat down near a group of American men in their early twenties who were being loud and boisterous.

'I have just had a good look at the station, there shouldn't be any problems, I expect Ramos will have people also watching.'

Lawrence nodded in agreement.

'Yes, we can pretty much guarantee it, how many and who, we do not know. Like I said we are on our own on this. I am going to check out Plaza de Armas bus station tomorrow in case they arrive by bus.'

Shaw pulled his cigarettes out of his pocket and lit one. Lawrence did the same and raised his glass to James who also raised his glass. They stood up and walked over to the swimming pool, and looked across the top of the city, La Giralda the cathedral bell tower was visible in the distance. Looking straight ahead, Lawrence said to

James.

'When you think about it, why are we here? The RAF could simply destroy those rigs that are being built and we would defeat Argentina in full combat. So why send us here to stop this Ramos deal happening, even though they want Powell to get the money as he apparently always pays his tax.'

James also kept looking ahead and replied.

'Strange isn't it, our people think that these rigs are going to be used for an invasion of the Falklands and a group of con men currently have the drilling permits for the area where the rigs are, these men also pay tax on the money they con out of people, you couldn't make this up, even Hollywood would turn that down. Let's forget all that. we will strategize tomorrow, tonight let's drink, smoke and have fun.'

Lawrence smiled in agreement.

Earlier, when James Shaw was dropping off the hire car at Santa Justa station; Lawrence Sharif made a phone call to his counterpart in Direction Generale de la Securite Exterieure or DGSE (The French equivalent of MI6) for assistance if it was required. Peter Bernard the director, and Lawrence are old friends, and Bernard agreed to help when required. When he was in the back of the taxi on his way back to the hostel, James called his brother John Shaw, a Major in the Royal Marines. James asked him if he could fly over and base himself in Triana on the other side of the river to Seville, he said that he would and that he would arrive the day after tomorrow. Shaw and Sharif let the other know what they had done, and they both agreed that they may well need all the help they could get, as they did not know how many people they were up against, or if it would just be Javier Ramos and a handful of goons.

After having a few more beers on the rooftop terrace, James and Lawrence headed along the river and settled on a bar that was just starting to get busy as the hot Andalusian sun was falling below the horizon. The bar was a mix of locals and tourists, who all seemed to be enjoying the ambience of the bar and city in general. Shaw and Sharif were drinking bottles of local beer and chatting to each other, then a group of ladies caught their eyes a few feet away. One in particular caught James's eye. They appeared to be in their early twenties and were either American or Canadian, both had had too many beers to be able to tell the difference. Shaw suggested that they go over, Sharif didn't think it would be a good idea.

'Come on Jim, they will think we are a couple of old sad cases.'
Shaw laughed and replied 'Don't be stupid, come on let's go say hello and stop calling me Jim, I have told you how many times.'
They walked over and introduced themselves to the five girls, who said they were from various parts of the USA. Shaw struck up a conversation with the one who had caught his eye earlier, she had introduced herself as Delinda Saint Germain.
'James Shaw. Delinda, I have not heard that name before it is a lovely name. Did you say Saint Germain?'

'I sure did,' Delinda said.

'Is that like Paris?' James replied but the joke fell on deaf ears.

'No, it is pronounced Saint Germane, not like the French way.'

'Very nice, have you been here long? This bar I mean?' Delinda was tall with light brown hair that reached halfway down her back, blue eyes, not dissimilar to James's eye colour, she had tanned skin and was wearing a pink lipstick, dressed in a black top with a jean jacket and jean shorts.

'What is your accent? Liverpool?'

'Liverpudlian or scouse. I am from Liverpool. I detect southern United States from you, is that right?'

'Yeah, Nashville, Tennessee. Liverpool that is so cool. I was there a few weeks back. Can I ask how old you are?'

'Thirty-Six,' James did not ask Delinda, he was always told never to ask a woman's age, she told him anyway.

'I am twenty-six.'

James nodded and took his cigarettes out of his pocket, he offered one to Delinda, which she accepted.

Delinda and her friends were on a backpacking trip around Europe after graduating from Harvard University. Seville was their last stop, before heading back to the USA from Malaga airport in a weeks' time.

'Are you and your friend here on vacation or are you travelling?' Delinda asked.

'No, just a City-Break to get away from the daily grind. How about yourself?'

'We have been to Italy, France, England, Germany and

now Spain. How long have you been here, you have a very nice tan?' Delinda asked.

Shaw could see no benefit in lying to Delinda so he told her a half-truth instead.

'I have been working in Cyprus for the last few years for the High Commission. What is it you do back home?'

'I have just finished a law degree at Harvard University, I am hoping to go in to commercial or financial law when I get back stateside. What do you do for work in Cyprus? I am not sure where that is?'

'It is an island in the Mediterranean, I work for the High Commission, which is what commonwealth countries have instead of embassies. I work as a trade advisor.'

Delinda laughed and asked. 'Is that like a spy or something?'

'If only it was that exciting.'

James Shaw looked over at Lawrence Sharif who looked to be enjoying himself talking to one of Delinda's friends, Ally Simmonds from Pittsburgh, Pennsylvania.

'My friend Lawrence seems to be getting along well with your friend.'

'They sure look like they are having fun.'

'Where are you going after here?'

'Do you mean tonight or for travels?'

'Both,' James answered.

'I am kinda enjoying myself here with you, and Malaga before our flight home next week,' Delinda replied.

James reached out and held her free hand and kissed Delinda slowly, she put both her arms around his waist and slowly worked her tongue around his, they held the embrace for a few minutes.

'I like it here too,' James answered, smiling at Delinda she returned the smile and kept hold of his hand.

'Would you like a drink?'

'Sure, a Jack Daniels and Coke please.'

'OK, I will be right back.' James said.

James left Delinda and motioned for Lawrence to join him at the bar. James ordered the drinks and turned to Lawrence.

'How is it going with Ally?'

'Yes, cannot complain, she seems like a nice girl. What about you?'

'Yeah, good, I am going to ask her for lunch tomorrow,' Shaw said.

'Just remember to keep your head in the game Jim.'

'Have I ever let you down?' And enough of the Jim.'

'I won't answer that.'

Shaw and Sharif jostled their way through the crowded bar with the drinks back to where the girls were standing waiting for them.

Delinda, Ally and the other three girls were staying in an apartment that they had rented on Air BnB a short walk away from the bar in the Santa Cruz area of the city. Backpacking certainly had changed since Shaw had done it years ago, for him back then it was all about hostels and sandwiches for dinner to save money for drinking, now it was Air BnB and three course meals, well for some people anyway.

Shaw and Delinda shared another kiss, this time without the awkwardness of the first time.

They held each other and looked deep in to each other's eyes.

'Would you like to have lunch with me tomorrow?' James asked nervously. This was the first time that he could recall being nervous around a member of the opposite sex.

'I would love too, thank you.'

They exchanged phone numbers and agreed to text each other the next day. The one thing Shaw had noticed when he first started talking to the girls was that they all had a copy of Rick Steves' Spain guidebook poking out of the top of their handbags. Shaw knew of Rick Steves, he is Americas premier travel writer and his guidebooks are famous.

'Do you mind if I borrow your guidebook until lunch tomorrow, it may help me pick a good place for us to eat?'

'Sure, no problem,' Delinda said. She handed the book over to James.

One of Delinda's friends asked James and Lawrence if they would like to go back to their apartment for a nightcap.

'No thank you, I don't wear them,' James replied.

The ladies laughed and Lawrence smiled.

'Thank you for the offer but we have to be up early, we have booked a time slot for some sights I am afraid,' Lawrence said.

'No problem, I am looking forward to lunch,' Delinda said smiling at James.

Lawrence had asked Ally for a lunch date and she accepted.

Lawrence offered to take a picture of James and Delinda with his phone. He motioned them in to position. The first picture he took completely missed them, instead taking a photo of the other side of the road along with the river bank.

'Sorry about that, let me try again,' he said, and took a picture of the two of them smiling with their arms around each other, he invited the others on and took a selfie of the seven of them.

Delinda and James danced together in the packed bar, patrons had now spilt out on to the street, the atmosphere was buzzing. After dancing for a short while, the group of seven decided to call it a night as they wanted to be fresh in the morning.

Javier Ramos was now at home, his wife had left before he returned from the hotel, maybe she had finally walked away from being a human punch bag every time he lost his temper. Ramos was about to retire for the evening when his phone rang, he answered it on speakerphone.

'Hello sir, there are two British men here, one of them is Royal Air Force, the other we are not sure about, they flagged up when they checked into a backpacker's hostel after their passport details had been entered into the police database.'

Ramos sighed and asked 'What are their intentions? Are they here about our deal or are they on holiday?'

'We are not sure yet but we will tail them tomorrow and see what they are up to, most likely nothing but thought you would like to know.'

Ramos thanked the soldier for letting him know and

asked to be kept updated, he ended the call.
'Brits, I hate them they better not interfere with this deal or it is game over for them,' he said to himself out loud.

James Shaw and Lawrence Sharif hailed two taxis, one to take Delinda, Ally and their friends back to the apartment they were staying in and the other to take them back to the hostel. James and Delinda kissed again. James then bid Delinda good night and said he will arrange lunch for them tomorrow, he climbed in to the back seat of the taxi alongside Lawrence, and both vehicles pulled away from the kerb.
'Nice girls, a good idea to go out Jim.'
James looked at Lawrence and said 'They are indeed, I look forward to lunch tomorrow, are you doing anything with Ally?'
'Yes, we are going to Museo de Bellas Artes de Sevilla then we will grab a spot of lunch Jim.'
James let out a small chuckle and replied.
'Living on the edge as always, and what have I told you about calling me Jim.'
'Sorry Jim, her idea not mine, I am just going to look interested in some paintings and then go for lunch. After which, we have got work to do.'
'I am warning you. OK but first of all let's go for a walk around the old town before we meet our dates. I would like for you to see the Real Alcázar.'
The taxi pulled up outside the hostel, both men went inside and grabbed a beer from the bar before it closed. Eventually they went to bed and after five minutes both were asleep.

NINE

In his Liverpool apartment; Lyndon Powell was fast asleep, that was until his phone vibrated on the bedside table and woke him up.

Who the devil is this he said to himself as he reached over to look at his phone, it was a text from Mike Williams. It read; ***Call me ASAP.***

Lyndon dialled Mikes number and before Mike could say anything he said.

'This better be important, do you know what time it is?'

'Sorry, I have just had a call from our friend Javier Ramos, asking if we have sent two people over to Seville early, obviously we haven't so I told him we haven't, and that we are arriving Sunday.'

Lyndon was more alert now.

'Why would he ask that, he is paranoid, I thought you told him we would be arriving on the Tuesday, oh what does it matter anyway, see you tomorrow, goodnight.'

He ended the call and fell back to sleep after ten minutes of trying to make sense of what Mike had said about people being in Seville ahead of them.

He must be getting nervous as the deal gets closer, just

paranoid. The sooner this is all over the better Lyndon said to himself.

TEN

'Right get up,' Shaw said as he was shaking Lawrence.
'What is the meaning of this, what time is it?' Lawrence asked groggily.
Shaw was already showered and dressed in a white Ralph Lauren polo shirt, white chinos with a brown belt and his Clarks Desert boots, and his sunglasses on his head ready to go out. Lawrence got up and headed for the shower.
'Hurry up.' Shaw shouted after him.
Sharif replied by sticking two fingers up as he walked down the corridor.

Sharif came back from the shower which was down the hall, dressed in a red Ralph Lauren polo shirt, grey chinos and grey Clarks Desert boots. The pair of them set off down the stairs and out of the front door. They turned left and headed towards the cathedral, which was at the centre of the city, and the main reference point for navigation. Sharif's phone made a beeping noise, it was a text message from Peter Bernard at DGSE in Paris.
'Our friends in Paris inform me that the man I took a

picture of last night is part of Argentina's special forces.'
'What picture and what man?' Shaw asked.

'The one I retook of you and Delinda, I noticed this man earlier on, and he hadn't moved all night, it was concerning me so I took a photo of him and sent it to Peter to find out who he is.'

Shaw smiled and said 'You don't miss a trick do you, can we assume he is a friend of Javier Ramos, and that he won't be the only one out here?'

'Yes, we must assume he isn't alone and that he is working for or with Ramos, this could create a problem, not so much for us but for Lyndon Powell and his people when they arrive. We have to seriously work this out before Sunday.'

James Shaw had the guidebook he had borrowed from Delinda open as he walked.

'Yes, instead of observing, then taking Ramos out, we may have to protect Powell and his crew from these Argentinian soldiers, assuming there is more than just one,' he said 'First let's check out the Real Alcazar, a Royal Palace still in use by the Royal Family, and its fabulous gardens, then we will meet our dates for lunch and art galleries.'

Sharif laughed.

'Good job you have got that guidebook, otherwise what would we be doing now?'

'Well, if it was up to you, we would still be in bed hungover, I got it for the maps, they are better than using my phone because they are zoomed in on the old town and the streets are named.'

They carried on walking and entered Avenida de la

Constitution, the main thoroughfare through the city centre, it runs alongside the cathedral, which was lined with shops, cafes and bars.

'Let us get a selfie together with the street behind us,' Sharif said.

He took the photo and looked at his phone for about twenty seconds.

'Can you find somewhere quiet?' Sharif asked.

'Yes, turn left here and up to the top of this street, I spotted him in Plaza Nueva we will go past the cathedral, pick up the pace, then wait for him to pass us.'

Javier Ramos answered his phone, 'Si.'

'Sir, I think they are tourists; I have just followed them, they have a guidebook open and were stopping to take photos of themselves, maybe they are a couple, I don't know but they look like tourists to me,' The soldier said.

'OK thank you, keep a trail on them for another hour, and if nothing happens that suggests otherwise, we must assume they are just tourists, keep me posted, I have to go, my wife has just returned.'

He ended the call and launched in to a tirade against his wife, for walking out on him. She apologised and said she will try to be a good wife from now on, like she had on many occasions. Ramos started beating his wife not long after they had moved to Spain, he had no excuse for it, no childhood trauma or abuse, he was a bully, picking on those weaker than him.

Shaw and Sharif were almost running, they were walking so fast. They quickly stepped into a shop selling tourist souvenir items such as magnets, post cards and a host of other tourist knick-knacks, opposite the La Giralda bell tower. They were looking at stuff in the shop whilst keeping a watchful eye on the street for the man that had been following them. They purchased some postcards from the cashier.

'Watch this,' James said.

He stepped out of the shop in front of the Argentinian special forces soldier, startling him.

'Hello do you speak English?'

'Yes,' the soldier replied.

'Good, I think I am lost. My friend and I are looking for the Real Alcázar, I think we took a wrong turn; can you help?' Shaw asked.

'Yes, walk past La Giralda, follow the cathedral wall and the Alcázar entrance is straight ahead,' the soldier answered.

'Gracias, thank you,' Shaw said.

He and Sharif headed off in the direction the man had explained to them.

'Turista's,' the Argentinian said to himself as he walked off before calling Javier Ramos.

Shaw and Sharif queued up for tickets to enter the Real Alcázar, and Sharif's phone began to chirp.

'OK, I see thank you for letting me know, not yet, we should be OK. I will let you know if things change, thank you again good bye,' he said to Peter Bernard in Paris.

'Now I know why we are on our own for this one,' Sharif said.

'Why, what are the French saying?' Shaw asked.

'The man who has been following us is not alone, there are twenty in total, all assigned to Javier Ramos personally two months ago, they all arrived with diplomatic bags so we must assume that they are armed,' replied Sharif.

Shaw stood in silence for thirty seconds deep in thought. 'MI6 and whoever else knew this too, that is why they sent us alone. So that Argentina and Britain did not play out a battle on the streets of Spain, I am going to give Will Ramsey a call, and see if he can help us out too, we both know him and can trust him, he can bring a car too. Right fuck this, back to the hostel now, we need to work this out.'

Sharif agreed and they jumped into a taxi back to the hostel to save time.

After getting out of the taxi and hustling into the hostel, they asked for some large maps and a pen from the receptionist, which he handed over. They rode the lift to the top floor, grabbed some water from the bar and took their drinks on to the terrace, they spread their maps out on the table. The time was 0930 and Shaw sent a text to Delinda. *Good morning how are you feeling today, still want to meet for lunch, how about we meet at the fountain outside Alfonso XIII hotel at 1300.*

'You might want to cancel your museum plans and just do lunch,' Shaw said to Sharif.

He agreed, and text Ally to rearrange plans.

Shaw's phone beeped first, with a text from Delinda. *Hey I'm good, you mean 1pm right I am sorta getting used to European times, look forward to seeing you*

again.
Yes 1PM see you soon, Shaw replied.
'DGSE are sending me a fix on the location of the twenty men working for Ramos,' Sharif said.
'Good,' Shaw replied with a nod of the head.
James Shaw circled Santa Justa railway station on the map along with San Bernardo station, which was the stop before Santa Justa on the line from Malaga. He also circled Hotel Ayre a hotel adjacent to Santa Justa, Hotel Alfonso XIII, and Triana where he had told his brother to stay, and also where Will Ramsey would stay.
Lawrence Sharif knew when James Shaw had a plan and he asked him.
'OK, what have you got and how much mess?'
Shaw lit a cigarette and placed the pack on top of the map, Lawrence did the same and put his pack next to Shaw's.
'Right then, we can forget about Plaza de Armas. They will arrive by train; I am going to wait for them at Santa Justa, and you will wait in Hotel Ayre's reception for them. First, we need to take care of some of these Argentinians and arm ourselves up, two Beretta M9's won't cut the mustard on this one,' he said. 'I assume that the meeting will take place in the Alfonso XIII Hotel, as it is the perfect setting for handing over fifty million pounds, John and Will could maybe be parked outside, if we need to make a quick getaway for some reason. Which reminds me what are we do to with Ramos?'
'He is expendable, we cannot let him get out of the hotel with those drilling permits. Good plan, what makes you

so sure they are getting the train and staying in Hotel Ayre. And what about the Argentinians, how do we get them alone?' Sharif said.

'Expendable makes things easier; they are getting the train; would you get a coach if you didn't have to. As for Hotel Ayre, they would have booked due to its location next to the station, no credit card use suggests they used a booking site, and will pay on arrival, once I spot them getting off the train, I will rendezvous with you and wait for them to check in, before we have a chat with them. As for the Argentinians, we will start with the one sat in that VW Polo down there,' Shaw said as he pointed over the railings of the roof terrace to the street below.

They looked over the edge of the roof top and could make out a figure sat in a blue VW Polo.

'Let's go, now', Sharif said.

They walked down to the floor below, where their bedroom was located. Shaw opened the door to their dorm, tossed the maps on to one of the lower bunks and collected their Beretta's from the drawer under his bunk. They tucked the pistol's in to the waistband of their trousers, underneath their polo shirts, and walked down the rest of the stairs to the reception area.

They burst outside into the street and were fifty yards from the car which was blocking the same road they had stopped on the day before. They strolled towards the car, splitting up so they would approach on either side of the vehicle. James Shaw approached the driver's side and smiled at the man inside and motioned for him to open his window.

'Hello, you're the man who helped me earlier.'

The soldier looked at Shaw and pressed the button to lower his window. As soon as the window lowered to the halfway point, Shaw punched him full force in the face, causing his nose to break, spraying blood everywhere and leaving him dazed.

Shaw opened the door, dragged him out and kicked him in the stomach, causing the soldier to double over in agony. Shaw slammed the door on his head, and the soldier slumped to the cobbled floor, barely breathing but still alive. Sharif opened the boot and helped Shaw lift him in before closing it.

'I wasn't expecting that,' Sharif said.

'Neither was I. The opportunity just arose when he opened the window, get in,' Shaw said.

Shaw got in behind the wheel and moved the seat back, whilst Sharif got in the passenger side.

'What now?' Sharif asked.

'Park it in an underground car park for now, then we will go on our dates,' Shaw replied.

As he checked his rear-view mirror, he noticed a black holdall on the back.

'What's in the bag?' Shaw asked.

Lawrence reached behind him and pulled the holdall through the gap in between the seats, and unzipped it to find a Steyr AUG assault rifle with 5.56mm rounds, a Browning pistol and 9mm rounds.

Sharif inspected the weapons as James navigated the tight turns of the narrow-cobbled streets. A few minutes later they arrived at an underground car park and Shaw parked up, and took the Browning pistol off Sharif. He stripped it down and told Sharif to bring the bag. They walked over to a pay machine and Shaw inserted sixty euros for twenty-four hours.

'Outrageous the cost of parking here,' he said to nobody in particular.

The machine dispensed his ticket, and he dropped the stripped Browning Pistol in to the bin, he kept the ammunition as it could be used in their Berettas. After placing the ticket in the windscreen, they walked back towards their accommodation to drop the holdall off, and get ready for going out for lunch with Delinda and Ally.

'I managed to pick his phone up, luckily it was unlocked, I have taken the phone numbers of his comrades so we should be able to track them using our iPhones instead of relying on Peter at DGSE,' Sharif said.

'Good work I wouldn't have thought of that,' Shaw said.

'Exactly, that is why you are in the Military, you are the Brawn and I am the Brain,' Sharif replied.

'You are more like Pinky, anyway who came up with the plan for Sunday. Now all I want to do is meet the lovely Delinda for lunch,' Shaw said with a smile.

They got back to the room, and put the holdall along with their Berettas in a drawer under the bed and locked it with a heavy-duty padlock. They freshened themselves up and headed to the roof terrace for a smoke. They were chatting with a young couple from Lincolnshire who were travelling around Spain before they went to University, Shaw told them that he would soon be moving to Lincoln for work.

'It's time to go Jim,' Sharif said.

Shaw looked at his watch, they had been talking to the

young couple for almost two hours. Shaw apologised to the couple.

'We have dates, hopefully we will see you later.'

'Or hopefully not,' The man replied with a wink.

His partner gave him a disapproving look but Shaw smiled and headed off with Lawrence. Shaw's phone pinged in his pocket; it was a text from Will Ramsey it read.

I am at Jerez just about to get back on the road, I will call when I arrive.

'Good, Will is on his way, he is just about to leave Jerez, and John will arrive tomorrow just in time for Powell and his crew on Sunday,' Shaw said to Sharif.

'Excellent in the meantime we need to neutralise as many of these Argentinians as possible without affecting the deal next week,' replied Sharif.

ELEVEN

In the underground car park where Shaw had left the VW Polo, the Argentinian soldier they had put in to the boot took his last breath and passed away. The combination of a broken nose, the heat and having his head smashed against a car door, had taken its toll on his body, and it finally gave up the fight to stay alive.

Lawrence Sharif had thrown the Argentinians phone into a bin on his way to the roof terrace, it had been called multiple times by Javier Ramos.
 Another of the special force's soldiers found its location on a tracking app, he and Ramos concluded he was still at his post, and maybe had turned his phone on to silent mode. Even though Ramos thought nothing of it, he still sent another soldier to patrol the area, to check everything was in order.

Fifteen minutes later; another Blue VW Polo drove past the location of the mobile phone three times, the driver could not see any sign of his comrades' car, he called Javier Ramos from his mobile.
 'Sir, no sign of his car but his phone is still saying it is here what should I do?'

'Can you follow the phone to an exact location.'
'Yes, I can do that,' said the soldier.
He entered the hostel where Shaw and Sharif were staying and walked upstairs, following the signal of the mobile phone. He stopped and could see its light in a rubbish bin as Javier Ramos was calling it, the soldier reached in and answered the phone to Ramos.
'Sir, the phone was in a bin, there is no sign of Juan, maybe these men are not tourists after all.'
'Try and find those sons of bitches and bring them to me, alive,' Ramos said.
'OK, Sir I will find them and bring them in.'

It was too late, Shaw and Sharif had found him first, as the soldier turned around, Shaw reached into the small of the man's back and took out his Browning Pistol and asked.
'Do you speak English?'
The soldier said nothing, and went to grab Shaw but Shaw was too quick for him, he punched him in the chest, knocking the wind out of him and causing him to double over in pain. Shaw and Sharif took hold of an arm each and dragged the soldier down the stairs towards the reception area. The man behind the desk seen them and shouted.
'I am going to call the police.'
'Put him in the car and I will speak to our friend here,' Sharif said to Shaw.
Shaw dragged the soldier out to his car and struggled to put him in the boot, after fishing the keys out of his pocket, Shaw punched him in the stomach to stop him

fighting back and grabbed the phone out of his pocket, before slamming the boot shut on him.

Sharif explained to the man behind the desk that this was an important matter and the police need not get involved. He promised the man five hundred euros when he returned later, he seemed more than happy with that, and said to Sharif if you need anything at all just ask. Sharif went out to Shaw in the VW Polo. This time they decided to leave the car on a street a couple of streets away with the soldier still in the boot.

Shaw put the soldier's phone in his back pocket, and he and Sharif headed off to meet Delinda and Ally. Sharif was meeting Ally in a restaurant alongside the river, he bid Shaw farewell, telling him to keep an eye out and to let the other know if they find anything suspicious, or see any more Argentinian soldiers following them.

TWELVE

James Shaw being the cautious type, was slumped on a bench looking at his phone near to the Puerto de Jerez metro station, where he had a full view of the fountain in the centre of the plaza and the six streets leading up to it. Shaw could see Delinda approaching from the Avenida de la Constitution end of the plaza, she was dressed in a white vest top along with pink denim shorts and black gladiator type sandals, what caught Shaw's eye though was not her long toned legs but the bum bag or fanny pack as Americans call them, she was wearing around her waist.

Who wears one of those these days? he asked himself. He looked at his watch it was 1257, he started walking the hundred yards to where Delinda was waiting for him at the fountain.

Shaw said 'Hello, how do you do?' And kissed Delinda on the cheek, which she returned.

'Hey James, so glad you made it. How has your day been so far?' Delinda asked.

'Quite busy actually. How about you, have you done much?'

'We got some breakfast at McDonalds, then just sat

around the pool at our apartment.'
'I skipped breakfast, early start, shall we get lunch?'
'Sure,' Delinda said.
They dawdled towards the restaurants and bars on Calle
San Fernando, which was home to the Alfonso XIII hotel
and the University of Sevilla on their right-hand side,
along the left side were eateries and bars with tables and
chairs outside. They chose a place that had a chalkboard
specials menu and was occupied by locals, they sat down
at a table. Less than thirty seconds later a waiter came
over and handed a menu to each of them, he took a
drinks order, James ordered a large Cruzcampo, Seville's
local brew and Delinda ordered the same as her date.

The waiter brought out their drinks and took an order of
Paella, Jamon, tortilla patata and patatas bravas.
'Are you really from Liverpool?' Delinda asked.
'Yes, why would I make that up', James replied.
'Oh, I don't know maybe to impress me.'
James had a sip of his beer and looked into Delinda's
eyes with intrigue.
'Interesting, and why would that impress you?' he asked
with a smile.
'Because it's so cool. The Beatles are from there, they
are like the best band ever and my family are huge
Liverpool fans, I was just there a few weeks back. I went
to Anfield for the first time, my pop was so proud, and
we beat Arsenal three zip, it was awesome.'
James smiled at her and could not help looking into her
beautiful blue eyes.
'I watched that game, we played well, has your dad been

to Anfield?'
'Yes, many times,' Delinda answered.
'I remember now you mentioning it, I didn't really take much notice, I am sorry.'
'Don't apologise, it was very loud in that bar.'
James nodded.
'What is Nashville like, will you be living there when you go into Law, it was Law wasn't it?'
'No, Nashville is great, but I have applied to Law firms all over the states mostly in New York City and Chicago.'
'I see, well I hope you get what you want. What other things are you interested in apart from music and football?'
'Reading, travel and cycling but that is mainly to stay fit, I am not a fan of the gym'
'Me neither, I cycle quite a lot myself. What do you like to read?'
'Anything really, I like thrillers and horror. Do you like reading?'
'Yes, I have just finished the latest Jack Reacher thriller, I love him.'
'Oh my, so do I. Lee Child is a great writer. Have you travelled much yourself?'
'Here and there, I actually came here around ten years ago, I have been to the US a handful of times too.'
'Has it changed much since you were last here?'
'Not really, the tram is new, but apart from that it is still as charming as it was. Even more so this time,' Shaw said with a smile.
'Where did you go in the US and what for?'

'Work and holiday, I went to Pittsburgh, Chicago and Detroit for the Superbowl in 2006 to watch the Steelers, the opportunity arose so I had to take it. I have also been to Las Vegas. Have you seen much of the US yourself?'

'Steelers fan huh, I don't really follow football, my Pop is a Packers fan but Liverpool take priority over them. Mom doesn't really get sports,' Delinda said. 'We travelled around some when I was little. Obviously being at Harvard I have seen Boston and most of New England, New York City and Florida. We vacationed in Europe too.'

'And now you are here without your parents, is it liberating?' Shaw asked.

'For sure, I can do things at my own pace, instead of being dragged around museums bored. What was it you do again I can't remember, but I remember you saying you live in Cyprus, where is that?'

'It is an Island in the Mediterranean, the gateway to the Middle East. I am an officer in the Royal Air Force, currently awaiting to return to the UK for my new post.' Delinda smiled at him and flicked her hair back, even though it had not moved out of place.

'What is your new post? What made you and your friend Lawrence come here for vacation?'

James stroked his chin before answering.

'My new post is the station commander for an Air Force base in Lincolnshire, as for why are we here? It is a long story that hopefully I will tell you one day if we see each other again.'

'I would like to see you again; would you like to see me again?' Delinda asked.

'Most definitely, this has been the best date I have had, not that I go on many dates,' James said getting flustered. 'I am sure you go on plenty of dates.'

He was saved by the waiter bringing their food to the table. James and Delinda tucked in to the various dishes that they had ordered. As they sat eating, drinking and laughing James's phone was ringing in his pocket.

'Excuse me,' he said to Delinda before answering, it was Will Ramsey.

'Hello Sir, I have just arrived and checked in to my hotel, let me know when you need me.'

'Ok Will thank you again, go and enjoy yourself, speak soon.'

James hung up and had a puzzled look upon his face.

'Sorry, I have to make a quick call then I am all yours.'

He dialled Lawrence's number who answered after five rings.

'Will just called, he has just arrived and checked in to his hotel, he is standing by.'

'Good news, I will speak with you later enjoy your date.'

'You too,' Shaw said and hung up.

'Sorry about that, now were where we?'

'You were about to tell me what you are really doing here, coz you sure ain't on no vacation.'

Her southern accent really came out as she said it, which James smiled at; he had a thing for the southern United States accent on women.

'OK, Lawrence and I have been sent here to ensure that a sensitive business deal doesn't happen.'

'I see, do you often do this type of work?' She asked.

'No, this is the first time I have done anything like this.

It's a nice change from flying a desk,' he lied.

They each took a sip of beer and said nothing for a minute. He had to say something to rescue the date. 'What has been your favourite place so far then?' Delinda thought for a few seconds, James looked at her in a way he could not remember looking at a woman before. Delinda stirred him from his day dreaming as she answered.
'Umm, Florence, Italy was awesome and Paris too, but I really like it here it's so charming and beautiful, and I met you', she said with a smile.
Shaw laughed and asked 'So it doesn't bother you that I am ten years older than you are?'
She looked at him the same way he had just looked at her.
'Of course not, why would it? You don't look thirty-six anyway.'
'Thanks,' He replied.

At the tram station on Calle San Fernando, adjacent to where James and Delinda where sat, was another of Javier Ramos's Argentine soldiers who was keeping a close eye on James Shaw and Delinda Saint Germain. Shaw noticed him as soon as the pair sat down at their table earlier. Six trams had passed and the man had not got on any of them. Shaw planned on leaving him where he was, as he did not want to cause a scene in such a public place and more importantly in front of Delinda.

James excused himself, left the table and walked inside the restaurant, firstly he used the toilets then the cigarette machine. After he retrieved his cigarettes from the machine, he dialled Lawrence's number who answered after about a minute.

'How is your lunch? I surmise that you are aware you have company?'

'Yes, we are at a place on the riverbank, and he is just sat on a bench about fifty yards away, not very good, are they?' Lawrence replied.

James laughed 'No terrible, they aren't even half competent, we need to address them before Tuesday ideally, incompetent or not they will still cause us problems.'

'Agreed. We will meet with Will and your brother tomorrow when he arrives.'

'Yes, see you back at the room later' Shaw said, and ended the call before he stepped back out into the heat. The restaurants in Seville have a spray system to cool the patrons who sit outside, it was needed on a day like today with the mercury reaching thirty-eight degrees. James cooled himself off before sitting back down.

James and Delinda finished their food, and asked for and paid the bill. They left the restaurant and strolled hand in hand past the Puerta de Jerez fountain where James had waited earlier and towards the riverbank to meet with Lawrence Sharif and Ally Simmons.

The Police had arrived on a street a few blocks away from where James and Lawrence where staying. They were responding to a call about shouting coming from the boot of a blue VW Polo. Two officers approached the car, they could hear muted screams coming from the rear of the car. One of the officers smashed the back window with his truncheon and lifted the parcel shelf to reveal a man cramped in to the small space. The police officers helped the man out of the car and asked him who did this to him. The man responded by saying he did not know but there were six of them and it just happened so fast he did not get a good look at any of them. The police said they would look into it and be in touch. They got back in to their patrol car and drove away from the scene, they would not look into what happened, there was no point in chasing a lost cause. The soldier knew this and was glad they wouldn't be looking in to it as he wanted to get revenge on Shaw and Sharif himself. He looked for a taxi to take him back to Javier Ramos's house, as James Shaw had dropped the car keys down a grid.

James stopped and turned to look at Delinda.
'Thank you for a lovely afternoon,' he said.
'No, thank you,' she replied and kissed James, he put his arms around her, they embraced for a full minute before letting go and smiling at each other.
'I just have to make a quick phone call,' James said apologetically and walked to a nearby payphone, he put his hand in his pocket and pulled out a handful of change, he picked out all the one and two Euro coins, and inserted ten euros worth into the coin slot, he dialled a number from memory.
A female voice answered 'MOD operator.'
Shaw asked the female 'Can I have a secure line to Major John Shaw, Royal Marine training centre Lympstone

please?'

Shaw heard keys being typed, then the voice asked 'Who is calling please?'

'Wing Commander James Shaw, Royal Air Force Intelligence,' he heard more keys being typed then he heard a click and then a dial tone. After three rings he got an automated voice saying *This line is secure* then John Shaw answered.

'Major Shaw.'

'John its Jay,' James Shaw said.

'What's with the secure line.' John asked.

'Things have changed, not safe on the mobile, if I call you on it, assume we are being listened to. What time are you arriving here tomorrow?' James asked.

'Flight lands about fourteen hundred, I should be at the hotel for fifteen hundred,' John answered.

'Change of plan, after this phone call get on the road to Birmingham, a flight leaves at five this evening, pay cash, no cards. Get a taxi or bus to Santa Justa train station when you get to Seville, I will meet you there,' said James.

'OK, you will tell me what's going on when I get there I suppose.'

'Exactly, now go, I will see you tonight.'

With that James ended the call and walked back to Delinda, and took her hand again as they carried on their way to meet with Lawrence and Ally.

After crossing the main road that runs alongside the Guadalquivir River, James and Delinda met with Lawrence and Ally at a riverside restaurant. They had just settled the bill and were ready to leave. The four of them sauntered along the riverbank with the famous Torre del Oro behind them. Delinda and Ally chatted to each other a few paces in front of James and Lawrence, James took the phone he had taken off the second Argentine soldier from his rear pocket and dropped it into the calm Guadalquivir.

'John is arriving tonight, I am going to meet him at Santa Justa, he is staying at Hotel Ayre, where Powell and his chaps will be staying when they arrive Sunday.' Lawrence asked 'Why the change of plan?'

'We need to turn our phones off and get new ones. Ramos has Will, or his men do anyway,' Shaw answered.

'What makes you think that. If that's the case we need to get him back, what is their angle as they haven't let us know or anything?'

'Well, that's why John is coming in early, I called secure to tell him the change of plan. Will called me Sir, which he never has done, he knew I would pick up on it. We just need to find out where he is being held,' he said. 'Ramos and his men will be waiting for John tomorrow, so that will give us the upper hand, hopefully they will crack and tell us where Will is. Mistakes coming back to haunt us Lawrence, we should have left that solider alone at the hostel, plus we have got two goons about a hundred yards behind us.'

'Yes, that is a problem, twenty to start with, two down. That in my eyes leaves nine active and nine resting, I surmise it would have taken five or six to take Will, so we can expect a similar number for John tomorrow, we need more firepower, we need these goons to take us to their car, hopefully they have the same weapons as the first one we took out.'

'What about the ladies?' Shaw asked.

'We must assume they are in danger too, hopefully we can get these two somewhere quiet and relieve them of their side arms, the one rifle will be enough, I don't want to use that ideally, let's talk with our dates we can sort this later,' Sharif said.

Shaw and Sharif hurried to catch up with Delinda and Ally.

'How did you enjoy your lunch?' Shaw asked Ally.

'It was very nice; your friend is a real gentleman,' She replied.

' He is indeed.'

'Did you enjoy your lunch?'

'I did, very much so, thank you for asking.'

Delinda took hold of James's hand as they wandered along the riverbank which was full of walkers and cyclists enjoying the afternoon sun, as the city carried on about its business above.

In Barrio Santa Cruz, the old Jewish quarter with its winding narrow lanes and orange trees, another Argentine special forces soldier was on point outside of Delinda and her friends' apartment, he had been sent there thirty minutes ago after Delinda and Ally had been spotted with Shaw and Sharif. The man had called in to base and said that nobody had arrived or departed the building since he had arrived, he was told to stay where he was and await further instructions, which he did.

James and Delinda dropped back a couple of paces from Sharif and Ally as they stopped to get a photo together with Calle Betis on the opposite riverbank in the background.

'I am sorry that I have to work.' Shaw said. 'I would like to spend more time with you, get to know you better.'

Delinda squeezed his hand. 'I would like to get to know you some more too. Can I help at all?'

'No thank you, we will be fine. Be careful though as the men about one hundred yards behind us are following us.'

Delinda gasped in horror. 'Why are they following us and who are they?'

'Just a game we play, they follow us and we follow them, no harm, nobody gets hurt, they are glorified body guards, nothing to worry about. Where are your friends, are they out?'

'No, they took a trip to Grenada and they will be staying for a couple of days so it is just me and Ally in the apartment,' she said to James with a seductive smile.

'I hope your meeting me hasn't stopped you going to Grenada?'

'No not at all I am glad I stayed. I have had an awesome day with such a handsome man from Liverpool. Would you like to come back to our apartment, no nightcaps,' she said with a giggle, remembering his joke from the night before.

'That would be great, first we need to get some stuff from our hostel and I have to meet my brother later but then I am all yours.'

'I was hoping you would say that. Your brother, is he working too or vacation?'

'Work I am afraid,' he replied.

James and Delinda scurried to catch up to Ally and Lawrence who were chatting to each other oblivious to the world around them, as Sharif stepped in to the path of an oncoming bicycle and nearly got ran over.

The four of them took the next set of stairs back up to street level at Puente de Isabell II. James spotted a taxi with its for hire light on and flagged it down.

'Go back to the apartment, we will be with you shortly,' Shaw said to Ally and Delinda.

'Are you going to be alright?' Delinda asked.

'Of course, just some work stuff we need to take care of we won't be long.'

Ally looked at Sharif with concern but he waved her away.

'See you soon,' Sharif said.

The taxi pulled away from the kerb and merged in to the traffic.

As the taxi drove out of sight, Sharif said to Shaw 'Ready?'

'Let's do this.'

They sped back down the stairs to confront the Argentines, they dodged people who were strolling along the river enjoying the peaceful ambience, as they got closer panicked looks spread across the faces of the Argentinians, panic turned to pain as they were each hit in the face with a fist at full speed, sending them tumbling to the cobbled ground unconscious.

Shaw and Sharif carried on running until they reached the next set of steps up to the main road, which they breathlessly ran up and managed to stop a taxi. They got into the taxi struggling for breath and told the driver where they wanted to go.

'This is a monumental farce, supervise the deal the orders were, and here we are with four Argentine special forces soldiers beaten up, one of them possibly dead, one of our own possibly kidnapped or worse, have you tried to call Will since you last spoke to him?'

'Phones switched off,' Shaw answered.

'Not to mention the girls are now caught up in this, if this deal doesn't happen you will be Group Captain of a stationary cupboard never mind a flying station and I will be sent to a research station on Antartica.'

'Not looking good, is it?' James said.

'But it's us, we always get the job done in the end and we have had some pretty big setbacks, once John gets here, we can sort a few of those goons out, then go and get Will, then hopefully we can oversee this deal, if not then we are done for but what can you do, they put us in this position knowing full well what we were up against?' Sharif said just as the taxi pulled up at the hostel.

James asked the driver if he could wait for five minutes as they were just grabbing some bags then they would be back. The two of them ran up the stairs and into their room, Shaw grabbed the bag with the weapons and ammunition in along with his black holdall, after two minutes they closed the door and ran back down to the waiting taxi, they clambered in to the back of the taxi with the bags. James text Delinda for the address of her apartment, she texted back a few seconds later, and James told the driver the address in Barrio Santa Cruz. In a few hours' time, John Shaw would be boarding his flight at Birmingham, and would be landing around eight thirty local time. James would expect to meet him at Santa Justa around nine o'clock.

THIRTEEN

John Shaw stared out of the window on the back row of a Ryanair Boeing 737-800. He was all twisted, as the legroom was not enough to accommodate his six feet three inches frame. He was taller than James, had blonder hair but instead of the icy blue eyes his were a dull blue colour. The aeroplane was flying over Madrid and had begun its descent towards Andalucia.

At ground level in Seville, James Shaw was aware that two men were following him, both of which were dressed in the same combat trousers, long sleeve t-shirts, fishing vest and boots, as the others he and Lawrence Sharif had encountered.

James walked out of the Barrio Santa Cruz area after leaving Delinda and Ally's apartment. He powered past the Cathedral and the entrance to the Real Alcázar, where he had been earlier in the day. As he marched past the General Archive of the Indies, James picked up the pace in to more of a power walk. As he approached the Puerta Jerez Metro station he picked the pace up again to a slow jog and hurried to the entrance, the Argentines quickened the pace too.

Shaw entered the metro station, he ran and jumped on to

the escalator, taking two steps at a time, taking care as not to lose his footing, as he reached the bottom the Argentines were at the top and running down after him, also two steps at a time. James sprinted through the ticket concourse, his crepe soles gripping the polished floor the best they could, and he vaulted the ticket barrier; he then ran down the next set of escalators to the platforms.

The passengers are protected from the track by a glass partition, which opened when the train arrived and the doors were lined up. Shaw waited on the platform amongst a crowd of people. The Argentines had arrived on the platform a few yards away. They both looked at Shaw, he did not look back but he knew that they were watching him. Ten seconds later the air turned cold and the noise of the metro train approaching the station got louder as it screeched into the platform area, and came to a stop with the train doors aligned with the doors on the platform.

Eventually they opened, and James stepped onto the train and stood up by the doors. The Argentines boarded further down but started moving toward James's end of the train. They were forcing their way along the packed carriage towards Shaw. He looked at them as they were getting closer and closer. Shaw counted to five in his head. As they squeezed past passengers in the centre of two sets of doors, Shaw made his move.

He jumped off the train back on to the platform as the doors began to close. The train moved off and James smiled and waved at the soldiers who were now stuck on the train heading to the other side of the river.

On the opposite platform; the train James actually wanted to get on, approached the platform. He stepped on, found a seat and took a deep breath. The train headed off towards San Bernardo, where he would get off a couple of minutes later.

James got off the Metro at San Bernardo, again vaulting the barrier and ran up the escalator to street level. The sun was slowly setting and the light fading but the temperature did not drop. James was sweating through his polo shirt. He took a breather before looking around to make sure he hadn't been followed. He hadn't. James untucked his polo shirt from his chinos and walked over towards the San Bernardo train station, which was adjacent to the metro station. He stopped short as a bus pulled up at one of the sheltered stops. San Bernardo is a major transport hub, with multiple bus stops, a mainline train station, tram station and the metro station that James had just left. The bus that had just pulled up was a city circular, and it called at Santa Justa railway station. James stepped on and paid the driver, taking his ticket, he walked to the centre of the bus. It was a bendy bus, and he stood in the bendy section so he could not be seen from the outside but he could see out. He was not expecting to be followed at this point though, after he had given the soldiers the slip earlier on.

At the Plaza de Cuba metro station on the Triana side of the river, the Argentine Soldiers stepped out onto the street, and one of them called Javier Ramos. When he answered they explained what had happened. Ramos was not angry but he left instructions for the men, and they began walking back towards Seville determined not to be fooled by Shaw and Sharif again.

James Shaw stepped out of the back door of the bus at the stop before Santa Justa so that he could walk ahead and scout out the area, it was an old habit of his that had always proven useful. If people were waiting for him, he would have the advantage. But nobody was waiting for him, he casually walked into the station and waited for his brother. James took a seat at a bar in the station and ordered a beer, with his view fixed on the side door at the other end of the station, which he expected John to walk through. As this was the side were the airport bus stopped.

At 2100 exactly he caught sight of John Shaw's towering figure strolling with purpose through the main entrance of the station, he spotted James straight away and headed over towards him.

'Good to see you and thanks for this I owe you one,' James said.

John who was dressed in a navy-blue shirt, jeans and the same Clarks desert boots as James replied.

'Don't worry about it, the Colonel was not happy with me just getting up and leaving, he wanted to know what was going on.'

James set his beer down and stood up to leave.

'Well bit of a story that, firstly a change of hotel we are putting you in Hotel Ayre over the road. It has got a nice pool and all the amenities you need.'

'OK so what about the one I have booked for tomorrow?'

'We will get to that.'

'I am going to enjoy this aren't I?' John said.

James and John left the station and crossed the road to Hotel Ayre, which was opposite the station.

They walked in to the lobby and James booked a room for John, paying in cash.

After receiving the room key, they went up to the room on the fifth floor, and John set his bag down and sat on the double bed. James sat on the chair under the window.

'Lawrence and I will move in here tomorrow so that we are all together.'

John asked 'Where are you staying now?'

'A backpacker's hostel but we are staying with some young ladies tonight, in their apartment.'

John laughed and said 'You never change. Go on, a bit of background please.'

'Basically, Lawrence and I are here to stop a business deal happening. A group of men based at home in Liverpool are selling permits for oil drilling in the South Atlantic, to a man called Javier Ramos who is CEO of ESPoil, he has links to Argentine special forces soldiers, some we have encountered and dealt with, there are still some on the loose.'

John nodded and said 'Well sounds pretty straight forward, how do you get involved in these things?'

James stood up and looked out of the window at the sunset.

'That's not all, remember my friend Will Ramsey, they have taken him as a hostage, we hope anyway, so we need to get him first before we stop this deal, but we need to try and take out as many of these soldiers as we

can, before we all end up dead.'
John looked at James and said 'For fuck's sake, do you and Lawrence have a plan?'
'Yes, that's why we decided to put you up in here, tomorrow we will wait at your original hotel and ambush them there, we must assume that they are listening to our communications, which is how they managed to grab Will, also we are on our own with no official help due to the sensitivity around the area in question. But we are getting help from the French when we need it.'
John looked at James in disbelief, just a few hours ago he was at his desk looking busy, now he was in the middle of a secret war on the streets of Seville.
'Do you have goodies?' John asked.
'Yes, plenty we will meet you here tomorrow at 1100, go get some sleep, and thanks again for helping out.'
'Don't worry about it,' John said.
And with that James Shaw left the room and went to the reception desk, he asked for them to call him a taxi, which they did.

FOURTEEN

James Shaw relaxed in the back of the taxi as it wound its way through the narrow streets of Seville. The sun had now set and the city was illuminated by orange and yellow light. He told the driver to stop on Calle Ximenez de Encisco, a few streets away from Delinda's apartment building, as he felt like a stroll in the night air. He paid the driver, who then drove off looking for another fare.

Shaw ambled through the streets, taking in the quietness and the citrus smell in the air from the orange trees, he was the only person on the street.

He turned a corner on to the street with Delinda's building. Shaw spotted a VW Polo parked on the street, it was the same colour blue that himself and Sharif had come across earlier.

Shaw instinctively looked around, he could not see anybody and the car was empty. He shrugged and carried on towards Delinda's apartment.

Fifty yards from Delinda's apartment door, one of Ramos's soldiers lunched from a doorway and slashed at Shaw with a knife in a backhand motion. Shaw instinctively arched his back to try to avoid contact. However, the blade sliced his midriff, ripping his polo shirt and his skin, causing blood to pour out from his abdomen.

Shaw put his hands to the wound and looked at the warm blood on his hands in disbelief. He let the adrenalin take over the pain, he launched at the soldier and wrestled him to the floor, the blade narrowly missing him as he fell on top of the soldier. The Argentine fought back and tried to stab Shaw again, he sliced his polo but missed his body. Shaw jabbed the soldier in the top of the arm, causing the knife to spill on to the cobbled pavement. They both reached for it, but Shaw was both taller and quicker. He picked it up and plunged the knife into the soldier's chest, killing him instantly, not even a scream was managed, his body shut down straight away.

Shaw dropped the knife and struggled back to his feet, he took his top off and used it to apply pressure to the wound and ease the bleeding. He used his foot to knock the Knife down a drain, and he staggered towards Delinda's apartment building as if he was drunk. Feeling fainter with each step, he sat down to try and calm himself as the adrenaline wore out. James took out his phone and dialled Lawrence's number.

'I am outside, come quick,' He panted, and put the phone down.

Half a minute later Lawrence stepped out onto the street, and could see James sat on the kerb holding his abdomen. James now struggled for breath and said to Lawrence.

'Get him in the boot, and get me to the hospital quickly.' Lawrence dashed over to the soldier on the floor and searched his body, he eventually found the keys to the

VW Polo parked a hundred yards away. Lawrence ran over to the car, got in and drove up to where James was sat and helped him into the back seat, which he lay across. Lawrence opened the boot and moved the car to the side of the soldier, he dragged the Argentine soldier in to the empty space and closed the hatchback on him, he then stepped around to the driver's seat and set off for the hospital. Which took him ten minutes to get through the narrow streets and one-way system.

Lawrence slewed the car to a stop outside the hospital's emergency department, and helped James inside. He explained to the receptionist what the problem was and if he could be seen straight away. He was told to take a seat like everybody else.
 A Doctor walked by and seen James Shaw fading in and out of consciousness, he called for assistance and James was quickly assessed before being taken down to surgery. Lawrence walked outside to move the car to a parking space, the last thing they needed was the police crawling all over the car and asking questions that could not be answered.

James Shaw lay on the operating table in theatre under a local anaesthetic. A screen had been erected so James could not see what was going on.
 The surgical team had managed to stop the bleeding, and they stitched him back together with precision. The knife had cut deep but luckily did not cause any internal damage; however, he would be left with a neat six-inch scar for his trouble.

FIFTEEN

Two hours later; James Shaw felt a searing pain in his midriff as the effects of the anaesthetic wore off. He had been placed in a side room and had been asleep before the porter's had wheeled him in to the room. As he awoke fully, he could see Lawrence sat next to him in a visitor's chair. Lawrence had James's clothes and personal effects in a bag provided by the hospital, he passed them to James.

'Get dressed, no time to sit in here all night,' Sharif said.

As they walked slowly towards the exit, people kept looking at James and his blood-stained shirt.

'The doctors said you will be fine, just a flesh wound, so you are fit for duty,' Lawrence said half-jokingly and half serious.

James shot him a disapproving look, and his phone rang. He pulled it out of his pocket and looked at the screen which showed a local number, he swiped to answer, a voice said.

'James, it is Will, sorry that I haven't been in touch, my phone stopped working I had to buy a new one.'

'It is Will Ramsey,' Shaw mouthed to Lawrence, who mimicked a talking sign with his hand meaning keep him talking.

'In 2008, where did we serve together and what were our room numbers?'

'Camp Bastion, you were in twenty and I was in twenty-one, you punched a hole in the wall after I beat you at FIFA remember?' Will Ramsey replied.

James gave a thumbs up to Lawrence.

'I will call you back,' Shaw ended the call.

James spotted a phone on the wall next to the automatic doors, he put two euros in to the coin slot and dialled the number that Will had just called him from, and waited for him to pick up.

'Fucking hell, we thought you had been kidnapped, where are you?'

'Funny you should ask that, there are two VW Polos parked outside of my hotel, with three men in each. There was only one until around half an hour ago, then another pulled up.'

'Stay in the hotel and don't leave, we will be there tomorrow at one o'clock, the other car must be for my brother John. I am going to call you back on the mobile, they are tracing my calls so I assume they are waiting for me to call back.'

James hung up and dialled the same number from his mobile.

'Good to hear your voice, I thought something had happened to you,' James said.

'No, I am fine, just enjoying the city.'

'Glad to hear it. The plan is: John will be staying in your hotel, he will be arriving at about 1530 tomorrow, myself and Lawrence will be there to meet you at 1500

and we will wait for John, you can get some beers ready for us.'
'OK I will see you tomorrow at 1500.'
James clicked off the call.
James and Lawrence left the hospital, and Sharif told James to wait whilst he went and got the car as they could not get a taxi at the hospital as it had gone past two in the morning. Shaw helped James into the passenger seat and drove slowly to Barrio Santa Cruz.
'You got lucky tonight,' Sharif said.
'Yeah, you could say that. I will be fine in the morning after some sleep, where are we staying? Delinda and Ally probably think we have done a runner, I have had four missed calls and texts.'
'Don't worry. I spoke to Ally we can still stay; they are expecting us.'
'Oh good,' Shaw said, as he reached into his pocket for a cigarette.
'We will go get some sleep and then we can make a plan for tomorrow, Will says there are six of Ramos's men outside of his hotel in two cars. I am guessing they will rotate at some point, but now let's just go get some rest,' James said to Lawrence, who nodded in agreement.

James and Lawrence arrived back at the apartment building after first circling the block to make sure that there were not any more of Javier Ramos's men waiting for them. They could not see any, much to their relief.
'I think they are getting a bit thin on the ground now,' Lawrence said.
'I hope so, and if they still have six outside Will's hotel,

133

tomorrow that will leave just a few around Ramos, who will not let them go, he will want to keep them close,'
'Agreed'.

Lawrence parked the car as close as he could to where he took it from earlier.

'Stay there a minute.'

'Okay,' Shaw said.

Sharif got out and opened the hatchback, and he was back in the driver's seat a minute later with the dead soldier's phone.

'How is your Spanish?' Lawrence asked.

'Mierda.'

'It's OK, I will give it a go.'

Sharif scrolled through the text messages, he found Ramos's number and carefully sent a text message to him.

Los Ingleses han dejado el apartmento con las chicas. Tienen equipaje. Los seguire. (The Englishmen have left the apartment with the girls. They have luggage. I will follow them.)

Ramos replied a minute later.

Mantenme informado (Keep me updated)

Sharif pulled away from the kerb and turned right, then left into a small square. They got out of the car, and once again Sharif went to the boot, he was rustling around and rocking the car. He came out with the Argentines T-Shirt. He rolled it up and opened the petrol cap. He used his finger to open the flap and slide the T-Shirt in. He fed it down so a small bit was hanging out.

134

Taking the lighter from his pocket he lit the T-Shirt, which caught fire straight away. He and James hustled away. They were back on the street were Delinda's apartment was when they heard the explosion.

'That will probably draw some attention from the Police,' Shaw said.

'Yeah, it will, and then Ramos will shut them down. He will be panicking when he hears about this.'

'I need to get some sleep, let's go get our heads down, and see what's what in the morning.'

They arrived at Delinda and Ally's apartment, and Lawrence rang the buzzer with the knuckle of his right middle finger to the apartment on the top floor. Delinda released the door lock remotely to let them in, and they climbed the stairs. James began to feel pain in his abdomen with each step. Lawrence stopped and helped him to the top, where they were met by Ally and Delinda.

Delinda put her right hand to her mouth and gasped in horror as she seen James's polo shirt covered in blood, along with the pain etched on his face.

'Nothing to worry about just a flesh wound,' he said with a grimace.

'Oh my god what happened?' Asked Delinda not taking her eyes off the blood on James's polo shirt.

'Some joker tried to mug me; he is worse off, believe me. Thank you for letting us stay here.'

Delinda took hold of James's hand and led him to her bedroom. Delinda kissed James passionately, they kissed and held each other tight.

'I have been so worried about you but I am glad you are OK now; I hope this doesn't sound too forward. But I really like you and would like it if we could spend more time together.'

James sat on the bed and dressed down to his underwear, Delinda sat next to him and rested her head on his shoulder.

'I like you too and we can spend more time together, Lawrence and I just have a few things to sort out here, then you will have me all day and night.'

'I can't wait'.

Delinda fell asleep in James's arms, he lay awake for an hour with all sorts of thoughts swirling around inside his head, from the situation he was currently in to what he was going to do next. He eventually fell asleep next to a woman for the first time in a long time and he was happy about it.

James woke up around six hours later and could feel somebody sat on the bed looking at him, once he cleared his eyes, he noticed it was Lawrence Sharif who was sat looking at him.

'How are you feeling? Are you fit for duty?' He asked.

'Yes, I am fine and why have you been watching me sleep?'

'Glad to hear it, the girls have gone out to get some breakfast, we need to plan what to do this afternoon, and we need to go back and get the rest of our clothes if we are going to stay here.'

'I agree, we could really do with a car, we don't want to

be carrying weapons around in taxis when we go to hit Will's hotel. I need a top too before we go back to get our stuff, I can't walk around in a blood-stained shirt. I brought the bag without any tops in.'

'OK, I will go back to the hostel and get our stuff, if you go and hire a car. You can pick me up, and then we can plan when we get back here, get John whilst you are out, easier if we all stick together today, and Delinda said she will get you a t-shirt, I told her to get extra-large.'

'Cheeky bastard,' James said to Lawrence with a scowl. 'Don't forget, Spanish people are generally smaller than us.'

James got up out of the bed and headed for the bathroom. He turned the shower on and looked at his stitching in the mirror.

Good job, this will hold up, he said to himself.

James got in to the shower and did his usual routine of wash, rinse, repeat and clean his teeth.

He got dressed in to his trousers and shoes, and walked out in to the living area as Delinda and Ally walked through the door with cardboard coffee cups, croissants and a plastic bag which James assumed was his new top.

'Morning,' he said to them, which they said back.

Delinda put the coffee on the table and gave James a kiss before she handed him the plastic bag. James opened the bag and pulled out a white t-shirt, he unfolded it and pulled it over his head. On the front it said *I heart Sevilla* the kind that you see in all cities with a big red heart and bold black writing.

'Really, thank you,' he said to Delinda.

Lawrence could not stop laughing.

'You definitely look like a tourist now.'

'How much do I owe you for the top?' James asked.

'Oh, it's fine, my treat, especially since you look so cute in it.'

James smiled and quietly said 'Thanks.'

The three of them sat around the long table eating, drinking and laughing.

Lawrence walked back to the hostel, whilst James got a taxi to Santa Justa station with Delinda and Ally who were going to Cordoba for the day.

James was going to hire a car at the same place as they dropped the SEAT off when they first arrived in Seville. He was happy to get another SEAT Leon. After thinking about space, he decided a Range Rover would be better or some other kind of 4x4. The taxi pulled up at the station, Shaw paid the driver and the three of them walked inside on to the vast concourse. People were waiting for trains and hurrying about.

James waited with Delinda and Ally until their train arrived. He was not allowed to follow them down to the platform, as ticket inspections were taking place at the top of the moving stairs. James waved Delinda and Ally off and headed over to a payphone and dialled the number for Hotel Ayre, which he had googled on his phone. When the receptionist answered he asked to be put through to John Shaw's room, the receptionist patched the call through and John answered.

'Yes.'

'Get over to the station.'

James put the phone down and walked to a car rental

booth. He asked the clerk if he spoke English, he said he did. He asked if they had any Range Rovers, they did, and it was two hundred euros per day, which James paid for on his card and signed a load of paperwork. A copy of his driving license was taken for the rental company's records. The man handed him a set of keys and directed him to where the car was parked. James thanked the man and walked out of the booth, John walked in to the station and waved at James, who hurried over to his brother.

They stepped out in to the sun and scanned the rental lots for a black Range Rover Vogue.

'Did you have a good night?' John asked.

'Had better, I got stabbed and ended up in the hospital, but apart from that, how about you?'

'Yeah, I had a good sleep and breakfast is nice here, so what about today then, wait what did you just say, you got stabbed?'

'Yeah, nothing major, it is just a flesh wound which needed a few stitches, we are going to meet Lawrence now, he is picking up the rest of our things, and then we will plan for this afternoon, good job you are here. We could do with your Marines expertise.'

'Nice t-shirt by the way, good way to blend in, how many people are we looking at?'

'Six we think,' James said.

'OK, should be easy enough, and do you have any maps?'

'Yes, we have got all that, and Will is safe so a false alarm on that one, he will be helping from inside the hotel.'

'Well, that's good news for a start, how have you and Lawrence Sharif ended up in this mess, seems to me you have been left out to dry?'

'We have in a way but we have the upper hand,' James answered.

'Was it one of these who stabbed you?'

'Yes, right outside of the apartment where Delinda is staying as well.'

'Delinda, nice name. Where is she from?' John asked.

'America, Tennessee.'

'Nice, will I get to meet her?'

'Not today. I have just waved them off, they are going to Cordoba for the day.'

'That's good, at least we can plan in peace.'

'Exactly, one less thing for us to worry about, here is the car,' James said as he unlocked the doors with the remote fob.

James inched through the Saturday morning shopping traffic; he eventually reached the backpacker's hostel. Lawrence Sharif was waiting with the bags at his feet outside the entrance, smoking a cigarette. He walked over to the car, opened the back door and threw the bags in, and then climbed in after them. James put the Range Rover in to drive and drove off towards Calle Torneo, which ran alongside the river. It would be quicker driving around the city, than trying to navigate the narrow streets and the one-way system in the centre of the old town.

SIXTEEN

Lyndon, Mike, Chris and Jack were in Liverpool making their final preparations before flying out to Spain the next morning. All boarding cards and train tickets had been printed, and all passports had been double checked, all that was left to do, was to receive confirmation of their hotel booking by Hotel Ayre in Seville.

The four men were on their way to a Liverpool John Lennon Airport hotel in a taxi. Mikes phone pinged; it was the e-mail confirmation of their hotel booking.

'Well gentlemen, everything is in place, I assume you have all set an alarm for the morning?'

They replied that they had.

'Think, in just a few days we will all be multi-millionaires, we have deserved it too,' Mike said.

'A lot of work to do between now and then, let's keep our minds on the job, and then we can have the biggest party you have ever seen, believe me,' Lyndon replied.

The taxi pulled up outside the hotel, it was directly opposite the entrance to the departures, in the morning they could just walk straight to the terminal, no need to check bags, as they were only taking hand luggage, for ease of moving around. Even though this was the biggest job they had ever done, all of the men seemed quite at ease, and relaxed about the whole situation. All the hard work had been done, now all they had to do was sign the permits over and collect their money, which they assumed would be transferred in to their business account.

SEVENTEEN

James Shaw, Lawrence Sharif and John Shaw sat around the dining table in Delinda and Ally's Air BnB apartment, with a fold out map, along with smaller computer printed maps spread out on the table. Lawrence had printed close up maps off at the business centre in the hostel before he was picked up by the Shaw brothers.

James and Lawrence smoked Marlboro cigarettes, and John a café crème cigar, he had given cigarettes up two years ago, and only smoked cigars now and again.

Circled in a black sharpie pen was the hotel Will Ramsey was currently staying in, which was also the one Javier Ramos and his soldiers believed John Shaw would be arriving at, later that day.

'Major, what do you think is the best way around this, it's not ideal that the hotel is located in the middle of the street, two hundred yards from the nearest junction in each direction?' Lawrence asked John.

'Three of us climb to the top of the buildings opposite, and we take them out from up there, get Will to leave the hotel on foot so that they react, and then we will take them out. We approach the buildings from this alleyway and make our way to the top and wait,' John answered,

pointing with a pen to the buildings and the alleyway on
one of the close-up maps.

James Shaw stubbed out his cigarette and laughed.

'That won't work.'

'And why not Wing Commander?' John Retorted. 'You
are an intelligence officer, I am the Royal Marine, this
stuff is our bread and butter.'

James stood from the table and walked over to one of the
holdalls, opened it and pulled out one of the Steyr
AUG's, that they had captured from the Argentines, and
laid it on the table and pointed at it.

'This is why.'

'What the fuck is that, we can't use them from up on
those roofs we will cause all sorts of damage, the
accuracy is shit.'

'Exactly, what I propose is, we get Will to give us the
location of the two cars, if they still have two there. We
pull up, jump out and capture them, a smash and grab
basically, all over in just a few seconds, let me call Will,'
James said.

James walked over to the landline phone and dialled
Will's hotel and asked to be put through to his room. He
was put through.

'Will, its Jay, can you see how many cars there are, blue
VW polo's? And by any chance are you armed?'

'Yes, two cars, parked right outside the hotel and yes, I
brought my Glock with me, it is in my jacket, no checks
today, the Spanish seemed in a good mood, what's the
plan then?'

'That helps us a lot, you took a chance with that didn't
you, wait in the lobby with your Glock. I will text you

when we leave, we are going for the smash and grab, pull up, toss them in to our car and hopefully no shots fired. Then we will have the upper hand.'
'Excellent see you soon.'
James hung up.
'John and I agree with your plan and it will help that Will is armed, like you said hopefully no shots fired,' Lawrence said.

The three of them sat and checked over the weapons, to ensure they were clean and that they worked. They had two Steyr AUG's between them, a Browning pistol for John and the Berreta M9's for James and Lawrence.
'Whose place is this anyway?' John asked.
'The girls we met are staying here, they are renting it off Air BnB,' James said.
'Very nice, I bet it's not cheap with the pool as well, bit big for two people, isn't it?'
'There were five, three have gone to Granada, I am not sure when they will be back.'
'I see, true gent you are Jay, send the ladies away whilst you plot and store weapons in their accommodation.'
James stood up and lit a cigarette.
'They probably have more firepower in the cupboard under the stairs,' James said. 'There is no time like the present, let's do this.'
He picked up his Beretta, tucked it in his waistband, and grabbed the Steyr Aug's off the table, along with the keys for the Range Rover.
The others followed suit and they left the apartment building and climbed in to the Range Rover.

James was driving, Lawrence in the passenger seat and John in the back, he had the assault rifles in the footwell next to him. James put the key fob in cup holder and pressed the start button, he turned the dial on the centre console to drive, and put his foot on the accelerator. He was heading for Triana on the other side of the river. As James drove around the tight corners of the Barrio Santa Cruz, he noticed a police car in his mirrors. He drove on slowly, and came to the junction with Avenida de Menendez Pelayo, which led to the bridge they needed to cross the river to Triana. As James pulled the Range Rover on to the main Boulevard the police car put its sirens on and signalled for James to pull over.

'For fuck's sake, the stupid bastards what are they doing?' James Shaw said to nobody in particular.

'Stay calm, probably just a routine stop,' Lawrence said. John was kicking the Steyr assault rifles as far under the seats as he could. James signalled with the right indicator, found a place to stop and pressed the button to lower his window. Only one policeman got out of the police car and walked towards the Range Rover, he approached James's window.

'Buenos Dia,' he said, in a Seville accent.

James replied 'Buenos Dias, no hablo Espanyol, Ingles' The policeman replied in English 'Good Afternoon, can I see your papers and licence please?'

James reached in to his pocket and pulled his wallet out, without trying to expose his back where he had his Beretta, he asked Lawrence to get the rental papers out of the glove box, which he did, and James handed both over to the policeman. The policeman seemed happy

with what he had seen and handed them back to James.
'Thank you, you may go now.'
'Gracias,' James replied, he put his licence and wallet
back in his pocket before setting off again.
'What was that all about?' John asked from the back
seat.
'Who knows, boredom most likely,' Lawrence answered.
'That has put me off, I am going to drive along the river
and cross at the Isobel bridge and come at the hotel from
the opposite direction,' James said.

James Shaw drove the Range Rover across Puente de
Isabell II. At the end of the bridge, he pulled over to the
right, put the hazard lights on and rested his head on the
steering wheel.
'What is upon you James?' Sharif asked.
'Three of us in this car, Will in the hotel, six of them in
two cars, how the fuck are we going to do a smash and
grab, where are we going to put them. What are we
going to say to them "Please wait here we will be back
for you", for fuck's sake it's all going to pot, I should
have got a van, pile them all in the side door,' James said
whilst banging his hands on the steering wheel.
Lawrence put his left hand on James shoulder and said to
him in a reassuring voice.
'Two in here and two in each of their cars, John and I
will take one each, we will use the same underground car
park as before, John can you pass me that daysack
please?'
John passed a black daysack to Lawrence, who reached
in and pulled out a handful of extra-large cable ties and

handed some to John.

'Obviously we will restrain them, it won't take long, thirty seconds from pulling up to driving off in the different cars.'

'Thanks, I should have thought of that myself.'

'That is what teamwork is for.'

'Or Royal Marine Commando expertise,' John added.

'Royal Navy you mean,' said James.

'How many times, I am a Royal Marine Commando Major, not Royal Navy.'

'What does your I.D. card say at the top?'

John said nothing.

'Exactly it says Royal Navy, I am going to give Will the signal,' James said as he pulled his phone from his pocket.

He dialled the hotel from his recent call list and asked for Will Ramsey, he came to the phone a few seconds later, which meant he was in the lobby and waiting.

'In thirty seconds, run out of the hotel doors we will RV with you, we are in a black Range Rover.'

He put the phone down and took his seatbelt off, John and Lawrence did the same. James put the selector back in to drive. He held his foot on the brake whilst pushing the accelerator, he let go of the brake, and the car shifted forward, James pulled in front of the traffic and crossed on to Calle Pureza, which ran parallel behind Calle Betis, which was on the river front.

Calle Pureza was free from traffic, which was a good thing, just a few pedestrians but none within harm's way. James sped down the street, and he could see up ahead the rear ends of the two VW Polos parked up. It was a good decision to attack from the Puente de Isabel II as it was a one-way street with vehicles parked on the left and traffic flowing on the right-hand side.

Squadron Leader William Ramsey stepped out of the hotel doors, which was on their left-hand side of the road. James Shaw was doing almost sixty miles per hour when he took his right foot off the accelerator and pushed the brake pedal hard to the floor. The Range Rover slewed to the left, and the front end of the car dipped with the force of the braking. The big car came to a complete stop. James and John jumped out of the left-hand side, Lawrence got out of the front passenger seat and ran around the bonnet towards the rearmost VW Polo with James Shaw, whilst John Shaw and Will Ramsey took the nearest. All four men had their side arms out pointed at the cars shouting.

'OUT, OUT, OUT.'

All six of the soldiers got out of their respective cars, with their hands in the air. Lawrence Sharif handcuffed the three men from his car with the cable ties and directed the driver to the Range Rover. John Shaw did the same whilst Will Ramsey covered him, the soldiers from the driver's seat of both VW Polos struggled in to the back seats of the Range Rover, James helped shove them in and closed the door on them, he climbed back into the driver's seat. Will Ramsey got in to the front passenger seat of the Range Rover next to James. Lawrence and John had directed the other four prisoners into the back of the VW Polos.

James opened the passenger window and pointed with

his hand extended.

'Straight on, follow me,' he said.

He moved forward to allow John and Lawrence to move into the road. As they set off one of the soldiers in the back of the Range Rover said in broken English.

'You cannot do this; you will not beat us.'

'Well, we are doing a fine job so far.' James said 'Now be quiet.'

'English bastards,' the other spat.

'Right Will, change of plan.'

Calle Pureza ended at a T-junction, James Shaw turned left on to Calle Betis and drove along it until he got to the roundabout at Puente de S. Telmo. Instead of going around the roundabout and turning left to drive over the bridge back towards Seville, James turned right down Avenida Republica de Argentina.

'Look, this is your street, maybe we should leave you here,' James joked.

The soldier with the broken English said.

'Malvinas will be ours again.'

Shaw and Ramsey did not react, Shaw was focused on the road, he checked his rear-view mirror to ensure that the others were still following him.

'Where are we going Jay, are you ok?' Ramsey asked in concern for his friend, who looked angry, yet he was totally focused on driving the car.

'Yes fine, how is your hotel? How long are you staying for?'

'How long do you need me to stay for?'

'That is up to you, you can go back to Gibraltar if you want later.'

'I will drive back tomorrow if you don't mind.'
'Not at all thanks for all your help, we couldn't have done this without you,' James said.
'No problem, I was happy to help, nice to see a bit of action, maybe we should have gagged them as well.'
'Yeah maybe.'
The convoy led by James Shaw in the Range Rover crossed over the diverted part of the Guadalquivir which was at the end of Triana furthest away from the city of Seville.

Twenty minutes later they arrived at Embalse del Gergal, which is a reservoir providing water to the city of Seville.
James stopped the Range Rover, dragged the soldiers out of the back and threw them to the floor.
Lawrence and John did the same, whilst Will covered them with his Glock 17 pistol. James walked over to the Polo that Lawrence had been driving and opened the boot.
'Open that one John,' James said pointing at the other VW Polo.
Which he did.
James pulled his Beretta out and gestured to the men to get in the boot.
'Tie their legs together please Lawrence.'
James and Lawrence squeezed two of the soldiers into the first car boot and closed it on them. They did the same with two more. The remaining two men were tied with cable ties to the steering wheel of the VW Polos.
James tossed the keys overarm away from the cars.

'Come on let's get back.' James said.

The four of them climbed back in to the Range Rover with James and Lawrence in the front, Will and John in the back seats.

Lawrence asked James 'What was that about then?'

'Didn't fancy paying to park in that car park again, actually surprised we haven't seen anything about the first one, that ticket has expired now.'

'Maybe they don't check that often, what is the real reason?' Lawrence asked.

'They were pissing me off, from the moment we got here we have been followed. I even got stabbed last night, so I decided to leave them in the middle of nowhere, take them out of action.'

'OK, it should make our job easier now. I estimate the rest will stay close to Ramos with maybe only one on Surveillance duties. Which will double to two when Lyndon Powell and his team arrive tomorrow.'

John put his head in to the gap of the front seats and asked.

'Lyndon Powell that used to go to our school?'

'Apparently so, have you ever met him? I haven't.'

'No but I know the name,' John answered.

James drove off and headed back towards Seville.

James parked back in the lot where he had picked the car up from and walked to the booth, he asked the rental clerk if it was OK to park there, he said it was. The four men jogged across the road towards Hotel Ayre.

'I noticed earlier that they had swimming shorts for sale in the lobby, shall I get four pairs or have you got some

John?'

'No, get me a pair please.'

James paid the same price as a full course dinner for three people for four pairs of swimming shorts at the reception desk and asked for towels which they were given.

Lawrence walked towards the swimming pool and turned off in to the bar.

'Go and get changed I won't be long,' he said.

The changing rooms were located next to the swimming pool. The three men came out in their new swim shorts, with their clothes and towel over their arms. They found four sunbeds around the pool, put their towels down and sat on the sun loungers. It was 1700hrs and the temperature was still thirty-seven degrees. Lawrence Sharif came out of the hotel, walked up to the pool and found where the others were sat. He was carrying four beers and had two packets of cigarettes in his mouth, he and James kept forgetting to take more cigarettes out with them, he set the beers down on the little side tables and threw a packet of cigarettes to James. Each of them grabbed a beer and raised them, and said cheers to each other. James and Lawrence lit cigarettes.

'Job well done today, even if the end was a little off plan, but we succeeded in the end and well done. Thank you to Will and John for coming in on this one.'

'Good job we did,' John said whilst laughing.

James Shaw put out his cigarette, and jumped in to the pool, the others followed. They horsed around in the pool and chatted with each other and the other guests.

Lawrence had agreed to pay John and Will forty thousand pounds each for their help, himself and James would transfer it later. They refused at first but Lawrence insisted. Will said that he would be returning to Gibraltar the next evening, as he had important work to complete the following week. John said he would stay until the deal happened on Tuesday, as he wanted to help, and he liked the city but more importantly he was away from his Colonel who thought of John as a bit of a rogue.

James Shaw's phone rang so he climbed out of the pool, dried his hands and swiped to answer.

'Yes,' he said.

He listened to Delinda.

'If you step out the front of the station and look left you will see Hotel Ayre, we are in the pool at the back, do you have your swimming costumes?'

He listened again.

'Oh good, see you in a few minutes, Bye,' and he put his phone down.

'That was Delinda, her and Ally are back from Cordoba.'

'They did not spend much time there, did they?' Lawrence said.

'I know, well they are on their way here, to join us.'

EIGHTEEN

J avier Ramos had tried the mobile phones of all six
soldiers who were stationed outside the Hotel in Triana,
with no answer from any of them.

'What is keeping them, all they had to do was take the
Shaw brother hostage before he got to the hotel so that
the others wouldn't know what had happened to him,
maybe these Brits are smarter than what we gave them
credit for,' he said to the most senior Argentine soldier at
his disposal.

'I don't think so Sir, my men and I are Argentine special
forces soldiers.'

To which Ramos replied 'Well start acting like it, we
might not like them but the British are the best, that is
why I hired so many of you, just in case they became
involved in this which they have, you and your men
were supposed to be enjoying your selves instead you
are losing men. Maybe they have nothing to do with our
deal with Mr Powell and his company, perhaps we just
picked on the wrong people at the right time.'

'That is possible Sir, it was reported at first that they
were just tourists, maybe they didn't like being
followed.'

'Yes, perhaps you are right, from now on leave them

alone, do not give them a reason to attack your men or come after us, we cannot let this deal collapse, from now on your men stay here or if they go out, they go in normal clothes and no weapons, we do not want to antagonise the English any more, or our plan may well fall apart.'

'I agree Sir, the rest of us will stay back here and relax until you tell us otherwise.'

Javier Ramos walked out of his house in to the back garden where his swimming pool was and made a call to Argentina. The phone was answered at the other end and Ramos spoke.

'Everything is going ahead as planned here, soon victory will be ours.'

He listened and then said.

'I will you call as soon as the transfer has taken place, adios.'

He put the phone down and sat on his sun lounger with a half worried, half happy expression on his face. He was excited to get the deal done, thus beginning a fresh invasion of the Falkland Islands, but nervous also, as he did not know what the British men in Seville were going to do. He thought to himself, *hopefully nothing now we are going to leave them alone.*

NINETEEN

It had gone seven o'clock in the evening, and James Shaw, Lawrence Sharif, John Shaw, Will Ramsey, Delinda Saint Germain and Ally Simmons had gotten dressed after spending time in Hotel Ayre's swimming pool. They had decided to go out for dinner in the old town.

James Shaw's pleas to go and get changed out of his *I heart Sevilla* t-shirt went unheard, and he was convinced to enjoy himself and relax. They decided to get the bus back in to the old town, as there were six of them, they didn't want to wait too long for two taxis on a Saturday night. After a short wait at the bus stop on the other side of the road to Hotel Ayre, they got on to the number 32 bus, which a few minutes later dropped them off in the old town at Plaza Del Duque de la Victoria.

Delinda suggested a restaurant that she had read about near to the cathedral, which served a mix of local food and steaks. The group agreed to try it out, they walked down the narrow-cobbled streets that were full of people on the evening paseo, they arrived at the restaurant, it was located on a street that split off in three directions, all of which were lined with restaurants that had outdoor

157

tables with a view of the gothic cathedral. A young waitress dressed in all white came over and spoke to them, she was tall with blonde hair and blue eyes and very attractive.

James thought to himself *Must be German or Scandinavian.*

The waitress spoke perfect Spanish with a Seville accent, she sensed James questions and said in English.

'My great grandparents moved here in the 1930's from Germany, that is why I have blonde hair.'

'I see, Andalucia is full of surprises,' he said.

Delinda looked at him disapprovingly.

The waitress sat them down at a table for six and asked if they would like any drinks. James asked if everybody was happy with wine, they were, he ordered a carafe of house red and one of white.

James sat opposite Delinda, Lawrence opposite Ally and John and Will sat opposite each other. The waitress brought the wine out and started pouring red for the men and the ladies had white. They ordered a selection of Tapas and James ordered a side of fries, he said.

'I need some grease after the day we have had.'

Lawrence asked Ally and Delinda how their day had been in Cordoba, they answered that they had enjoyed it but wanted to come back to Seville early.

'Why did you want to come back early?' James asked.

Delinda reached across the table and took hold of James left hand.

'Because I missed you,' she said.

James Shaw's face turned crimson.

'I missed you too,' he said to her with a smile.

The six of them conversed and laughed before their food arrived.

'What time are you setting off tomorrow Will?' James asked Ramsey.

'Around five, if that is, ok?'

'Fine by me, no need to ask, it's been good to see you, when are you due a posting? You should move to Waddington.'

'What, and have you as my boss, I am happy in Gib if I am totally honest.'

'Yeah, I don't blame you what's not to like, same with me leaving Akrotiri, but service before self and all that caper.'

'How many years until you pension out Jim?' Lawrence cut in.

'Five, and what have I said about that Jim business.' Everybody laughed.

'What are you going to do when you do, you could always work with me?'

'I work with you now, I don't know. Maybe that is a good idea, I wouldn't mind going back to Liverpool for a short while and relax. I will probably extend and do 30 years, maybe get promoted to Air Commodore, you know how things are.'

'When do you have to go back to England?' Delinda asked James.

'Technically, not until July, why do you ask?'

'Would you like to come back to the US with me for a vacation, I could show you around Nashville?'

James didn't quite know what to say.

'Yes, I would love to, thank you,' he replied.

He wasn't sure if he meant it or not. However, for now he was enjoying himself, even if the circumstances were not ideal, he wished he had met Delinda whilst he was here for leisure and not business.

It was clear that Delinda Saint Germain was beginning to fall for James Shaw, and he for her but he tried to supress the feelings, until the job he was there to do was complete, he could then give her is full attention.

I will go to America he said to himself smiling at Delinda as he ate a piece of lamb off his fork.

The conversation flowed between the six of them, Will Ramsey said that he had an announcement to make after tapping his glass with his fork.

'Well, what is it?' James asked.

Ramsey was clearly nervous about what he wanted to say, after ten seconds he finally answered James Shaw's question.

'I am going to be a father, Nadine is six months, a little girl.'

Everybody said congratulations and James got up from his seat and shook Will's hand.

'I am very happy for you, I cannot believe you didn't tell me, well done.'

'Thanks mate,' Will replied.

James caught the waitress's attention and asked what champagne they had.

'None of that Cava either, the real French stuff,' he said.

She went away to check, then a minute later came back.

'Sir, we have Bollinger or Moet and Chandon,' she said.

'Thank you, Bollinger please, three bottles please.'

'Sir, it is one hundred euros per bottle.'
'No problem, we have good news to celebrate.'
'Very well Sir,' the waitress said, and she went off to get the champagne and glasses.

The champagne flowed, along with the conversation. Once all the food had been cleared away and the bill had been paid, they sat some more, and James and Lawrence smoked some cigarettes.

Eventually they left the restaurant with the waitress happy after being left a very handsome tip. James and Will held back whilst the others walked on ahead.

'I really am happy for you mate, why don't you think about moving back to the UK after the baby is born, get settled in Lincoln,' James said.

'Thanks mate, I think you may be right, it would be good to get settled somewhere, what's the deal with you and Delinda anyway?'

James looked at his friend and said.

'I don't know, obviously it is good at the moment, I will just see what happens. I will probably have forgotten about her this time next week.'

Will Ramsey laughed 'You never change.'

They both laughed and hurried to catch up with the others, who were about to walk in to a bar in the Alfalfa area of the city, it was busy with young locals and backpackers.

There were people inside and outside drinking, smoking, talking and laughing. Spanish pop music played out of the speakers, people were dancing to it and enjoying themselves. John was at the bar ordering some drinks.

Lawrence nodded to the door that James and Will had just walked through, and pointed at James, motioning him outside. James Shaw stepped back out on to the noisy street followed by Lawrence Sharif who offered James a cigarette.

'Thanks, what's the matter?' he asked.

Lawrence lit James's cigarette then his own and asked.

'What is your plan for tomorrow, for when Powell and his people arrive?'

James took a drag of his cigarette.

'Well, I have two, the first one is based on Ramos not having any eyes on us, or a single entity at best. I will board the train at San Bernardo and observe them.'

Lawrence nodded and said 'OK yes, and second plan?'

'Assuming somebody will be watching them, I will be at Hotel Ayre with John, waiting for them to arrive.'

At that moment John walked out and handed James and Lawrence a plastic glass of lager each, they thanked him and then John asked.

'Did I just hear my name?'

James answered 'We are just talking about tomorrow.'

At that point Delinda, Ally and Will joined them outside. They continued drinking and enjoying themselves for another hour. James said that he wished to retire for the night. The others agreed so they flagged down two taxis. John, Lawrence and Ally in one and James, Will and Delinda in the other.

Will Ramsey had been dropped off at his hotel in Triana first, and the taxi drove back across the river to Seville to drop James and Delinda at the Air BnB in Barrio Santa Cruz. Lawrence and Ally were not back yet. James Shaw and Delinda Saint Germain walked up the stairs hand in hand, the alcohol had a numbing effect on James as he could not feel any pain from his wound. Delinda opened the door and they stumbled in to the living area kissing passionately. As they worked their tongues around each other's mouths Delinda lifted James's top up, taking care not to catch his stitches. They moved in to Delinda's bedroom where she got his top off and he took hers off. She pressed her body against his and reached her arms around his waist whilst kissing him hard.

After they were finished, James lay next to Delinda and closed his eyes; she did the same and took hold of his hand.

Day had broken and they made love again, this time was better than the first. *How is that possible* Delinda thought to herself.

After they had finished, James kissed Delinda and went to the bathroom to get a shower and freshen up, Delinda got up and walked into the bathroom behind him.

'Do you really want to come back to the US with me or were you just saying that to get me in to bed?' She asked. James opened the shower cubicle door turned it on and waited for it to heat up before stepping in.

'Of course, I do, I would not have said otherwise, when is your flight back?'

'It's an open return, I just have to ring a couple of days in advance and pick a flight.'

'I see, well how about Thursday? Lawrence and I will be

wrapping things up here on Tuesday, then Wednesday head to Malaga and fly over Thursday.'

Delinda was excited that James wanted to go back to America with her, she got on the phone to the airline immediately. Five minutes later Delinda walked back in to the bathroom.

'Damn, Delta just sold their last two seats a half hour ago.'

'Not to worry gorgeous, we will sort something out,' James said from the shower.

'When are your friend's due back from Granada anyway?'

'Oh, they are going to Valencia, then Ibiza to party.'

'Do you and Ally not want to go with them?'

'Nope.'

'Fair enough,' James said and carried on with his shower.

On the ground at Liverpool John Lennon Airport; Lyndon Powell, Mike Williams, Chris Hampshire and Jack Reuben sat in their seats on a Ryanair Boeing 737-800. Which had been pushed back from the gate and awaited clearance to taxi to the runway. The four men felt awake and fresh, even though they had been awake since three o'clock. They were nervous, yet excited about the upcoming few days. Lyndon had tried to calm the excitement within the group but the others knew that he too was excited, how could he not be, this was to be their biggest payday and without much effort compared to previous cons they had pulled off. Even though weeks of planning had gone in to this job, they had changed their strategy. Usually they met with potential marks, along the con they would give small returns to the mark in order to keep them investing, finally once the big amount was invested, the mark would be told that things had changed in the market, or some other excuse and the four men would be away with the money. This time it was different, there were no investments to lure the victim in, it was just a couple of meetings and telephone calls, the next of which would be made later that evening, once they arrived in Seville. As the aircraft lined up on the runway ready for take-off, Lyndon looked across from his window seat to the other three.

'Gents, this is it no turning back now, in a few days we will be millionaires and set for life thanks to all your hard work.'

The others looked back and said in unison.

'Let's do it.'

The aircraft inched forward, and the engines roared to life and they sped down the runway, a few seconds later they were in the air on their way to Malaga, from where they would complete their journey to Seville.

TWENTY

James Shaw stepped out of the shower and shouted through to Delinda in the bedroom.

'What about the next morning?'

'That's booked up also, I hope we don't have to wait too long.'

'Have a look to see if there are any other airlines that we could fly with, I will pay for the flights.'

'Don't be silly sweetie, I will see if I can arrange something with Delta.'

'OK, sort Delta later. Let us get a flight booked first.'

Delinda picked up her phone and began typing as James walked in to the room.

'Air Transat have a flight leaving at one thirty p.m. to Montreal, we could change there to New York and maybe spend a few nights there, and then fly down to Nashville.'

'OK, we can do that, let me get my card, I will book a hotel too.'

James got his card from his wallet and handed it to

Delinda, whilst he got busy looking at hotels on his phone, he booked The Plaza Hotel in New York City. Delinda finished up booking the flights and sent James's boarding card to his phone.

They walked in to the living area to find Ally sat at the breakfast bar drinking coffee whilst Lawrence Sharif was making scrambled eggs. He made James a cup of tea and Delinda a coffee.

'Ally and I are flying to America Thursday, are you two wanting to join us?' Lawrence said whilst focusing on the stove.

'Yes, we are flying to Montreal first, and then to New York, we are going to stay there for a couple of nights,' James replied.

'Good, how come you are flying to Montreal?'

'Flight was sold out, I assume you have not long booked tickets?' James said with a scowling grin.

'Yes, sorry about that.'

'Forget about it, I am hungry and after breakfast we need to talk.'

'Right you are,' Lawrence replied.

Lawrence Sharif served breakfast which they all ate, and thanked him for making it.

James and Lawrence walked out to the swimming pool, where they both lit cigarettes. They leant against the rail that overlooked the city towards Plaza de Espana.

'I remember the day I first met you,' Lawrence said.

'I remember that day too.'

'I told you about my family connections to T.E. Lawrence and Prince Faisal, and you said you were a fan of T.E.'

'Yes, one of my heroes, where are you going with this?'

'What would you say is the most relevant thing he said, that reflects our current situation?'

'That is a bit heavy for a Sunday morning Lawrence, I don't know "We can't all be lion tamers" maybe,' James said whilst laughing, he took another drag on his cigarette.

'If you stop being a clown for a minute, maybe we could all be lion tamers, now think and tell me your plan, after you think of what he said that is relevant to this mission.' James extinguished his cigarette and lit another one.

'I have got it "All men dream: but not equally. Those who dream by night in the dusty recesses of their minds wake up in the day to find it was vanity, but the dreamers of the day are dangerous men, for they may act on their dreams with open eyes, to make them possible" Javier Ramos is the latter I presume?'

James took a big drag on his cigarette and turned to Lawrence waiting for his reply.

'Exactly right, he has the most to gain and will do anything to make sure it goes his way, hence surrounding himself with Argentine special forces soldiers, who much to our annoyance have been following us to keep us out of the way, this deal is big James, if he gets his hands on those drilling permits and gets away, the Falklands will be under threat, he is working with the Argentinian government, using his oil platforms as a staging base to launch an invasion.'

'How, he has not gotten the permits yet?'

'Lyndon Powell and his friends don't know either, I

doubt very much they care. They fall in to the former part of what you have just quoted, they have one aim, which is to get money, they don't know what Ramos's plans are, they have just set up a bogus company in order to relive Javier Ramos and ESPoil of a sizeable amount of money.'

'Is there any evidence to suggest this is what he is planning?'

'The RAF are flying past once a day on reconnaissance flights, that is one of the reasons you were supposed to be there, but I wanted you here instead to tackle Ramos and stop this planned invasion.'

'Tricky one for us as well, the government don't want to start a war with Argentina surely, so they want us to hold it up here secretly?'

'No, they want this doing with as little fuss as possible, but we will if we have to.'

James and Lawrence extinguished their cigarettes and James said.

'There are two trains from Malaga, they both leave within a few minutes of each other. The later one arrives half an hour earlier and comes from the north, I want you at Santa Justa, if they are not on the early train, you go to Hotel Ayre and wait there with John until I arrive, I will wait for them at San Bernardo, get on to the train and follow them over to the hotel.'

Lawrence agreed to the plan and they walked back inside to Delinda and Ally who were waiting for them.

'The day is young; shall we relax by the pool for a couple of hours?' James said.

The others agreed and they went off to get changed in to

their swimming attire.

James was lying on his sun lounger in his blue swim shorts next to Delinda who was wearing a white bikini that showed off her bronzed body, James couldn't take his eyes off her and Lawrence noticed this.

James Shaw stood up and jumped in to the water splashing everyone else, he started swimming, and his phone chirped.

'Bloody hell, can they not ring a minute earlier,' he said to nobody in particular.

He climbed out of the pool and dried his hands on his towel, Delinda passed him the phone and he swiped to answer 'Yes,' he said and listened.

'Ok, stop by here before you go, I will text you the address, see you soon mate.'

James put the phone down after texting Will Ramsey the address.

'That's Will, he is heading back to Gibraltar now, but he is going to stop by here before he sets off.'

'OK, good, he has done well,' Lawrence said.

The buzzer to the apartment rang, James and Lawrence walked inside and pressed the button to open the door. William Ramsey walked in to the apartment thirty seconds later and was greeted by James and Lawrence.

'Thank you again for you helping with this, now go back to your missus and have a nice relaxing Sunday, I will come and see you soon,' James said.

'Thank you and see you soon too mate,' Will shook James's hand then Lawrence's who said.

'Good luck, have a safe drive back.'

After that Will walked towards the door followed by James.

'I will see you out.'

They walked down the stairs together and out in to the street.

Will got in to his car and said 'Well, thanks again and see you soon, keep in touch.'

'I will, and think about moving to Waddington, especially with a baby on the way.'

'I will let you know,' and with that Ramsey started the engine and Shaw banged his hand on the roof. Ramsey pulled away from the kerb, with James waving him off as he drove off down the street on his way back to Gibraltar.

James turned back to the apartment building door that had closed behind him, he rang the buzzer but Lawrence opened the door startling James

'We need to talk,' Lawrence said.

'About?'

'You and Delinda.'

'Interesting, what do you mean?'

'I see how you look at her.'

'So, what is the problem, you like Ally, don't you?'

' Yes, I do but with you it's different, you both look at each other with those puppy dog eyes. I just don't want you to be distracted.'

'I can assure you I am one hundred per cent focused on this job, any suggestion otherwise is an insult to my professionalism, how many times have we worked together?'

'Yes, your right I am sorry, we just cannot mess this up,

there is too much at stake.'

'And we won't, I will speak to Delinda and ask her and Ally to go to Malaga tomorrow afternoon, we will bunk in with John at Hotel Ayre.'

'Good idea that will ensure we have no distractions, is that a good idea with Powell and his people staying there, Ramos will have it under surveillance surely, what about the Alfonso XIII?'

'Your right, yes good idea I will make the booking when I get back upstairs.'

'No need, I have already done it.'

'What did you ask for then?' James asked, shaking his head in annoyance at Lawrence.

They went back upstairs and out to the pool. James gave Delinda a kiss before jumping back in to the pool, she followed him in as did Lawrence and Ally. The temperature outside was forty degrees Celsius so the pool was a good idea. James Shaw felt pain in his abdomen from his stitches, so he decided to stop swimming and leant with his back on the side of the pool. Lawrence Sharif's phone pinged to indicate an incoming text message, which he ignored.

TWENTY-ONE

Squadron Leader William Ramsey joined the A4 motorway to take him south to Gibraltar. The A4 would take him past Jerez de la Frontera where he had decided to stop and have a short rest, before continuing his journey.

As he reached cruising speed on the A4, he caught a glimpse of a blue VW Polo a few car lengths back in his rear-view mirror, Will Ramsey kept looking in his rear-view mirror, the car appeared to be getting closer to his Volvo S60. He dropped his speed to sixty miles per hour and the VW Polo sped past him, without the driver or passenger even looking at Ramsey's Volvo. Thirty seconds later the VW was out of sight. Ramsey let out a sigh of relief.

As Will Ramsey drove towards Gibraltar; in the air to the east and south of him Lyndon Powell, Mike Williams, Chris Hampshire and Jack Reuben had their seatbelts fastened and were ready to land at Malaga Airport. After a short descent they touched down with a bump and screech.

After taxiing to a stop and disembarking with their luggage, the four men found themselves outside the arrivals lounge in the heat of southern Spain in suits. The four men jumped in to a taxi which was a White SEAT Toledo.

Ten minutes later the taxi had dropped them off at Malaga's Maria Zambrano Railway station. Mike Williams used a self-service ticket machine to purchase four return tickets to Seville, the next train was due to depart in an hour. The four men decided to have a quick bite to eat in the vast station concourse whilst waiting for their train. They were anxious to get to Seville so they could find out the location of their meeting with Javier Ramos ahead of time and get prepared. After finding a restaurant serving Spanish food, the four of them were chatting and relaxing.

'Let this be the start of the rest of our lives,' Lyndon Powell said.

The others agreed and raised their glasses in unison. After finishing their food and drink it was time to head to the platforms and get on to the train. They took their seats and the train pulled away from Malaga on its journey through the mountains to Seville.

TWENTY-TWO

James Shaw climbed out of the swimming pool and lay down on his sunbed, still wet. Lawrence Sharif followed him out and walked over to his phone, he read the message that he had just received.

'That was from DGSE, the Argentine president wants to meet with our PM, but he has declined of course,' Sharif said.

Delinda and Ally stayed in the swimming pool and paid no attention to James and Lawrence's conversation.

'What does that mean, do you suppose they are trying to start talks before taking action?' James asked Lawrence.

'Could be, or could just be diversion tactics, it is an irrelevance anyway if we do our job here, which we will.'

James Shaw checked the time on his phone and said to Lawrence.

'Powell and co are on their way, we will get in to our positions in an hour, do you want to walk to San Bernardo with me and then you can get the train to Santa Justa?'

'Yes, that will work, bring the car keys with you, we will bring the car back here, we can then drive the ladies

to Malaga tomorrow.'
Delinda overheard and said 'Oh my, we will be fine on
the train, a ride to the station would be nice though.'
　'Well, if you are sure? We will be with you Tuesday
night or Wednesday,' James replied.
　'Yes, we are good, you do what you have to do here,
then you are all mine mister.'
　'As it is your last night in Seville what would you like
to do tonight?'
　'How about we get some food, then go to the bar where
we first met the other night?'
The others agreed. James and Lawrence went back inside
the apartment to get changed before setting off on their
scouting mission.

James Shaw stepped out of Delinda's room dressed in
another pair of white chinos, a white cotton oxford shirt,
a navy-blue blazer with gold buttons, and of course his
Clarks desert boots. Lawrence stepped out from Ally's
room dressed in blue jeans with a navy-blue Ralph
Lauren polo shirt, he laughed at James's attire.
　'You look like you are about to go yachting, what is the
blazer for? It is forty degrees outside.'
James Shaw opened his blazer to show Lawrence the
butt of his Beretta M9 sticking out of the left hand inside
pocket.
　'OK, well if you think you need it,' Lawrence said.
　'Well, you never know what is going to happen, do
you?'
　'I suppose you don't,' Lawrence replied as he revealed
his own weapon, which was tucked in to the waistband

of his jeans, and was covered by his un-tucked polo shirt. James opened the fridge and took out two bottles of water, he threw one to Lawrence, who thanked him. They stepped outside to the pool area to re-join Ally and Delinda. Delinda asked James if he was feeling alright, he replied that he was and they kissed passionately. James's blazer had a wet mark from Delinda's bikini top, where they had held each other whilst kissing.

Delinda said to him 'I am sorry, why don't you take it off to dry.'

'It is no problem; it will be dry after a five-minute walk.'

'OK, well if you are sure.'

'Yes, it will be fine, thank you, I will see you later on.'

'I will be here waiting for you handsome,' Delinda said. James smiled at her and gave her another kiss, he stepped away and said to Lawrence 'Let's move.'

They walked inside and left the apartment, walking down the stairs and stepping out on to the street.

James pulled his Oakley *Frogskins* sunglasses out of his outer jacket pocket and put them on as he and Lawrence set off in the direction of San Bernardo station. It was more or less a straight walk, once they got out of the little streets and on to Calle San Fernando, which was home to the Hotel Alfonso XIII, where they would be staying from tomorrow night. They could have gotten the tram but decided to walk, as they still had time to waste before either train was due to arrive at Santa Justa. As they walked past the University of Seville, Lawrence turned to James and asked.

'What is your plan after America. Go back to the UK, assume your role of Station Commander at RAF Waddington and go back to normal, or does Delinda feature in your future plans?'

'Hard to say, we will just have to see how America goes, we are only going for a few days she will probably grow tired of me, also it is not likely that she would move to England as she has only just finished her Law Degree. I don't know how that stuff works with transferring it over, I don't know.'

They crossed over the road to walk alongside the Prado de San Sebastian Park, and bus station. They were on the side covered by the shade of the trees, and carried on their conversation.

'Do you love her? Because it is clear that she is falling for you.'

'What is with your questioning Mr Sharif? What is the deal with you and Ally?'

Lawrence answered 'No deal we both agreed that it is just a bit of fun, are you going to avoid my question.'

'Yes. I have not seen any of our Argentine friends since we have been out, have you noticed any?' James said with a smile.

'No, I have not but I doubt it is the last we have seen of them. I would not be surprised if we see them today, I am sure they will be waiting at the station for Powell and his men, and they will report to Ramos when they have arrived.'

James agreed with Lawrence, he stopped walking and leant against the park fence and lit a cigarette, whilst scanning the area for any followers. They could not see any, and doubted they would be in the park behind them. The two of them leant against the fence smoking and observing all around them, seeing who was getting on and off the buses, and the tram across the road, there was nobody of interest, so they stubbed their cigarettes out in the ashtray of a bin, and set off towards San Bernardo station. Big red buses rumbled past them as they walked, making a conversation difficult without shouting, so they walked on in silence.

They arrived at San Bernardo station ten minutes after they had left Prado de San Sebastion. James tilted his apple watch towards his eyeline revealing the clock face.
 'They are about half an hour out on the fast train; do you want to get in position now ahead of the Argentinians or should we have a beer in that bar over there?' Shaw said.
 'No, I will get to Santa Justa now, I will have a beer waiting for you in Hotel Ayre.'
 'Your right, let's go.'
They hustled in to the entrance of San Bernardo station, and ran down the escalator to take them to the booking hall, where they purchased tickets as it was the only way to gain access to the platform. James had done enough barrier jumping over the last few days and did not want to end up getting caught and locked up in a Spanish police station, that would be no good at all. It would compromise the whole operation for the sake of one euro fifty. After descending a small staircase, they arrived on the platform. After two minutes a Renfe Cercanias commuter train pulled up at the platform. Sharif stepped

on and Shaw waved him off. As soon as the train was out of site James walked back up to the booking hall and crossed over to the platform on the other side and boarded another Cercanias commuter train towards Dos Hermanos, a small town located about ten miles to the south of Seville. That was where James was going to get off and wait for Powells train to arrive, if his instinct of them getting the slower train was right

Lyndon Powell, Mike Williams, Chris Hampshire and Jack Reuben sat at a table with four seats and where in good spirits. They only had three more stations to stop at before they reached Seville, one of which was Dos Hermanos. They sat around the table on the Renfe Media Distancia train going over the presentation for Javier Ramos, they had finally decided that they were now happy with what they had and not to amend it before their meeting. The location of the meeting was still unknown to them, as Mr Ramos had not yet disclosed those details. The crew just thought that he was trying to keep the upper hand and trying to be smart. Lyndon had said he did not mind what tricks Ramos played because he did not care how or where it took place as long as he walked away with the fifty million pounds for him and his partners, that had previously been agreed. Lyndon had brought it up earlier in the journey that he anticipated Ramos trying to pay a lower price but he was determined to stick to his guns and would not accept anything less than what had already been agreed. The others knew Lyndon well and that he was no push over, if Javier Ramos thought he was then he would soon be proven wrong. For Javier Ramos was about to finally meet his match.

James Shaw sat on a bench in the blazing sun on the Seville bound platform at Dos Hermanos station, his phone buzzed in his pocket. It was a text from Delinda which read. *I miss you; I am so happy we met the other night. It has been amazing spending time with you.* James looked up at the electronic information board, it told him that a Media Distancia train was the third train due and would arrive in twenty-seven minutes, he was happy to wait and sit in the sun, and he decided to text Delinda back.
Me too, we have had a good time I hope it continues, he pressed send, he then found his brothers number and called him.

'Get into position in fifteen minutes we will be there in forty-five, I will see you back at the hotel for a beer, see you soon,' he ended the call.
Before he could put his phone away it buzzed again with another message from Delinda it read *I hope so too.*
James smiled to himself and thought *Is Lawrence right, am I falling in love?*
He had no time to answer, his phone was ringing in his hand, it was Lawrence Sharif.

'Yes.'

'Am I right in assuming you are not at San Bernardo since you have just answered your phone,' Lawrence said.

'I came out to Dos Hermanos, I had time to burn, I thought better to be in the sun than underground.'

'Good move, one of our Argentine friends is here, he is alone and hasn't yet spotted me, he arrived not long ago and keeps checking the arrivals board, and looking towards platform eleven, which is where the fast train from Malaga arrived four minutes ago, they must be coming in from your end as the last of the passengers have now surely walked out.'

'Interesting, they must be, the other Argentines must be with Ramos because nobody has been following us.'

'He will be keeping them close until all this is over, send me a text when you get on the train and have spotted Powell and his crew.'

'I will do, see you in a short while and don't forget those beers,' James said.

'I won't.'

James ended the call, and put his phone back in to his pocket, and sat back on the bench waiting for the train to arrive, he took a sip of the water he brought with him and spat it out as it had gone warm in the sun, he put the bottle in the bin, sat back down and lit a cigarette.

TWENTY-THREE

Squadron Leader William Ramsey slowed down as he approached the end of the slip road for the service station outside of Jerez de la Frontera, he had not seen the blue VW Polo since he had left Seville, nor had he seen any others.

Ramsey decided to stop here for a toilet break and to get himself a cold drink, before continuing his journey to Gibraltar. He parked his Volvo in the car park that was farthest from the service station, as he wanted the short walk to stretch out after being seated for the last hour. The car park was almost empty, it seemed not many people moved about on a Sunday in Spain. He sent a text to his partner Nadine to that say he would be home soon. After putting his phone back in to his pocket, he found himself face to face with two men who looked familiar, but he walked past them without hindrance or any words exchanged. Will put it down to coincidence and walked inside the service station.

Four minutes later he walked out in to the sun with a bottle of ice-cold water and a can of diet Pepsi, as he walked across the almost empty car park, the two men from earlier approached him from either side, but Will

Ramsey ignored them and continued towards his car, opening it via the key in his pocket so that when he got there, he could get straight in and drive off. What he was not aware of was the two men that were also following him from behind, as he had become preoccupied with the two coming from the side.

Will managed to get himself into his car, he started the engine and headed for the slip road to re-join the motorway, as he made the turn on to the slip road, he slammed his brakes on.
Blocking the slip road was a Blue VW Polo, which was parked across the lane. Ramsey put the selector in to reverse and screeched the car backwards performing a j-turn, he headed towards the slip road that he had earlier left the motorway from, he did not care that he would be facing the wrong way, he decided to handbrake turn at the bottom so that he would be facing the right way. This road was also blocked by another blue VW Polo, he was cornered.

Using his quick thinking, he decided to j-turn again and head back to the first Polo with his foot on the accelerator. With the speed climbing, he aimed for the rear of the VW knowing that his Volvo was a far superior car in strength and safety, as he approached the car, a shot was fired.

It hit his windscreen cracking the glass, making it impossible to see. Instead of hitting the rear of the VW he smashed right into the side of it, causing an almighty bang from the metal on metal collision. Which was followed by the bangs from the detonation of three airbags. The driver of the VW was killed instantly, the Volvo making his head slam violently into the side window, the passenger who was on the side that had been hit had his legs amputated by the crushed metal and was bleeding out and unable to do anything about it.

Will Ramsey was temporarily deaf from the explosion of the airbags. He put the selector in to reverse to try and pull out of the wreckage, with a screech he slowly reversed out of the wreckage, he was unharmed and got out of the car to check the damage and to see if he could still drive it. The only damage was that the front bumper had come off along with some minor dents.

'Volvo one, Volkswagen nil,' he said out loud.

Now he knew why they were called the safest cars in the world. After inspecting the damage, he swiftly got back in to the driver's side, reaching across to the glove box he pulled his Glock pistol out and shot the windscreen from the inside so that the glass would fall on the outside. After firing a second shot, the glass finally shattered and fell onto the bonnet.

A third shot was fired sending glass in to the Volvo and exploding the head rest behind where Wills head should have been had he not been leaning over to put his pistol back in the glove box. One of the Argentines from the other VW Polo had heard the loud bangs and went to investigate, he fired a round from his rifle into the Volvo. Will Ramsey feeling lucky to be alive put the car in to drive, and mounted the kerb to get around the VW that was parked across the lane, and he drove down the slip road and back on to the motorway, with the wind in his face, due to the new air conditioning system he had created.

Unknown to Ramsey, his car was leaking oil and blue smoke started coming out of the engine compartment, just five miles on from the service station. Will decided to pull over on to a small country road which he noticed up ahead. Three miles down the country road was the city of Jerez de la Frontera but the tarmac stopped after a mile and the road became a dirt track, for farm traffic he assumed. After taking his pistol out of the glove box and tucking it in to his waistband, Will set off in the direction of the city, to find some transport either to Gibraltar or back to Seville. After walking for five minutes, he turned around to see the other VW coming towards him, he ran off the road and in to the field on his left-hand side, which was full of olive trees, knowing that they could not get the car through the trees made it a level playing field.

Running amongst the trees he heard rifle fire and the sound of the rounds ricocheting of the tree trunks around him, he kept on running, zig zagging through the trees to try and lose the Argentines. Five more rounds were fired, more in hope than actual aiming, then a sixth hit Will Ramsey in his left calf sending him to the ground, he struggled back to his feet and tried to carry on running but was unable to, he even tried on one leg but to no avail.

Deciding to sit at the base of an olive tree in the hope that he would not be seen, he ripped his shirt off to use as a bandage on his leg, this helped ease the bleeding. As he lay with his back resting against the tree, he could hear the Argentines getting closer, he looked around the base of the tree and fired at one of them, the round grazed his right arm, Ramsey fired again, hitting him in the hand. The other Argentine appeared in front of Ramsey, and said in broken English.

'You leave me for the death, I will leave you to the death.'

He shot him with his pistol in the stomach, before Ramsey could fire back.

The Argentines left Ramsey where he was and walked back towards their car, where they had a first aid kit to bandage up the wounded soldier.

Will coughed up blood and kept pressure on the wound, but he knew deep down that the end was nigh, he reached in to his pocket with the last of his energy and got his phone. He sent a text to his partner Nadine saying *I love you*.

The phone fell out of his hand as he took his last breath, his lifeless body slumped down the olive tree and his head came to rest on the hard-sun-baked earth.

TWENTY-FOUR

James Shaw looked south down the tracks, and could see a white Media Distancia train approaching the station, the electronic board informed him it was the one he needed. As the train neared, he walked further down the platform so that he could look through the windows as it passed, before coming to a stop. The train passed him and he had spotted Lyndon Powell in the front coach on a table with four seats, they had left the sun shade open, he was sat with Mike Williams, Chris Hampshire and Jack Reuben. James remembered the others from the picture that Lawrence had sent to him when they first arrived in Seville. The train came to a stop, and James Shaw boarded the train at the rear most of the three carriages, the train was only half full.

Sunday really is the day of rest here, he said to himself, as he began to make his way through the coach to the front, where Lyndon Powell and his crew where sat. As he walked through the second coach, he sent a text to Lawrence Sharif saying.

On way, they are on here, he put his phone back in to his pocket and walked through the dividing doors in to coach one. After letting the door close behind, him, he

walked towards where Powell was sat and smiled a
greeting at them before sitting on one of the table seats
across the aisle from them.

TWENTY-FIVE

Lawrence Sharif had finished reading the text from James Shaw, and he watched the Argentine soldier he had been keeping an eye on walk to the end of the station and in to the male toilets. As he watched him enter the facilities, he was shocked to see John Shaw walk in behind him. Lawrence took his phone from his jeans pocket and dialled James's number; it rang and rang but he did not answer.

In the facilities; John Shaw walked over to the urinals, where Argentine special forces soldier Rodriquez was relieving himself. John grabbed him around the neck with his left arm and put his right arm around the top of his head, Rodriquez struggled, but John pulled his right arm and with a crack Rodriquez's neck was broken, he had taken his last breath.

  John put his arms out to catch the dead weight of Rodriquez's body and dragged it across the floor to trap four and sat him on the toilet, with his lifeless body slumped against the side wall of the trap. John closed the door on him and grabbed a handful of coins from his pocket, picking out a penny he used it to turn the lock from the outside to the occupied position, he put his change back in to his pocket, and left the toilets just as somebody was walking in. John Shaw left the station and walked back to Hotel Ayre to wait for James and Lawrence.

Lawrence Sharif watched as John Shaw left the station, and after two minutes concluded that the Argentine would not be leaving the toilets any time soon. After another unsuccessful attempt to contact James Shaw on the phone, Lawrence decided to send him a text.
Well done, good move, that will make are lives a bit easier, see you when you get here.
As he looked up at the arrivals board it said that James's train was due to arrive in five minutes. Lawrence decided to wait for him at the top of the moving ramp.

The train from Malaga came in to view underneath Lawrence as it pulled in to the station, once it stopped, about fifty people disembarked and headed for the moving ramp, some had suitcases, some had backpacks and some just themselves. Lawrence spotted Lyndon Powell and his men exiting from the furthest coach to him, all four men were dressed in suits and were pulling small suitcases on wheels. As they moved towards the ramp, he noticed James Shaw about ten paces behind them. The moving Ramp brought Lyndon Powell and the others to the concourse level, they walked right past Lawrence without paying him any attention and walked into the main concourse looking for the exit. Moments later James stepped off the moving ramp and walked to Lawrence.
'Shall we allow them time to work out where they are

going first?' James asked.

'What for, we know where they are going, we could get there before them if we wanted to. Would you care to explain what John was doing here?'

'It makes life easier for us, the last thing we need is eyes on that hotel whilst we are in there, then being followed to our new hotel, we need the advantage here.' Lawrence smiled and said 'Good work, you are wasted in the RAF, now let us go and meet John for that beer, before we introduce ourselves to Mr Powell and his friends.'

They hustled out of the station in to the heat and the bright sun, ahead of them Powell and his crew were walking towards Hotel Ayre, James and Lawrence kept themselves a short distance behind.

James and Lawrence walked in to the lobby of the hotel and right past Lyndon, Mike, Chris and Jack who were speaking with the desk clerk, who was checking them in. Shaw and Sharif walked outside to the pool area, where John was waiting for them with three large beers.

When he saw what James was wearing, he laughed and asked.

'Where are you going, yachting?'

James laughed with his brother.

'Just for that you can get the next one as well, did everything go OK with what we discussed?'

'Yes, we won't be having any problems from him.'

Lawrence cut in. 'Where did you come from? I didn't even see you in the station, only when you walked in to the toilets.'

'I wasn't in the station, I was outside, then I see that

Argie walk towards the toilet and I decided to strike.'

'Good work, thanks for the beer, I am sure our guests will be out here once they have checked out their rooms.'

'What are you doing tonight, John?' James asked.

'I have signed up for a tapas tour with a load of backpackers. What about you? Are you going out with Delinda and Ally?'

'A tapas tour, that sounds fun, yes, they are going to Malaga tomorrow, we should meet up when we have finished our meal.'

'Yes, good idea, I think it turns into a pub crawl after the food, so you four can join in with that.'

'Sounds like a plan, wouldn't you say Lawrence?'

'Yes, we have nothing to do tomorrow, well once we pack our stuff up and drop Ally and Delinda at the station around midday.'

Lyndon Powell, Mike Williams, Chris Hampshire and Jack Reuben walked out to the pool area around thirty minutes after they had checked in to the hotel. They each had a pint of lager in a plastic glass in their hands as they looked around the unfamiliar surroundings, trying to take it all in. The four men were all dressed in light coloured suits and had removed the ties that they were wearing earlier. Lyndon looked over to where James, Lawrence and John were standing like he recognised them but he looked away and carried on talking to his friends.

'Let us go and introduce ourselves,' Lawrence said to James and John

The three of them paced over to the other side of the

pool area to introduce themselves. Lawrence took the lead and stretched a hand out to Lyndon Powell.

'My name is Lawrence Sharif and this is James and John Shaw, we are here to oversee your business deal with Javier Ramos and ESPoil.'

The seven men all shook hands and exchanged pleasantries.

'I was not aware of this, who are you overseeing for?' Mike asked.

'The British government sent us to make sure that Mr Ramos plays fair and does not try to dupe you.'

What Lawrence had said was not a complete lie but also not the truth.

'Why would the government be interested in this deal, we are just a small company selling to a bigger one, this sort of thing happens every day,' Lyndon said matter-of-factly.

'They do indeed, however the government do not like the idea of its business owners being taken advantage of by foreign business's, thus taking away income and revenue from the UK.'

James looked at Lawrence with a look that said what are you going on about, but he let him carry on.

Lyndon looked confused.

'Well, that is very concerning of them, I was not expecting this, will you be in the meeting? Ramos is not very fond of Brits as we have found out'

'No, we will be nearby, we do not want to interfere, we are just here in case things don't go as planned, where is the meeting taking place anyway?' Lawrence asked.

'We have not been told yet, Ramos said to contact him

when we arrive and he will inform us of the location of the meet,' Mike answered.

'I assume you have not informed him of your arrival yet, give it another couple of hours, get settled in here go and see the city first,' James said.

Lawrence handed a business card to Lyndon Powell, the card read *Lawrence Sharif, Director of Foreign Trade* and it had a foreign office logo in the top left corner and at the bottom his mobile phone number.

'As soon as he tells you the location, call me on that number and we will make the necessary arrangements, enjoy your first night here, this is a great city, I look forward to hearing from you.'

He shook Lyndon's hand and then the others. James and John did the same, and Lyndon asked the two of them where they were from, as he detected a Liverpudlian accent in them a bit like his own, washed out over the years from living out of the city but still underlying. James answered him and said 'Crosby, originally.'

'Small world, so am I,' Lyndon said.

'It is a small world, we will see each other again soon, have a nice night, nice to meet you lad,' James winked at him, acknowledging their shared home town which they were brought up in.

James, Lawrence and John walked away from the pool area back indoors.

'Enjoy your Tapas tour, and text me when you have finished and we will come and meet you for a drink,' James said.

'I will do, enjoy your meal, see you later.'

John walked over to the lifts to return to his room, whilst James and Lawrence left the hotel walking out on to the traffic heavy street.

'I will get the car,' James said.

'You have had a drink.'

'Only one. I will be fine'.

'It only takes one,' Lawrence said.

'Your right, let's get a taxi, dibs not in the paying seat.' They stood on the pavement looking in both directions for a taxi, a few drove by but were occupied.

'We will just get one at the station it will be easier,' James said.

'Good thinking Batman.'

They finally managed to cross the road after waiting for the lights to change and headed towards the main entrance to Santa Justa station, where all the taxis would be parked up waiting for their next fare. They got in to a SEAT Toledo taxi, which seemed to be the car of choice for taxis in the city, and they told the driver that they were going to the Barrio Santa Cruz.

After getting out of the taxi a street away from the apartment they were staying in, they split up and walked in opposite directions to make sure that they were not being followed. They met each other at the street door to the apartment building, nobody had been following them.

James Shaw led the way in to the building, taking each step one at a time as he did not want to stretch more than he had to, as his stitches had been causing him pain since he had gotten off the train at Santa Justa. James led

Lawrence through the front door of the apartment, there was no sign of Delinda or Ally and the apartment was spotless with two roller bags by the door they had just walked through.

'I wonder where they have gone?' James asked.

'Not sure but they are coming back because their bags are still here.'

James nodded in agreement with Lawrence, he stepped in to the bedroom he was sharing with Delinda. His bag was still under the bed where he had put it, he turned back around to walk out of the bedroom, the front door to the apartment opened, James Shaw instinctively reached for his Beretta. Delinda and Ally walked through the door with Ally holding a cup holder containing four cups, and Delinda was holding paper bags with something hot in them he assumed as Delinda was holding them by the top of the bags.

'Hey guys, I grabbed us all some churros and hot chocolate, take a seat,' Delinda said as she placed the bags of hot churros on the table along with the drinks Ally put down.

James and Lawrence took a seat opposite Delinda and Ally and they dipped churros in to the hot chocolate.

'That was good timing, wasn't it? I wasn't expecting to come back and find you all packed and cleaned, I will do the same once we have finished these, they are delicious by the way, thank you,' James said.

'I like to be organised that's all, we have got an early start in the morning.'

Before he could say anything in return James's phone vibrated in his pocket, it was his brother John, he swiped the screen to answer the call.

'Hello John,' he said, and listened, then Lawrence's phone was ringing and James motioned him to pick it up before continuing his own conversation.

'OK, they are calling him now, thanks John. I will text you later and let you know where we are, see you later' James hung up the phone at the same time as Lawrence.

'Was that them? John said 1400 Tuesday at the Alfonso XIII hotel, that's good for us, no travelling.'

'Yes, that's what Powell just told me too, very good indeed, we can plan tomorrow when we are there.'

'Yes, sorry ladies, thank you again for the churros, how do you fancy some Tapas tonight?'
'Sounds good to me,' Delinda answered.
Ally and Lawrence also agreed with him, they all sat laughing and enjoying their Hot chocolate and churros, before going to relax by the pool for a few hours.

TWENTY-SIX

The hot Andalusian sun blazed over the City of Seville; James Shaw lay on his sun lounger lost in thought. Many thoughts raced through the dusty recesses of his mind in regards to the next day, and how it would play out with Lyndon Powell, his men and the unpredictable Javier Ramos.

Ramos was the one variable in all of this that James Shaw felt he could not control or second guess, as the man was clearly some kind of lunatic from what he had read and been told about him. However, James Shaw's thoughts started to drift as they had since he was about fourteen years old to the subject of females, more specifically this time to Delinda Saint Germain. He had enjoyed the past few days that they had spent together, and he was looking forward to his impending trip to the USA with her. The problem was what he was seeing beyond that trip, it was something he had never envisioned before, it involved himself and Delinda having a future together. *Was this the time for James Shaw to finally settle down*? He asked himself.

James was awoken from his thoughts by Lawrence Sharif placing an ice cold can of beer on his forehead, this caused James to jump up in shock.

'You're an absolute arsehole,' he shouted.

Lawrence laughed and sat next to him, he put Delinda and Ally's beers under his lounger out of the sun as they were chatting to each other in the pool.

James turned to look at Lawrence and lifted his sunglasses up.

'Do you think Ramos knows that we are staying at the Alfonso tomorrow? It seems a bit coincidental that he has arranged to have his meeting there with Powell and his men the day we decide to book a room there.'

Lawrence sat up and held his beer in both hands.

'I must agree with you, but on the other hand it is the cities top hotel so it makes sense that he would choose to meet there, to make Powell feel important yet intimidated, it is all about power with Ramos.'

'Sounds the most likely reason, maybe I am just overthinking this,' James said leaning over to his table to reach for his cigarettes, he lit one and threw the packet to Lawrence who took one.

'Thanks, you have been doing a lot of thinking, recently haven't you?'

James Shaw took a long drag on his cigarette before he answered Lawrence with.

'Well don't all people think?'

'Don't get smart, we both know what I meant.'

'Not my fault it's just the way things are,' James said as he put his cigarette out in the ashtray.

He stood up, ran and jumped in to the swimming pool, sending the water splashing over Lawrence, who said to himself *I am losing him, he is all grown up now,* like he was James's father.

Whilst daydreaming earlier Shaw had switched his phone onto silent mode from vibrate, as he swam towards Delinda he was unaware that a number unknown to him had tried to call his phone. James swam up behind Delinda and put his hands around her waist and kissed her neck, she responded by turning her head and kissing him slowly.

'I will leave you guys to it.' Ally said as she swam over to the edge of the pool near to Lawrence.

He was shaking his head at the man, who since the moment he met him, had been the consummate professional, of course he had his moments, he was a joker and a womaniser, somebody who his juniors looked up to and respected, but he had never let a female interfere with his work. It wasn't at the moment either but he could see that Delinda had feelings for James and that he felt the same way about her.

Hold it together for a few more days Jim Sharif said to himself, just as Ally got out of the water to sit next to him.

James and Delinda were still in the pool with their arms around each other and still kissing passionately.

'Shall we go inside?' She whispered in his ear.

'That would be a good idea, come on let's go.'

They climbed out of the pool and grabbed a towel each, drying themselves as they made their way back to Delinda's bedroom. James closed the door behind them and kissed Delinda again as he undid her bikini top, she moved her arms out of it as it dropped to the floor, he moved his hands down her tanned body as she moved hers down his before falling back on to the bed pulling James on top of her.

After it was over, she looked up in to his eyes lovingly and said,

'James Shaw, I love you; you are amazing, it feels like I have known you so much longer than just a few days.'

'It is strange, isn't it? I am having an amazing time with you and I love you too.'

He had said it and he meant it, Delinda smiled at him and kissed his tanned chest.

James lay there looking at the ceiling and said in his head *I cannot believe I have just said that but I meant it, I really love her.*

Everything seemed right for him at the minute, promotion, money, nice car and now a beautiful woman, who adored him as much as he adored her. He drove these thoughts from his mind to focus on the real reason he was in Seville.

'Shall we freshen up, and re-join the others,' he said. She agreed and chased James in to the bathroom. James turned the shower on and took his razor out of his soap bag and put it on the little soap dish in the shower stall, he stepped into the hot steamy water. Delinda joined him and said 'I hope you don't mind.'

'Of course not, we can wash each other.'

He grabbed the shower gel off the shelf and squirted some in to his hands, and he worked it in to a lather as he rubbed it over Delinda's body, she took the bottle and returned the favour to him. She noticed that he was getting in the mood again so she kissed him.

They eventually got showered afterwards and James had a shave as the clock moved around to 1900hrs.

'Shall we get ready?' James asked.

Delinda agreed and opened the closet, as James fished out some clothes from his bag.

'Would you like me to iron anything for you?'

'No, I'm good,' she said.

James took out of his bag a khaki pair of Ralph Lauren chinos and an orange Ralph Lauren polo shirt, the ones with the big logo and number three on the sleeve, James went off to the living area to iron his clothes.

In a world of his own ironing, James failed to notice Lawrence sneak up behind him

'Ally and I are going to dine together tonight, you and Delinda can do the same, is that OK?'

'Yes, why though, I was under the impression we would all be going out together.'

'We just thought that it would be a good idea to dine alone, as it is their last night here, we will meet later for drinks.'

'OK mate, if you are happy with that.'

'Yes, Ally is good company.'

James finished ironing his clothes.

'Shall I leave this up for you?' He said pointing at the ironing board.

'Please mate, thank you.'

James picked up his clothes and carried them back to the bedroom, where Delinda was finishing putting her make up on, her hair was down and she had bright red lipstick on, and a light eye shadow which she was just finishing. *Wow* James said to himself, as she was sat there in black underwear and black patent leather high heels.

'Are you going out like that?' He quipped.

'No silly,' she replied.

James put his chinos on and his desert boots, as he tied them, he thought to himself.

I should have brought another pair of shoes, but then again, I was expecting to be in the Falklands.

After tying his shoes, he stood up and put his polo shirt on, he was ready after a quick spray of Paco Rabane aftershave. Delinda got dressed into a knee length black dress, which was sleeveless and showed off her tanned skin perfectly. James looked at her, then himself in the mirror and felt under dressed *Why is she with me?* He asked himself. Sensing his thoughts, she said to him.

'You look nice, very handsome and smart'.

'Thanks, you look amazing. I forgot to mention that Sharif and Ally wish to dine alone, so it will be just you and I for dinner.'

'Oh OK, I look forward to it, shall we go then?'

' Yes, we can meet the others for drinks later, where shall we eat?'

'I really don't mind, how about you?'

Typical female response James thought to himself.

'How about one of those restaurants near where we went last night, they all looked nice?'

'OK, sounds good.'

'Shall we get a taxi or can you walk in those shoes?'

'I am OK, later I will need a taxi home though.'

They said goodbye to Lawrence and Ally, and left the apartment, heading towards the cathedral.

TWENTY-SEVEN

Thirty seconds after leaving the apartment, Lawrence Sharif came out chasing after James and Delinda. James turned around and asked 'Are you OK?'
'Yes, you left your phone by the pool.'
James took the phone from Lawrence and said 'Thanks mate, I will see you later, yes.'
'You will, enjoy your dinner,' and with that Lawrence turned on his heel and jogged back to the apartment.
James checked his phone, it showed that he had a missed call from a number he did not recognise.
'More PPI shite,' he said aloud before putting his phone in his pocket.
'What is PPI?' Delinda asked him.
'Oh, just some nuisance calls everybody in the UK gets, even though I haven't lived there for years.'
They strolled together hand in hand along the sun-soaked streets of Barrio Santa Cruz, the sun still burnt brightly even at seven thirty P.M.

Ten minutes later after an uneventful walk through Barrio Santa Cruz they arrived at the little street where they had dined the night before with the others. They looked over a few menus displayed outside various establishments, before settling on a restaurant with rooftop seating, that served local dishes. The waitress had seated them at a table for two along the roof wall with a view of the city.

James Shaw excused himself from the table and asked Delinda to order him a beer if the waitress came over. He headed back towards the lift, that they had just come up in, he pressed the call button and waited for the lift to arrive. He turned around and looked at Delinda who was partaking in some kind of selfie pose with her phone, she was not looking in his direction. The motor and cables from the lift stopped and the doors opened, before they could open fully James Shaw launched at the lift with his right fist, using his whole body for speed, his fist connected with the man's face who was preparing to step out. The man was slammed into the back wall of the lift, as the speed and power of James's punch knocked him off his feet. The sound of bone crunching could be heard as the man's nose was shattered, along with a few teeth that fell out of his mouth. The man slumped to the floor unconscious, then James relieved him of his phone. The man was dressed in combat trousers, long sleeve t-shirt, fishing vest and boots, the same throw together uniform all the other Argentines had been wearing, when himself and Sharif had first encountered them. James pressed a button on the lift panel to take it down to the next floor, where the facilities where located. When the doors opened, he dragged the soldier out of the lift towards the gents, hoping that they were not occupied. They were not.

He dragged the soldier into one of the traps and sat him on the seat, and he locked the door behind him. James Shaw took the laces out of the Argentines boots and tied his hands and legs together and stuffed his mouth with one of his sweaty socks, so that when he came around, he would be unable to call for help. Shaw climbed up over the locked door and dropped down the other side on to the bathroom floor. He dropped the phone he had taken, in to the bin on his way out and made his way back upstairs. On the way he sent a text to Sharif saying. ***Watch out, Argentinians about.***

Lawrence Sharif replied ***Copied*, thanks**.

Shaw took his seat opposite Delinda, she had ordered a pint of lager for him which was on the table waiting for him, he duly took a sip. Delinda spotted the redness on James's right hand.

'My god look at your hand, what happened?' she asked. He spread his fingers out and looked at them.

'I caught it in the door of the toilet, it will be fine.' Delinda put her hand on his and tenderly stroked his hand, he looked up at her and smiled.

Shaw had spotted the Argentine with his peripheral vision, when himself and Delinda were studying the menu downstairs, and he had deduced that he was following him. Deciding to deal with him would make the end game a lot easier.

'What can I expect in Nashville then?' James asked.

'I will have to take you to a Honky Tonk on Broadway,

and try the hot chicken.'

'Hot chicken sounds good, what is a Honky Tonk. I have heard them mentioned in country songs but have no idea what it is?'

'It is just a bar that plays country music, but everyone joins in and dances.'

'I look forward to that, I need to let my hair down after this week.'

Their food was brought out and they ate in between conversation.

They did not want to be anywhere else at that moment in time.

Lyndon Powell, Mike Williams, Chris Hampshire and Jack Reuben were sat at the bar in Hotel Ayre with a city map laid out on the table. They were trying to decide where to go for the night, firstly for food and then later on drinks. Mike suggested somewhere near to the Alfonso XIII hotel so that they could check it out before their meeting with Ramos on Tuesday. The others agreed with him, and they would leave once they had finished their drinks.

After meeting with James, Lawrence and John earlier, the four men had gone up to Lyndon's room and went over the presentation for the meeting with Javier Ramos on Tuesday afternoon. As they sat there going over each detail with a fine toothcomb, they were unaware that Ramos had already manoeuvred floating platforms and people into the areas that they had earmarked for drilling. They also had no idea that Ramos just wanted the permits and did not care one bit about a sales pitch, he just wanted a swift exchange, the fifty million pounds to Lyndon and his men, and the permits for drilling for himself. This was the biggest job they were about to pull off, yet it would be the easiest, usually they would pull this sort of con off with fake stock certificates, fake permits and the like, but they had done their homework on Javier Ramos and they all decided to do everything properly so as not to end up as part of the Seville metro expansion.

James Shaw and Delinda Saint Germain stepped out on to the cobbled street, and were surrounded by people sat outside of restaurants eating and laughing, generally enjoying themselves, it was mostly tourists on desert and locals just getting started, as they went out to eat later than the tourists. Shaw had a good look around to see if anybody else was planning to surprise them, there wasn't which he was happy about. He took hold of Delinda's hand, and they walked along the cobbles. Delinda taking each step with care in her heels. They reached a road, and James flagged down a taxi, asking the driver to take them to Maria Luisa Park.

After a short taxi ride, they got out at the gates to Maria Luisa Park, which was home to the awe-inspiring Plaza de Espana, the plaza consists of a semi-circular building with a canal separating the building from the plaza, four bridges cross the canal from the buildings, leading to a big open tiled space with a fountain in the centre. It was built for the Spanish exposition in 1929 and has been used as a filming location for various films, including *Lawrence of Arabia*. It was now home to government offices. James and Delinda walked through the park gates towards the vast Plaza de Espana, and they took some pictures together in the square. The canal had rowing boats for hire, a handful of people were struggling around the canal in the evening heat.

'Would you like to go on a boat?' Delinda asked.

'Yes, why not. I will have to take it easy with my stitches though.'

'I will row sweetie, you relax.'

'No, it is ok, I will just take it slow.'

'Well, if you are sure,' Delinda said.

'No problem at all, let's do it.'

James got in to the boat after paying the attendant, and he helped Delinda in before he set off rowing. Even at this late hour the temperature was well above thirty degrees. Delinda offered to take an oar but James declined, as he powered the boat along the canal with his arms. Delinda was posing for selfies whilst James had control of the boat, unaware that she was also taking photos of him. After twenty minutes, James turned the boat around to head back to the starting point.

'Are you sure that you want to come back to America with me, I wouldn't want you to feel as though you have to?' Delinda asked him.

James rested the oars.

'Of course, I want to, why would I not, do you still want me to come?'

'Yes of course I do, I suppose I am not used to this, having only met you a few days ago and feeling like this, it is crazy.'

He smiled at her

'It is crazy you're right, but then the world is crazy.'

He picked up the oars again and rowed through gritted teeth, as he was in pain from where he had been stabbed a few nights earlier but he continued on through the pain. They eventually reached the end and the boat owner helped Delinda out of the boat, James stepped out without any help.

James was now in some pain and struggled to walk. However, his luck was in, as he spotted a horse and carriage, they got in and asked the rider to take them to Bar Chile. Bar Chile was where they had first met, and they thought it ample that it should be where they would spend their last night in Seville together. As the coachman controlled the horses Delinda rested her head on James shoulder and held his hand tight.

'Thank you for a lovely night, you really are a gentleman.'

'Thank you too. The night is still young.'

'It sure is.'

They sat in silence holding on to each other for the rest of the journey.

They arrived at Bar Chile, and Delinda took the initiative and ordered them both a bottle of the local lager Cruzcampo.

'When we get to New York can we go to Central Park? I have always wanted to walk through Central Park.'

'It is right opposite the Plaza Hotel, so we can do that for sure,' Delinda replied.

'I look forward to it, my first ever trip to New York.'

'It will be great, just me and you in the big apple.'

'Then on to Nashville, I have only been to the north and Las Vegas.'

'You are going to love Nashville, you will enjoy the southern way of having fun, and meeting my folks.'

'Yes, I am looking forward to it.'

Truth was, James Shaw was nervous about meeting Delinda's parents, even though they were getting along great, in reality they had only known each other for a few days. What were her parents going to think of him? Delinda had not mentioned meeting her parents earlier. James was saved by a text from Lawrence asking if they had finished eating. James replied saying that they had and told him where they were.

Ten minutes later, Lawrence and Ally stepped out of a taxi and walked over to James and Delinda, taking a seat at the table. Lawrence motioned James over to the bar and they got up from the table to go and order some more drinks.

'In the morning, after we have dropped the ladies off at the station, we shall go get ourselves some new suits suitable for tomorrow,' Lawrence said to James as the barman put four bottles of beer on the bar, which James paid for.

'If that is what you want to do, why suits?'

'It is a nice hotel full of people on business dressed in suits, so we need to blend in.'

'OK, that is fine, I will get a new shirt as well.'

They walked back to the table to re-join Delinda and Ally. The four chatted over more beers for another two hours, and Delinda and James danced to a couple of songs.

James received a text from his brother John saying that his tour was finishing in a night-club called Bilindo, which was about five hundred yards along the road that they were on. They finished up their beers and left to go meet with John and the tour at club Belindo.

TWENTY-EIGHT

The sun had set long ago, but the air remained hot as James Shaw, Delinda Saint Germain, Lawrence Sharif and Ally Simmons queued up outside the Bilindo night-club. Bilindo is a favoured night spot in the city, it backs on to the Maria Luisa Park, and has an outdoor dancefloor and bar. The perfect venue for a hot night. Eventually they got in to the club and walked over to where John stood chatting to a man and two women at the bar, they introduced themselves to each other, one of the women and the man excused themselves, leaving John with a woman of about twenty, who said she was from Australia.

After dancing and drinking for the best part of three hours, James and Delinda decided to go back to the apartment. Lawrence Sharif and Ally Simmons followed, and the four of them left the night-club to go and get a taxi. John Shaw said that he was going to stay out with the Australian girl, whose name James could not remember.

TWENTY-NINE

The Guardia Civil had received a call from a farmer
who owned an olive grove, just off the A4 motorway,
near Jerez de la Frontera at 0600hrs. The caller had said
in a panic that he had found a man dead on his Olive
plantation with lots of blood around him that had dried
up, suggesting that maybe he had been there since
yesterday, as the farmer did not do any work on
Sundays. The farmer also said that there was a car on the
side road from the motorway, he said it was damaged,
like it had been in a crash with another car.

Two Guardia Civil officers arrived at the farm on the
same road that Squadron Leader Will Ramsey had used a
day earlier. They parked their marked Nissan X-Trail
behind the battered Volvo that Ramsey had been driving.
They got out of the car and looked around the Volvo,
they noticed blue paint chippings that were embedded
into the front wing.
  'Looks like a bad crash,' one of the officers said.
Before the other officer could reply, the farmer came out
to meet them. They introduced themselves and the
farmer took them through the Olive trees to where
Squadron Leader Ramsey's body was resting. One of the

officers called for an ambulance, he could see straight away that Ramsey had been shot in the abdomen and most likely had bled to death out in the sun as one side of his face was burnt. As they waited for the ambulance to arrive the first officer looked through Ramsey's pockets, and told the second officer to put his gloves on and check the Volvo. The first officer found Will's wallet in his back pocket, the wallet contained bank cards, a couple of hundred euros cash and his Royal Air Force Identification card, which had his picture, date of birth, height and rank alongside his name. The officer swore out loud, the farmer asked what was the matter, but the officer said nothing and called his garrison, as the British consulate in Malaga would need to be informed, who would in turn inform the next of Kin.

The second officer came back from the car with a passport in his hand and handed it over to the first officer, who was in charge. The name on the passport matched that of the Royal Air Force ID card.

'What else is in the car?'

'Just a bag with clothes,' the second officer answered. The Argentinians had taken Ramsey's Glock with them.

'OK, we will wait by the car for the ambulance.'

They thanked the farmer for his help, and said he could go back to his work.

As the officers stood by their car waiting for the ambulance to arrive, the officer in charge's phone rang in his pocket. It was the Colonel of the garrison, he spoke at length, and the officer listened, he ended the call. The British consulate was sending somebody up to the hospital from Malaga and they would inform the next of kin, the British had been promised a full investigation and all progress will be reported to them.

'Why do you think he was killed?' the second officer asked.

'That is what we need to find out. This looks like a professional job, whoever shot him knew he would bleed to death, the who and why, we will find out later.'
As he finished his sentence, he could hear the sirens of the ambulance as it turned onto the road. After a few minutes struggling through the olive trees, the crew had bagged Will up and put him in to the ambulance and took his body to the nearest hospital with a morgue.

After seeing all the documentation and the body, the British delegate from Malaga called Squadron Leader Ramsey's commanding officer in Gibraltar to inform him of the news. Wing Commander Gibson was upset about the news as he and Ramsey were good friends, as were both of their wives. Gibson wiped tears from his eyes, and grabbed his hat from his desk, he would personally go and tell Ramsey's partner Nadine the worst possible news at 0830hrs on a Monday morning.

THIRTY

At 0830hrs in Seville, Wing Commander James Shaw sat up in bed, with Delinda Saint Germain resting her head on his chest, they spoke about the next couple of days, and their impending trip to America, once they had rendezvoused in Malaga. In the other bedroom down the hall, Lawrence Sharif awoke to a series of missed calls and a text message from his boss saying *Call me now Sharif.*

'This cannot be good,' he said out loud, he called the number that had text him, it was answered after one ring, the voice at the other end said to Sharif.

'What is going on down there?'

'Sir, what is the problem?'

'Had you enlisted the help of an RAF intelligence officer, Squadron Leader Ramsey?'

'Yes Sir, Wing Commander Shaw brought him onboard, why?'

'Well, he is dead, the Guardia Civil received a call at 0600 local time this morning, they found him on a farm, gunshot wound, he bled out.'

'Shit,' Lawrence gasped.

'Yes, his next of kin will be informed, and the official

line is that he was on his way back to Gibraltar after visiting friends in Seville. Make sure nothing like this happens again, once tomorrow is done get out of there, take some leave, and come back in a few weeks well rested, do you understand?'

'Yes Sir, thank you for informing me, I will let Wing Commander Shaw know, and no more mistakes, thank you Sir.'

'Good, inform me tomorrow when you have completed your task, then don't come back here for four weeks.'

'Yes Sir,' and at that Lawrence Sharif's boss ended the call.

Ally Simmons lay in bed still asleep, so Lawrence decided to go wake Shaw up and tell him the bad news about Squadron Leader William Ramsey. He banged on Delinda's bedroom door.

'UP,' He shouted.

James Shaw got out of bed to see what the problem was, he answered the door in his underwear.

'Out here,' he said pointing to the lounge area.

'What is going on?' James asked.

'Sit Down,' Lawrence said.

James took a seat and Lawrence sat opposite him.

'I have just gotten off the phone with my boss, he told me that Will was shot and found on a farm this morning, he bled out, I am sorry.'

James said nothing.

About a minute later he spoke.

'Who?' he asked.

'We don't know.'

'Shit, what about Nadine and the baby, he should have told me, I would never have asked him to get involved if I had known.'

Lawrence stood up and put his hand on James's shoulder.

'It's not your fault, he wanted to help, I doubt he would have left if you had told him to.'

'Your right, he was one of my best friends, lets focus on the here and now, the time to mourn will be once we have finished here.'

James stood up and went back to Delinda's bedroom to get dressed, he felt bad for not fully mourning his friend's death but he would in due course. He was even more determined to get this job finished successfully, so that he could avenge Ramsey's death.

'Are you OK?' Delinda asked

'Will was found dead a few hours ago.'

'Oh my god, how awful, What about his baby? Are you OK?'

'I will be, are you all set to go, we will have to get a taxi the car is at the station, are you sure you don't want us to drive you to Malaga it is not a problem.'

'No baby, it is fine we will get the train, I feel so bad about Will, I love you, James.'

Delinda kissed and held him tight.

'I love you too,' James replied.

At this moment he felt happy and safe in Delinda's arms, he wished that she would be staying in Seville for tonight as he did not want to be alone.

Thirty minutes later James Shaw left the apartment and got in to the taxi that he had ordered on his phone. He asked the driver to take him to Santa Justa station.

At the station, Shaw got out of the taxi and walked over to the car park, to get in to the Range Rover he had hired a few days earlier. After a short but slow drive, he arrived back at the apartment, Ally buzzed him inside. He helped the ladies load the car with all the luggage, Delinda and Ally's went in last as it would be first out. The four of them got in to the car, and James put the selector in to drive and set off for Santa Justa station. James looked up in the rear-view mirror to look at Delinda.

'Are you sure you don't want me to take you to Malaga?' he asked.

'No, it's OK thank you for offering, we don't want to be any trouble,' Ally replied.

'We have already paid for our tickets it seems a waste not to use them,' Delinda added.

'OK then,' he said with a smile, and turned his attention back to the road.

Ten minutes later they arrived at Santa Justa station, James parked the car in the short stay car park at the front entrance and paid two euros for thirty minutes at the barrier.

James Shaw got out first and opened Delinda's door on his way to the boot, Lawrence did the same for Ally. James lifted their luggage out of the boot, but as he did, he felt a searing pain in his abdomen from when he had been slashed with the knife by the would-be Argentine assassin.

They walked out of the heat in to the cool station, and James winced in pain once again, Lawrence noticed this but said nothing. On the station concourse the arrivals board showed that the train to Malaga had just arrived at platform eleven. The departure board showed that it would leave in ten minutes time. The four of them walked under the boards and through the doors to the access ramps to the platforms. Delinda put her arms around James and kissed him.

'All being well, I shall see you Wednesday, if not Thursday,' James said.

'I sure hope it's Wednesday.'

'Me too.'

Lawrence and Ally had also finished saying their goodbyes. Two Renfe employees were checking tickets at the top of the moving ramp so there would be no romantic waving off at the platform this time either. As Delinda and Ally waited to get their tickets checked, James walked over to her.

'Send me a text when you arrive in Malaga.'

'I sure will baby,' she said and kissed James again before showing their tickets to the inspector.

Shaw and Sharif waited at the top as Delinda and Ally descended down the moving ramp, when they reached the train they turned, looked up and waved at them before boarding, Shaw and Sharif waved back and turned on their heel and headed back towards the car.

James Shaw looked at his watch, it said the time was 1128.

'What now Chief, we cannot check in to the hotel until 1400?' James said over the roof of the car.

'Maybe you should go see a doctor.'

'Oh, don't worry about me, a few pills and a nice hot bath and I will be fine.'

'Well, if you are sure, let us go and get something to wear for tomorrow.'

'OK, I will park at the hotel,' James said. 'Do you think that Ramos's men killed Will?'

'I hate to speculate, but yes, there is no other scenario I can think of, what are the chances of a random shooting at the side of a motorway in Spain. Please though James do not try to get revenge, we need to see this through.'

'Don't worry about me, I know what needs to be done, have I ever let you down before?'

'Yes,' Lawrence said laughing.

James pulled up at the Alfonso XIII Hotel car park and his phone rang in his pocket, it was his brother John Shaw, he asked Lawrence to answer it and put it on speaker phone.

'Morning,' John said.

James laughed and said 'Is it, what time do you call this, what time did you get back last night?'

'I have just got back now; I couldn't remember the name of the hotel so I had to get a taxi to the station then I saw the hotel opposite.'

James and Lawrence snorted with laughter.

'Hang on where have you been then, if you are only just getting back now?' Lawrence asked.

'Some backpackers hostel with that Australian girl I met in that outside nightclub.'

James took the key out of the slot and stepped out of the car; Lawrence stepped out of the other side with James's phone in his hand and walked around to where James stood.

'Do you want to meet us in the old town, we are going to buy some clothes for tomorrow?'

'Yes OK, can we get something to eat? I am starving.'

'Yes, we will meet you at Plaza Del Duque in around half an hour,' James said.

'OK, see you there.'

Lawrence ended the call and handed the phone back to James.

THIRTY-ONE

At the pool area of Hotel Ayre, Lyndon, Mike and Chris crowded around Jack's sun lounger. Jack showed them the final version of their presentation for their meeting with Javier Ramos tomorrow on his iPad.

'Leave it as it is now. If we keep going over and over it, we will miss something, check again in the morning, now let us enjoy the sun, I am going for a swim,' Lyndon said.

And with that he jumped in to the pool.

'Is he not being a bit to confident?' Jack asked Mike.

'No, like he said you can over analyse, by the way it is good, we will find out tomorrow wont we, enjoy yourself, get some sun, you need it.'

John Shaw clocked the four of them by the pool as he looked out of his hotel room window. He watched them for a few minutes, and he then left to meet James and Lawrence. John headed for the lift to take him down to the lobby, where he would get a taxi into the old town to meet his brother. His phone indicated a message as he stepped out of the lift.

We are sat outside a bar opposite Plaza del Duque. By a Burger King. James text him.

John hustled through the lobby doors and climbed in to a taxi that had just dropped a couple off at the hotel. John told the taxi driver to take him to Plaza Del Duque.

THIRTY-TWO

John Shaw got out of the taxi on the opposite side of the street to where James and Lawrence where sitting. He paid the driver and crossed over the road to join them.

'Beer?' James asked.

'God no, just a fresh orange please.'

James motioned the waiter over and ordered an orange juice for his brother.

'What are you two up to then?' John asked.

'Getting some new clothes to wear for this meeting tomorrow,' Lawrence answered.

'And your girlfriends?'

'On the train to Malaga, and she is not my girlfriend, I can't speak for him though,' Lawrence answered as he tilted his head towards James.

James reached in to his pocket and pulled out a packct of cigarettes and said help yourselves, John declined and Lawrence took one, and said thanks.

'Will is dead. Found this morning, shot on a farm off the motorway to Gibraltar,' James said.

'Shit, who was it do we know?'

'Not for sure but we can guess that it is Ramos's men,'

Lawrence replied.

John raised his glass of orange juice and said 'To Will, rest in peace.'

The others raised their glasses.

'Obviously we have to focus on the job in hand,' Lawrence said.

'I need to reach out to Nadine, see if she needs any help with anything. I cannot imagine what she is going through now, a child on the way, this was meant to be a good time for them. I have known Will since we first walked through those gates at Cranwell all those years ago. I could understand if he was killed in Syria or Afghanistan, but this, why did he agree to help me knowing he had a baby on the way?'

Lawrence cut him off 'Do not beat yourself up, it is not your fault, he wanted to help you as a friend, call Nadine when we get to the hotel.'

James nodded in agreement with what Lawrence had said.

'What are you doing after here John?' James asked.

'Not sure yet, I better call the Colonel before he blows his top, I just left and he wanted to know what was going on.'

'Just call him and I will speak to him,' Lawrence said.

John reached for his phone and dialled the Colonels number from memory, the phone was answered after three rings.

'Good morning, Sir, Major Shaw.'

James and Lawrence could hear the Colonel.

'Don't you good morning me Major, where the devil are you, I want answers or you will be back to a Captain before you know what day it is, do you hear.'

'Just hold one second Sir,' John said, and handed the phone over to Lawrence who spoke to the Colonel.

'Hello Colonel, my name is Lawrence Sharif and I work for the Foreign Office. I am sorry Colonel it was a last-minute thing; your Major will be returned to you in a couple of days.'

'I see, well next time tell him to inform me, goodbye,' the Colonel replied.

Lawrence ended the call and handed the phone back to John Shaw.

'Thanks for that, got me off the hook with that moaning bastard,' John said.

Delinda and Ally were an hour away from Malaga, the train they were on had just left a station called Bobadilla. Their conversation had turned to the subject of James Shaw and Lawrence Sharif.

'So, what about you and Lawrence?' Delinda asked.

'We are just having a bit of fun, no strings, how about you and James? You guys seem pretty serious huh.'

'Yes, I just don't know what will happen in the future, with me just finishing college and trying to start with a firm in New York.'

'Would you not move to England and maybe work there?'

'I could do I guess, it is something I could look at, if James wanted me to move to England, then I would, I guess,' Delinda said.

Delinda took her phone out and searched the process for working in England with a law degree from the USA.

The train passed through the mountains, tunnel after tunnel going the opposite way to which Lyndon Powell and his men had travelled the day before.

James Shaw had finished his beer and lit a cigarette, he sorted through his cash and left twenty euros under his empty glass, it was enough to cover the three drinks and for a handsome tip for the waiter.

'Come on then, let's go and do some shopping,' James said.

They headed off in the direction of the main shopping street, Calle de Velazquez with its narrow passageway and high buildings either side, it provided some nice relief from the searing sun overhead. Lawrence led them in to a shop that sold formal wear, he said something in Spanish to a man who had a tape measure around his neck, he motioned James over to him and the man began to measure him up. After they had all been measured and after some fittings, they left the shop nearly five hundred euros lighter, each. They each had purchased a stone-coloured linen suit, shirt, shoes and belt and James a tie. The three of them headed towards the Hotel Alfonso XIII, they sauntered past the cathedral, cafes and restaurants on Avenida de la Constitución. James's phone buzzed and he reached in to his pocket to get it whilst juggling the bags with his new purchases, he put all the bags in one hand and held the phone in the other. It was a text message from Delinda.

Hey, we have just arrived in Malaga, can't wait for you to get here. Love you.

After reading the message James put his phone back in

to his pocket and carried on walking with Lawrence and his brother John.

James Shaw felt fatigued, for he had not rested properly since his injury and the hot sun was not helping, he was glad once he arrived at the hotel so that he could take a seat in the lobby. Lawrence Sharif checked them in at the desk, he asked John if he wanted a room but he said that he was ok where he was.

'I will see you two later. I am going to have a walk around, see some sights,' John said.

'OK mate, have fun. I will call you later.'

'Yes, see you later,' Lawrence said.

John left the lobby and exited the hotel. Lawrence handed a key card to James and they got in the lift to the top floor.

'Have you got the car key?'

'Yes, here you go,' James said as he handed over the keys.

'I will be back shortly with our luggage.'

'OK, I will check my room out,' James said.

James opened his room door and stepped over the threshold, to see a king size bed with too many cushions, a plush rug and a desk area, he hung his new suit and shirt up in the wardrobe, and he put the shoes at the bottom. He walked over to the window and opened the glass doors to the small balcony, and looked out across the city. He turned back in to the room, and in to the bathroom, turning the tap on to fill the free-standing bath. James used the complimentary bubble bath and undressed. There was a knock at the door. James put the complimentary robe on and answered the door to Lawrence Sharif, he handed him his luggage and a bag with weapons in.

'I am going to take a long hot soak; I will let you know when I have finished.'

'OK, take as long as you need, I might do the same, see you soon,' Lawrence said.

James closed the door and put his luggage bag on the floor and the weapons at the bottom of the wardrobe. After hanging his robe on the back of the bathroom door he climbed in to the bath and the hot water soothed his wound, he reached down for his phone and typed a text message to Delinda in reply to her earlier message.

That is good, how is it? Love you too.

THIRTY-THREE

In the eastern suburbs of the city, Javier Ramos had finished giving his long-suffering wife her latest beating, this time for not making his coffee correctly. She could not understand why; he had seemed much happier over the last few days. As she went off to make another coffee for her husband, wiping the blood from her nose, she said to herself.

I need to leave this bastard; I am better than this.

Meanwhile, Javier Ramos was speaking on the phone to the President of Argentina, he was explaining that he would have the permits tomorrow and that the military would be able to send as many people as possible to the floating platforms in the South Atlantic. They only had a handful of men there now, so as not to attract to much attention from the British.

The President said that he had wrote to the Prime Minister of the UK asking for dialogue regarding the Falklands, he informed Ramos that until they had received a response, they would hold off on building troops up on the platforms so as not to provoke the British in to action before they were ready. Ramos was not happy but he could see the point that the President

233

was making, and he agreed that he would inform the President as soon as he had received the permits from Lyndon Powell the next day. He ended the call as his wife brought him a fresh cup of coffee, Ramos told her to get out of his sight and to leave him alone as he was busy.

THIRTY-FOUR

Soaking in the bath in his room at the Alfonso XIII
Hotel, James Shaw appeared very relaxed, his pain had
subsided, and he convinced himself that he would not
allow the thoughts of getting revenge for his friend Will
Ramsey to get in the way of the task at hand. Lawrence
Sharif had text him earlier to say that he was down at the
swimming pool.

James decided to go and join him. He got out of the
bath, towelled himself dry and put his swimming shorts
on. He headed down to the pool area at the rear of the
hotel. James found Lawrence relaxing on a sun lounger
with a beer in one hand and a cigarette in the other.

'I saved you a sunbed, the waiter will be here in a
minute to get you a drink.'

'Thanks, I feel much better now, I am a bit nervous
about tomorrow though.'

'Don't be, everything is in order. The only thing that can
go wrong is everything, you know what humans are
like.'

James laughed and said 'You are not wrong; I have just
been reading on BBC news that the Argentine president
has reached out to the PM, something about dialogue

regarding the Falklands.'

'Yes, it is all a ruse to throw everybody off, whilst Ramos rides off in to the sunset with his permits that allow for drilling within the exclusion zone, which in turn gives them a platform to stage an invasion. We are here to stop that happening.'

James took a cigarette from his pack, lit it and took a long drag.

'It would be better if we all just got along, wouldn't it?'

'It would, however we would then be out of a job,' Lawrence said.

A waiter came over and asked James if he would like a drink, he ordered a beer and Lawrence ordered another for himself.

They lay by the pool relaxing, drinking and smoking.

'Are you looking forward to taking command at RAF Waddington?' Lawrence asked.

'Yes and no. Yes, because it is a new challenge for me, and it is most likely the highest rank I will achieve in the RAF. No, because I have never been in command of so many people, and not to mention all of the paper work that goes with it. I never imagined myself to be a full-time desk jockey. My Dad said that about being a Captain, even though he was in charge of a ship, the amount of time he spent behind a desk doing paperwork he could never have imagined.'

Lawrence smiled at James and said 'How do you think I feel, apart from when I have been with you in the field, I spend ninety percent of my time behind a desk doing paperwork, why does the world need so much paperwork? You will do well with that scrambled egg on your hat, you will be the man other officers want to be, and a man the NCO's and junior ranks respect and admire.'

James laughed and said 'Thanks, I will do my best.'

'You are not the best officer; however, you are a great man and in a way that makes you a great officer, you will do well, and don't forget you will never be alone, you will always have Wing Commanders, Squadron Leaders, Warrant Officers and Sergeants to ask for advice.'

'Your right, I cannot be that bad if I have got this far. Fancy a swim?'

'Yes, come on.' Lawrence answered.

They left their sunbeds and jumped into the warm pool, other guests looked at them as if they should not be enjoying themselves, it was that kind of hotel. Mostly rich snobs who wouldn't know a good time if it hit them in the face.

'It would be nice if we stayed in hotels like this all the time, wouldn't it,' James said.

'We used to until all the budget cuts came in, if James Bond was based on real life, he would be staying in Motels, buying his suits in high street stores and fifty pounds expenses for the casino and he would need to kccp the receipts, wait till you see the palaver I will have to go through when I get back to claim for the flights for coming out here.'

'I thought this was all off the books?'

'It is, but I can still claim expenses, those MP's claim for everything so I should be able to, at least mine are legitimate.'

James laughed and replied 'Won't you have to answer to those MP's soon, when you get promoted?'

'Unfortunately, yes.'

James swam up to the edge of the pool and rested his arms on the tiled area and Lawrence joined him.

'I have just had an interesting thought.'

'Go on,' Lawrence said.

James paused for a moment.

'We arrived here Thursday, Ramos's men have more or less followed us everywhere around the city, in fact you could probably bet your last euro someone is staking us out right now.'

Lawrence cut in 'That's how this job works, you have done it long enough to know the score now, they follow us and we follow them.'

'Yes, I know that. I just don't think they expected us to be who we are, I think they thought we would stay in the shadows just to oversee the deal.'

'They obviously had not done their homework on us; don't poke a sleeping Bear I think the saying is,' Lawrence said.

'Yes, I know I know. But what happened on Thursday that changed the course of the last few days, which has led to me being stabbed, Will Ramsey being killed and not to mention what we have done to them. Thursday night, ever since then we have had nothing but trouble?'

Lawrence looked at James with a seriously puzzled look.

'What is it you are getting at?' he asked.

'Think about it, ever since we met Delinda and Ally we have had nothing but trouble, and what happened to the other girls? I think they are holed up with Ramos right now, and not in Valencia. Delinda seems too keen, what if they asked us to America so that Ramos or his men can finally get rid of us, think how easy it is to buy weapons over there, we get to New York, take a stroll through central park, and then, bang. The press will say *"tourists killed in a robbery gone bad".'*

Lawrence put his hand on James's arm and asked.

'What have you taken?'

He answered 'A couple of pain killers why?'

'No more beer for you, I have seen plenty of Femme Fatales and Delinda is not one, she has got it bad for you, it is genuine.'

Lawrence climbed out of the pool and returned to his sunbed; James followed.

'We will see when we set off for Malaga, I have a plan.'

'Ok, but I think they have nothing to do with this, anyway forget that now, just rest, have some water and clear your head before tomorrow.'

James agreed and asked the waiter for some water which he duly brought over in a bucket of ice, setting it down on the little table next to his sun lounger.

THIRTY-FIVE

The sun dropped in the sky as the evening set in; James received a text from Delinda as he was dozing off on his sun lounger.

Hey, how y'all doin' are you checked in at the hotel, we are just chilling and emailing home before we go get some dinner. Kisses.

'It's a text from Delinda asking if we have checked in to the hotel.'

'Throw away the key,' Lawrence said with a smirk.

'That reminds me, I forgot to call Dad back about going on holiday.'

'How did that remind you of that?' Lawrence asked.

'I was supposed to meet them with the keys, I was going to pick them up from the airport and go to the villa.'

'Your mind works in mysterious ways.'

'And yours doesn't? I will call him in a minute.'

First off, he replied to Delinda's text message.

Yes, we have checked in to the hotel, see you soon xx.

James dialled his parents' home number and after four rings his father answered.

'Shaw residence.'

James laughed and said 'Hello Dad, why do you answer the phone like that, you are not the butler? Did you get the message I left the other day?'

'No, the machine doesn't say anything,' his dad replied. 'Just press the play button, anyway I called to say I won't be able to go away with you and Mum, I am caught up with work.'

'OK son, I will let your mum know, see you soon.'

'Bye Dad.'

James put his phone down and said to Lawrence,

'John must of called them too, he didn't sound happy, oh well plenty of time for holidays when I get back from America.'

'Exactly,' replied Lawrence.

'The only way to find out what Delinda's game is, is to go over there and see what happens.'

'Oh, will you give it a rest, you were not complaining the other day when you were both all over each other.'

'Maybe, like I said we will see when we get to America, what their real intentions are.'

James lay back on his lounger with his sunglasses hiding his closed eyes as he rested. Lawrence Sharif scrolled through his phone, all was peaceful around them, the faint sound of traffic in the background was the only sound they could hear, until James Shaw received a text message which jolted him from his relaxed state.

I am so looking forward to seeing you, it feels like I have known you for so long, roll on Wednesday, read the text message from Delinda.

'Delinda is looking forward to seeing us, I bet she is.'

'She probably is mate, what do you feel like for dinner?'
James sat up and put his sunglasses on his head turning
to Lawrence.

'You know what? I feel like something fatty and greasy
like a big cheese burger and chips, then come back here
and have a good sleep before tomorrow.'

'Sounds good, let's do it, I will find somewhere for us to
go.'
Lawrence searched on his phone for somewhere to eat.

'How about the hard rock café, it is just opposite the
hotel?'

'OK, do we need to book a table?' James asked.

'I have just done it for eight o'clock.'

'Another half an hour in the sun then we can go and get
ready,' James said.
James picked up his phone and sent a text to his brother.
*We are going to the hard rock café for our evening
meal if you want to join us.*
James put his phone down and closed his eyes, and went
over the last few days in his head, from the moment he
left RAF Akrotiri up until now, he could not come up
with any reasonable explanation for how Delinda and
Ally would be involved with setting them up with the
Argentines, yet the nagging thoughts would not go away,
he was falling for Delinda and he did not want to believe
that she could be involved but could not think of any
other way the Argentines would know of their presence
in Seville.

Fortunately, Lawrence had not been taking pain killers,
and was thinking straight. He sent a text to Peter Bernard

at DGSE, asking if Javier Ramos had access to the Police passport log which was used by Hotels and Hostels to register guests. Lawrence had requested passports with alternate names for him and James but his request had been denied as the Foreign Office wanted plausible deniability, this meant they had to travel with their official passports. A few minutes later Peter Bernard replied to Lawrence, confirming that Javier Ramos did have access to the Passport log. Lawrence thanked him for his help and gathered his things together as did James and they went up to their rooms to get ready.

THIRTY-SIX

Dressed in lightweight trousers and cotton shirts; Lyndon, Mike, Chris and Jack left their hotel and crossed the road to get a bus to Plaza Del Duque. They had a table booked at the same rooftop restaurant James Shaw and Delinda Saint Germain had eaten at the previous night. They had chosen it based on recommendations from trip advisor, and planned to have a night of relaxation and fun with no mention of what lay ahead tomorrow for them. Lyndon often used this tactic before big jobs to relax everybody, not too much that they would sleep in the next morning and either miss the meeting or vital preparation time.

Despite turning down the wrong street three times and ending up back where they started, Lyndon found the restaurant and on time. They were seated at a rectangular table along the edge of the rooftop overlooking the Cathedral and the La Giralda bell tower. The waiter took their order for starters, main course and wine. Jack Reuben who was not used to seeing so much sun was enjoying himself in the heat of Seville. He vowed to get more active when he returned back to Britain, as even after a day, he felt a lot healthier and happier.

'Good to hear Jack, twenty years too late mind, all those years of being the indoors man, and now you want to come out,' Lyndon said.

'Well, you have never brought us here on a job before, it could have all been different, but here we are today, from now on I am going to get out more.'

'Indeed, well I would like to toast the best group anybody could ask for, to us,' Lyndon said raising his glass.

The others replied in unison 'To us,' and raised their glasses in a toast with Lyndon.

Their starters arrived, and everybody tucked in to their meals.

'When we return home, do you want to come and work for me?' Lyndon asked the group.

'We do work for you,' Mike answered.

'No, you work with me.'

'Same thing,' Chris chipped in.

'My Dad is handing the jewellery stores over to me, and I want you three to join me in running them.'

'How come your dad is handing the shops over to you?' Jack asked.

'He wants to retire and relax.'

'I am in, it will be good to do some honest work for a change,' Mike said.

'Me too,' added Chris.

'Count me in too,' Jack said.

'Thank you, we will discuss it further when we get back home.'

The four of them continued eating and supping wine,

laughing and talking. Surprisingly nobody had mentioned the job at hand the next day, which Lyndon was pleased about. He was doubly pleased, as everybody had agreed to work with him when they returned to the UK in the next couple of days. Lyndon wanted to expand the company to be the biggest jewellery retailer in the world, and he would have the means to do it in the next few days. R&A Powell Diamond specialists had an edge on its rivals because their quality could not be matched by the other high street jewellers. The more he thought about it, the more excited he became about getting started.

Anyway, that can wait for now, more important business to take care of first he said to himself.

The dessert menu came out as the fourth bottle of wine had been finished, all four declined a desert and decided to settle the bill and head back to Hotel Ayre for an early night. That way they would be well rested for the next day.

The four of them went in search of a taxi, and after five minutes they climbed into a SEAT Toledo taxi, which took them back to their hotel. After walking through the lobby and riding up in the lift, they said their farewells and each headed to their own rooms for the night.

THIRTY-SEVEN

Whilst Lyndon Powell and his partners were fine dining; James, Lawrence and John were being careful so as not to spill grease on to their clothes from the juicy cheeseburgers they were eating at the Hard Rock Café. The three of them had ordered the same meal, cheeseburger with fries and a pint of Cruzcampo. They were dressed casually, each of them in shorts and a polo shirt, James in yellow, Lawrence green and John white. John was being extra careful not to spill anything as he had white on. The three of them seemed very relaxed about the next day. All had been planned and gone over many times.

   John would sit in the lobby and text James when Powell and Ramos arrived, in which order they did not know yet. Once both parties had arrived, John would then join James and Lawrence in the courtyard, where they would wait for twenty minutes, as agreed with Powell the night before, fifteen minutes for them to get things wrapped up, and five extra minutes to allow for any questions or issues from Ramos. Lawrence Sharif had been sceptical at first but was assured by Powell that this meeting was just a formality, as all the necessary details had been sorted out beforehand. This meeting was to officially hand over the permits and money to formally rubber stamp the deal.

Javier Ramos had already met with Mike Williams and Chris Hampshire, and he knew what Lyndon Powell looked like, he had not yet met Jack Reuben but he would be attending the meeting, he never usually went to the final meeting, he was always the behind the scenes man. Posing as a member of Powells crew would not be an option for Sharif and the Shaw brothers, as Ramos would know to expect only four people. This was not lost on Lawrence Sharif who had planned for Ramos bringing two of his own people to the meeting, with maybe two more outside of the hotel for security. This is why he would sit in the courtyard with James, and John would join them after the others had arrived.

After the agreed twenty minutes they would walk in to the conference room and calmly take away the drilling permits and escort Powell and his partners out of the hotel, and to the railway station with nobody getting hurt. Well, that was the plan; there is no saying what variables could happen on the day. The three of them were all in agreement with the plan that they had set out. They finished up their burgers and left the Hard Rock Café. John walked to the tram station just outside of the Alfonso XIII hotel. James and Lawrence waited with him, and after two minutes the tram came around the corner. John got on it towards the Prado de San Sebastian, where he would finish his journey back to his hotel by bus. James Shaw and Lawrence Sharif walked over to their hotel, they walked up the stairs and in to the lobby.

'Good night,' they said to the night time receptionist, and they stepped into the lift to the top floor, they got out and walked down the corridor, stopping outside of James's room.

'Sleep in tomorrow, set your alarm for nine o'clock, we will have breakfast here before we go to Hotel Ayre.'

'Thanks, you are too kind, good idea, then get back here around twelve,' James replied.

'Go get some rest, good night.'

'Good night,' James said.

They walked in to their rooms and locked the doors behind themselves. James folded his clothes up and placed them over the desk chair, he climbed in to his four-poster bed. He shuffled to get comfortable and reached for his phone on the bedside table. He had two messages from Delinda, he had his phone on silent and had not checked it whilst he was out. Delinda had asked him how he was and what he was doing, the second text was more concerned asking if he was OK, and to send a message when he could.

Sorry, I left my phone on silent, how are you? I am just getting ready to go to sleep.

He put his phone face down on the bedside table and turned over to fall asleep, he turned back and checked his phone again and opened a message from Delinda which read.

Wish I was in there with you, I miss you, cannot wait to see you, talk tomorrow'.

James smiled and text back.

Same here, good night, speak to you tomorrow.
Setting his phone back on the bedside table, he rested his head down on the pillow and fell asleep within a minute.

THIRTY-EIGHT

The hot Andalusian sun appeared on the horizon to mark the beginning of a new day, the sun lit up the eastern side of the city, this included Javier Ramos's house. Already dressed, he stood next to his swimming pool feeling pleased with himself, as this was to be a day to remember. Ramos decided to leave his long-suffering wife to sleep, he wanted an early start so he could be relaxed at the meeting with Lyndon and the others.

West of Javier Ramos's house at Hotel Ayre, Lyndon Powell had just woken up and groggily stumbled to the bathroom as he could not see properly due to his room having blackout curtains, he sat himself down on the toilet and sent a text to the other three to see if they were awake. Within a few minutes they all replied to Lyndon that they were awake, and the four agreed to meet downstairs for breakfast in twenty minutes, this was going to be the day that changed their lives forever, and they wanted to get a head start even if it was only half past six.

'Up and at them,' Lyndon said as they met in the corridor before taking the lift down to the breakfast room.

Also in Hotel Ayre, John Shaw was fast asleep, as was his brother across the city in the Hotel Alfonso XIII along with Lawrence Sharif. They would not wake for another couple of hours, for them today was about getting the job done, it would make no difference to the rest of their lives.

However, it could potentially stop a war between the United Kingdom and Argentina, a war the British had no appetite for, yet they would defend the Falklands if provoked. The Argentines on the other hand had nothing to lose, they had presidential elections coming up in the next few months, and a successful invasion would guarantee the current president another term, not to mention a distraction from their shattered economy.

In Malaga, Delinda Saint Germain and Ally Simmons were eating breakfast together and planning their sightseeing for the upcoming day. They had guidebooks, maps and various leaflets spread out on the table as they ate their cereal.

'So, do you see yourself having a future with James, I know I keep asking?'

'Yes. Yes, I can, I have already looked at working in the UK, it is complicated but I can make it work, I will speak to James when we get back stateside,' Delinda replied.

Ally smiled at her friend and was slightly jealous that she had found somebody who made her happy, even if they had only just met each other, she may have been slightly jealous but she was also happy for Delinda.

THIRTY-NINE

The Foreign Secretary, Barnaby Lockwood walked in to Number 10 Downing Street, after being summoned by the Prime Minister; he wondered what was so urgent to be called in at this time of the morning. The Prime Minister showed the Foreign Secretary in to the cabinet room and they both sat down.

'You must be wondering why I called you here?' the PM asked.

'Well Sir, I was actually,' Lockwood answered.

'I want you to speak to the Argentine ambassador. Tell him, in no uncertain terms will the United Kingdom discuss the issue of the Falklands with the President of Argentina.'

'Yes Sir, I will get on it right away.'

'Good, and how are your men getting along in Spain? Any reports yet?'

'Not yet Sir, I will keep you informed, how did you know about that?'

'I am the Prime Minister, it is my job to know these things, keep me in the loop.'

'Yes Sir, I will type a draft up for the Argentine ambassador before heading over to their embassy.'

The Prime Minister stood up and leant over the table with his hands holding his weight up, and said to Lockwood. 'That will be all, thank you for coming over so early.'

'No problem, Sir, I am here to serve.'

'One more thing, your men in Spain better succeed or you will be on the backbenches, never again do something like that without informing me, now off with you.'

'Sir,' Lockwood said before leaving the cabinet room and the house, he got back in to his ministerial car which would take him to the Foreign Office, from there he would then meet with the Argentinian ambassador in Mayfair.

FORTY

Javier Ramos decided that two of his men would proceed ahead of him to the Alfonso XIII hotel exactly one hour before he was due to arrive, this was to ensure that nobody had any tricks up their sleeve to disrupt the meeting. Once Ramos arrived, they would accompany him to the conference room. He was very relaxed, for a man who was about to complete a deal of such magnitude. Cigar lit and in hand, he was relaxing by his swimming pool, whilst his long-suffering wife slept. His security detail had been given the morning off, as he felt no threat from the British who were in Seville. The clock on his phone read 0758, his wife walked out of the house into the garden in her swimwear, she dived in to the water, and swam to the surface. Ramos ignored her as he was busy reading the local news on his phone. After finding nothing of interest to read, he stood up and said to his wife 'I will make my own coffee then shall I, stupid bitch.'

His long-suffering wife pretended not to hear him and carried on swimming whilst he went inside to make his coffee.

James Shaw had been awake for ten minutes.

'So much for a sleep in,' he said after looking at the time on his watch. His head was much clearer than it had been the day before; he sent a text to Delinda saying, *Good morning.*

He got up out of bed and walked in to the bathroom, turning the taps on to run the bath, he decided to relax for half an hour before getting ready and going for breakfast. Delinda sent him a message back.

Good morning to you too, we have a busy day today, I will call you later if that is ok?

Of course, it is, have a nice day. James replied before stepping in to his bath.

After a long bath; James put on fresh underwear along with the clothes that he had worn the previous night.

It is only breakfast he said to himself.

Closing the door behind himself and checking that it was locked, he walked over to Lawrence's room and knocked loudly. Lawrence Sharif answered after about three seconds already dressed.

'Did you sleep in too,' Lawrence said with a laugh.

'Not enough booze last night, I feel fresh today and my stitches feel good too.'

'Glad to hear it, what do you want for breakfast, shall we eat in here or go out?'

'Let's eat here shall we, I feel like some goodness, a croissant, fruit juice and some fresh fruit,' James said.

'What is wrong with you? Oh, I know you are trying to look after yourself for your new love,' Lawrence said answering his own question.

'Don't start me,' James whispered under his breath.

They walked towards the lift which would take them to the dining room on the ground floor.

'Do you still think Delinda is working for Ramos? Or have you realised what an idiot you were being?'

'Maybe.'

'Well, which is it?'

'That, my friend is for you to decide isn't it,' James answered, as the lift doors opened and they stepped out towards the breakfast room. They could smell the freshly baked pastries before they set foot in the room. It was a self-service breakfast but staff came to the tables with tea and coffee. They sat at a table for four, and straight away a waiter came over with the hot drinks, they both chose tea, the waiter explained the rules of the buffet and what was on offer, they thanked him and he was on his way to another table. James walked over to the fruit and picked a selection of melon, grapefruit and pineapple, he poured a glass of orange juice and returned to the table, Lawrence opted for the same and joined James at the table.

'A pink grapefruit, winner,' James said as he cut the fruit in half, he ate the bitter flesh with a spoon.

'I hate waiting for these things, why can't they have a nine o'clock meeting like normal people, what are we supposed to do for the morning, doss around the pool?' James said.

'I know, I have a deck of cards upstairs, I will bring them down to the pool after breakfast.'

'Why are you only just telling me this now, good idea though, somebody who knows how to play blackjack, and if John comes over, we can play some poker, we better set an alarm otherwise we will miss the meeting,' James said with a laugh.

He enjoyed playing cards, especially when he made Lawrence pick up a load of cards at blackjack, he was actually a feared poker player at RAF Akrotiri. On many occasions he had cleaned up with poor hands but he never let anything show on his face, his expression remained the same if he had a royal flush or a pair of fours. Lawrence was almost as good as him.

Lawrence left the table and returned with two croissants, one each for him and James, along with some strawberry jam and butter.

'How do you feel then?'

'About what?' James answered.

'Well, this, the last time we will work together on something like this.'

'There is always one last time.'

'Maybe you are right, but I do not think there will be after this, what with me becoming deputy director of operations and you a Group Captain, our faces will be in the public domain. As soon as somebody goes on to the RAF Waddington website, there will be a picture of you on there all smart in your blue uniform, standing in front of the ensign, same with me, if you log on to MI6, I will be there front and centre with a nice suit on smiling for the camera.'

'I don't understand that, MI6 is a secret organisation, yet the big cheeses names and pictures are in the public domain, so anybody that knows you but they don't know what it is you actually do, will all of sudden know. You will have all those meetings with the Foreign Secretary and any other clown poking their nose in to look forward to,' James said.

'Please don't remind me, every job has its downsides.'

'You are not wrong,' James said.

Two more cups of tea later, and James and Lawrence finished up and headed back upstairs to get changed into their swimwear. They wanted to go to the pool to relax before they had to get down to business.

FORTY-ONE

In a few months' time; RAF Waddington would be under the command of Group Captain James Shaw, but at present an E-3D Sentry powered down the runway, the wheels lifted off the ground and the pilot made a left-hand turn before keying in a heading of 210 degrees, towards Ascension Island. The E-3D Sentry is a surveillance and airborne early warning and control aircraft, it is a custom-built Boeing 707 with a big circular disc on top of the fuselage which is the main radar.

One and a half hours earlier the night staff in the operations room of 8 Squadron had received a secret transmission, stating that an E-3D was to get airborne immediately and that further instructions would be given once the aircraft arrived at Ascension Island. After receiving the orders, a young SAC arranged for an aircraft to be fully fuelled and he went about informing his officer in command, who in turn contacted the crew for the assigned aircraft, and arranging Air Traffic Control to open the tower before departure. Ten minutes after getting airborne the night shift was relieved by the incoming day shift who had been told what had happened, they asked what was going on but since nobody knew exactly what was going on, no answer could be given.

Foreign Secretary Barnaby Lockwood stepped out of his ministerial car and walked into the Argentinian Embassy in Mayfair, London. He was shown to the Ambassadors office by the secretary. The Ambassador shook Lockwood's hand and motioned for him to have a seat as he walked back to his own chair behind a big mahogany desk.

'What can I do for you Mr Lockwood?' The Ambassador asked.

'I have a message for your President, from our Prime Minister.'

'I was expecting this; I was advised that dialogue had been opened by our President.'

'Well, our PM is closing it, as the United Kingdom of Great Britain and Northern Ireland has no intention of discussing the sovereignty of the Falkland Islands, which are a British overseas territory and will remain so, consider this matter closed,' Lockwood said firmly.

'I understand and I will relay your message, thank you for coming to see me,' The Ambassador replied, standing up to shake Lockwood's hand.

Lockwood left the embassy, and got back in to his car to take him back to the Foreign Office. As Foreign Secretary, Barnaby Lockwood had top secret clearance and was privy to all goings on with diplomatic matters. However, on this occasion, he was not aware that the Prime Minister had directly contacted the chief of the

Air Staff to issue the order for surveillance of the reported oil platforms within the exclusion zone in the South Atlantic. The PM had decided to take action himself, as he knew how cunning the Argentines could be, especially since he had been briefed by Lockwood about Javier Ramos and his dealings with four British men in relation to selling drilling permits in the south Atlantic. The PM wanted to make sure that the Argentines were not planning to use these platforms for an invasion, he also knew that only British companies could drill within the exclusion zone, but that was another matter for another day. What the PM did not know was that, not only were Lyndon Powell and his associates selling the permits for drilling, they were selling the entire company, a British registered company. This would enable Ramos to drill and explore as he pleased in the south Atlantic. The Foreign secretary knew all of this but had not divulged the information to the Prime Minister, he had faith that MI6 would get things done in Spain.

FORTY-TWO

The digital hands on James Shaw's Apple watch
moved to 1200hrs, he was dressed in the clothes that he
had purchased the day before. He stood and looked out
of Lawrence Sharif's room window, which overlooked
the main entrance to the hotel. They figured that Ramos's
men would suggest to him that somebody go ahead to
check that everything was secure for the meeting. Not to
be outdone, James had suggested that John sit at one of
the bars opposite the tram stop, as the view from the
window was partially blocked by the palm trees that
lined the perimeter of the hotel.

Two minutes later, James spotted a tram approaching
from the direction of Prado de San Sebastian, he tracked
it until it stopped at the station but his view was
obscured of who was getting on or off. His watch buzzed
and it showed a message from John.

Two of them.

James spotted them with his own eyes about ten seconds
later as they walked through the gate to the hotel.

'We got two goons coming in,' James said to Lawrence
who was sitting in a chair doing something on his iPad.

'Right on time, we will stay up here, there is no point in

us getting involved now, let them check the place over, they will walk back out in around twenty minutes, and will return about half an hour before the meeting is scheduled to start.'

'Shall I call John in?' Shaw asked.

'No leave him there for now, call him back around 1345 so he can be in the lobby when the goons reappear,' Sharif replied.

'No problem, what are you doing anyway?'

'Typing up a report.'

'For what, I thought this was all hush hush, a black bag job?' James said.

'It is, but it never stays that way for long, this is to cover our arses in case things don't go our way, or worse the government find out and launch an inquiry, we know how they love an enquiry at the minute.'

'That could well be the last time you write a first-person report for field work.'

'I would rather do this than be the one reading and signing off on them, and then hiding them away forever, or at least until some new government starts wanting to know what we have been getting up to over the years, they are always suspicious of the intelligence agencies.'

'You can't really blame them. Why are you taking the job if you are going to miss doing this type of stuff?' Shaw asked.

'It is a young man's game now, and the same reason you are a Wing Commander soon to be Group Captain, and not a Flight Lieutenant, time moves on and you have to move with it, and our time has come to sit behind desks shuffling paper, reading reports and offering words of wisdom to younger men and women,' Sharif answered.

'I guess you're right, drink?' James asked pulling two cans of Fanta from the minibar.

'You know I am right. Thanks, you can pay for those, I can't believe people actually still use those things, I have paid less for a bottle of wine.'

'That isn't that hard out here is it, I have seen bottles for one euro,' James said, taking a seat next to Lawrence drinking his Fanta, awaiting the text from John saying that the Argentines had left the hotel.

James and Lawrence said nothing to each other for the next half an hour, they were used to waiting around so they both relaxed, no point using up energy when there is no need to.

Lyndon Powell, Mike Williams, Chris Hampshire and Jack Reuben left their hotel in a taxi with a nervous excitement about them. Ten minutes after leaving, the taxi dropped them off at the rear of the hotel Alfonso XIII, they decided to walk around to the main entrance.

'We need to make an entrance, show that we are ready,' Lyndon said.

'Let's do this,' Chris said.

'We still have half an hour,' Mike interjected.

'Well, we will check in and see if the room is available, we can then get everything set up before Ramos gets here,' Powell said to the other three.

Chris spoke to the man at the reception desk, who said that the room was available and he asked concierge to show them to the conference room. They walked through the lobby area and were taken through the courtyard and past the fountain that was in the centre. In the corner to their left, James Shaw and Lawrence Sharif sat at a table drinking what looked like water, the six men nodded at each other. As Powell and his associates were shown in to the conference room, James Shaw left Lawrence to use the toilet, which conveniently was past the conference room, he walked past and glanced in to the room but did not go inside. He carried on towards the toilets and past display cases of various artefacts from the old Spanish Empire.

Stuck in traffic on Paseo de las Delicias which ran alongside the Guadalquivir River was the Ferrari California which belonged to Javier Ramos. He was in the driving seat and alongside him was his head of security. Ramos was growing inpatient, sounding his horn in annoyance and edging his car in to the oncoming lanes to try and get around the cars in front, but to no avail. Eventually the traffic eased off and Ramos managed to arrive at the Hotel Alfonso XIII with ten minutes to spare before the scheduled start of the meeting with Lyndon Powell and his associates.

Ramos's men who were on point at the hotel had failed to spot John Shaw sitting in the lobby, he had however spotted them and alerted his brother and Lawrence. As the Argentine special force's soldiers walked around the courtyard and not through it, they failed to notice James Shaw and Lawrence Sharif sat in the corner as their view was blocked by a corner post for the support of the glass sliding windows surrounding the courtyard. The two soldiers were standind guard outside of the door to the conference room as Javier Ramos approached with his head of security.

James and Lawrence sat looking at each other bewildered that the Argentines had walked right past them.
'How did they not see us, the fools!' James said.
'As you well know, the best place to hide is in plain sight, either they have gotten complacent and do not think we are here or they have decided to deal with us after the meeting so as not to upset their paymaster.'
'I wouldn't upset him either, he sounds like a piece of work.'
'Right, twenty minutes starts now, as of my watch.'
'Roger,' James said checking his own watch.
Both men were dressed in the new stone coloured linen suits that they had bought the day before, inside their jackets they had their silenced Beretta M9's, hoping that they wouldn't have to use them. Plan for the worst, hope for the best.

Three thousand one hundred miles away on Ascension Island; The E-3D sentry that had left RAF Waddington at dawn that morning was preparing for the second leg of its journey, the flight crew swapped over and the new captain opened his orders on the flight deck. Squadron Leader Kent showed the orders to the other crew members in the main compartment of the aircraft, their role was to monitor the images and footage from the onboard cameras. They had been instructed to survey and monitor a series of oil platforms that were under construction, one hundred miles to the North of the

Falkland Islands. After completion they were to land at Mount Pleasant Airfield and await further orders. The E-3D was scheduled to arrive on target at 2100hrs Zulu which was 1800hrs local.

Javier Ramos extended his hand to Lyndon Powell and said 'Pleased to meet you at last Mr Powell, how are you enjoying your stay in Sevilla?'

'Pleased to meet you too, very much it is a wonderful city,' Powell replied shaking Ramos's hand.

'Excellent, shall we get down to business,' Ramos said.

'Indeed, if you don't mind, I would like to introduce Jack Reuben our head of research and technology, who will go over in detail what the company consists off assets wise and what we have found so far in the south Atlantic.'

'Thank you, Mr Reuben, I am sure you have prepared a well detailed presentation designed to wow me and convince me to hand over fifty-six million euros, but I have a better idea.'

'What is that?' Powell asked.

Powell and the others looked at each other nervously.

Ramos motioned for his head of security to bring the bag over that he had brought with him. Lyndon Powell motioned for the others to stay calm, even though his heart rate was accelerating rapidly. Javier Ramos pulled an iPad from the bag and touched the screen; he handed the iPad over to Lyndon.

'Please enter your account details here then hand the iPad back to me.'

Lyndon typed in the details, and he handed the iPad back

to Javier Ramos, he motioned to Chris to pass him the briefcase, which he did. Lyndon opened the briefcase and took out a stack of papers, he separated them in to two piles.

'Transfer complete,' Ramos said as he looked up from his iPad.

'Excellent, now if you could just sign here and here,' Lyndon said pointing to two separate boxes on the pile of paper closest to him, his heart rate was easing. Ramos signed and then asked if he needed to sign anywhere else, Lyndon said that he did not.

'These belong to you now, these are the drilling permits, in the document is all the access codes to the company systems, accounts and files. Congratulations you are now the proud owner of South Atlantic Oil and Gas, these guys said you were the right man for this and I have to agree.'

'A pleasure doing business Mr Powell, Mr Williams, Mr Hampshire and Mr Reuben,' Ramos said as he passed the paperwork to his head of security, who put it into the bag with the iPad.

As the men were shaking hands and congratulating each other, the door to the conference room swung open.

Foreign Secretary Barnaby Lockwood sat in his office, in the Foreign Office building on Whitehall. He was awaiting a phone call on his pay as you go mobile, that had been given to him by the head of MI6 for the sole purpose of being able to contact him without anybody listening in to their conversations down at GCHQ, as they both knew their personal mobiles and office phones were more than likely being monitored, they knew this as they both had been strong voices in favour of all government departments being monitored. Lockwood kept looking at the phone, urging it to ring but for some reason it did not.

Have they been delayed, what is happening he said to himself, he stood up and walked over to his coffee machine to pour himself a fresh cup, telling himself to stay calm.

'They are professionals, doing things properly. I will call him if I don't hear anything in an hour,' he said aloud.

Four Spanish police officers filed in to the conference room with their pistols drawn. Lyndon, Mike, Chris and Jack stood frozen to the spot, unsure of what was happening. Ramos's head of security stepped forward towards the lead officer to ask what the problem was, he was told not to speak by the officer. The lead officer signalled with his free hand to one of his colleagues, who stepped over to Ramos and handcuffed him.

The lead officer said 'Javier Ramos, estas bajo arresto por el asesinato de Vicente Garcia. Usted tiene dercho a permanecer en silencio.' (Javier Ramos, you are under arrest for the murder of Vicente Garcia. You have the right to remain silent).

'No puedes hacer esto,' (You cannot do this) Ramos's head of security said to the police officers.

The officers said nothing in return and dragged Javier Ramos out of the conference room to the van waiting outside the hotel entrance, Ramos's head of security followed.

'The bag?' Chris said to nobody in particular. Lyndon reached in to the bag that Ramos had put back on the floor and relieved the paperwork from it before handing it over to Jack. One of the officers returned for the bag and asked Lyndon if anything else belonged to Mr Ramos.

'No, that is everything, what is going on? Lyndon replied.

'Mr Ramos has been arrested for murder, please leave the hotel as Mr Ramos will be detained for some time.' They did not need telling twice, and they headed for the door.

'Gracias,' Lyndon said as he walked past the officer. The policeman closed the door and squeezed past the four men in the corridor to re-join his colleagues. Javier Ramos was thrown in to the back of the van and onto the floor, he shuffled himself to sit upright which was no easy task with his hands cuffed behind his back. The officer with the bag climbed in behind him and closed the doors. Ramos smiled to himself when he seen the bag.

This will all be over in a few hours once my lawyer explains everything, and I will be on my way to Buenos Aires he thought to himself.

He did not say anything to the officers, as the police had a way of hearing things that were never said and twisting things that were.

That bitch did this to me he said about his wife to himself.

Ramos' head of security ran out of the hotel to the

Ferrari so that he could follow the police van to the station.

In the courtyard five minutes earlier. Lawrence Sharif said to James Shaw.

'This is us, let's go.'

As he finished that sentence, four police officers ran through the courtyard in the direction of the conference room where Powell was meeting with Ramos. Sharif decided not to follow so as not to get himself arrested for possession of a firearm, which would lead to questions that they did not want to answer. Around four minutes later they watched Javier Ramos being led through the courtyard in handcuffs, everybody who was sat in the courtyard turned their heads to see what was going on. The fourth officer followed with a bag a few minutes later, who in turn was followed by Lyndon, Chris, Mike and Jack who joined James and Lawrence at their table.

'Well gentlemen, did you get your money?' Lawrence asked.

'We did indeed, he was very happy to pay us, then his face changed when those police officers stormed in, murder he has been arrested for,' Lyndon replied.

'Really,' Lawrence said surprised.

'Have you got the permits?' James asked.

'Yes, here you are,' Lyndon said as he pulled them from his own bag and handed them over to James Shaw.

'Thank you, now get out of here, go home and don't let me see you again.'

'Yes Sir, and thank you,' Lyndon said as he shook James's hand and then Lawrence's, as did the other three, they hustled out of the courtyard and the hotel to look for a taxi to take them back to hotel Ayre to collect their luggage. They were going to board a train to Madrid, from where they would stay overnight and fly back to Liverpool the next day.

Lawrence caught a waiter's attention and ordered three beers as John Shaw had just joined them from the lobby.

'What was all that about then?' John said.

'He was arrested for murder apparently,' Sharif answered.

'Murdering who?' John asked.

'Vicente Garcia, the man who was in the position Javier Ramos is in now, it would appear he removed him so he could take his place,' James answered.

Lawrence looked at him with a half concerned half smiling expression and asked James Shaw.

'How do you know this?'

'Lyndon Powell told me the other day.'

'How, we met them together.'

'I met them on the train on Sunday, I said to them to act as if they had not met me before when we meet again, they did very well actually.'

'So, they called the police? Did they have any proof?' Sharif asked.

'No, it was me that called them, I thought let's make this easy for ourselves. Yes, they had a mobile phone trace that puts Ramos in the same place at the same time of Vicente Garcia's death, it is only circumstantial but it will be enough for the police to ask some questions and make him confess hopefully. Well, that is not our problem now is it.'

Lawrence sent a text to a number from memory saying *Done*.

Barnaby Lockwood received a text from the director of MI6 on his pay as you go mobile saying *All clear; I told you they would get it done.*
He smiled and replied *Good.*
He took the back off the phone and took the sim card out of its holder before snapping it in two and putting it in the confidential waste bin at the side of his desk, he put the phone in his top left desk drawer and locked the drawer. Lockwood was relieved that this secret mission had succeeded; he would inform the PM in the morning. *No need to bother him now,* he said to himself.

Putting their empty beer glasses on the table, James and Lawrence lit a cigarette each, they exhaled and tilted their heads back.
'What now then?' John asked.
'I say we get out of here, no point in hanging around.' James answered.
'Same here,' Lawrence said in agreement with James. Cigarettes were extinguished in the ashtray, and the three of them stood up, James picked the papers up off the table, he reached into his jacket pocket with his free hand and pulled out the car keys and said to John.
'Bring the car to the front.'
John nodded to acknowledge James, and he set off for the car park whilst James and Lawrence headed for the lifts up to their rooms. Once in their rooms James and Lawrence threw everything in to their bags including the weapons and left in about a minute, they were in the

lobby another minute after that. Lawrence explained to the receptionist that they were checking out early, the receptionist said she would not be able to refund him for that night's stay, Lawrence said this was not a problem and handed the key cards over. James asked the receptionist if they had a shredder, she said that they did. James handed the drilling permits to the receptionist and asked.

'Can you shred these for me please?'

'Si senor,' she replied fed the sheets into the shredder. James watched as the strands of paper dropped into the bin below.

'Thank you.'

He and Lawrence picked their bags up and walked outside to where John was waiting in the Range Rover.

'I am driving,' James said to John.

'Suits me,' John replied and got out of the driver's seat and climbed in the back.

'Have you got a flight booked?' James asked John.

'Not today.'

'Book one now, from Malaga.'

John looked on his phone, as did James but he was typing, he sent a text to Delinda saying.

Call me when you get this message, please.

John leaned on both of the headrests and said 'Malaga to Liverpool at nine o'clock tonight, I will call in on mum and dad, the Colonel can wait until next week.'

'You got lucky there, seatbelts on let's go,' James said.

The two Argentine Special Forces soldiers that had been sent in to the Alfonso XIII ahead of Javier Ramos were

275

walking around the corridors upstairs at the time of Ramos' arrest and had only just been informed by their commanding officer that Ramos had been arrested. They had seen James Shaw and Lawrence Sharif getting in to the Range Rover at the main entrance, unfortunately their own VW Polo was parked at the Prado de San Sebastian bus station, as they decided it would be easier to park up and get the tram the rest of the way than trying to park in the small hotel carpark or risk a ticket on the street. The two men ran down Calle de San Fernando in the hope of being able to catch the Range Rover as they hoped it would get stuck in traffic along the river.

FORTY-THREE

Held up in traffic was exactly where they were, having barely moved two hundred yards since turning onto the Paseo de las Delicias. At a junction three hundred yards up the road, a blue VW Polo joined the queue of traffic from Avenida Maria Luisa, which led from the Prado de San Sebastian to the river front. One of the advantages of being in a high car was that the Shaw brothers and Sharif were able to see over the smaller cars and they spotted the VW Polo joining the traffic up ahead.

'Did you see that?' Lawrence asked.

'Yep, got them, they will be able to see us also but not to worry,' James replied.

As the traffic slowly moved forward, James noticed the Argentines VW Polo had stopped at the kerb and put its hazard lights on.

'Nice try,' he said aloud.

'What are you going to do?' John asked.

'On the next light change watch.'

They were about fifty yards from the lights which at the moment showed red. James Shaw waited patiently. As soon as the traffic lights changed to amber, James pulled the Range Rover out of the traffic and sped past the waiting cars along the opposite side of the road and pulled a hard left onto Avenida Maria Luisa, where the Argentines had just come from, he did not slow down until he reached the next set of lights, which were at the far end of the road, near the Prado de San Sebastian bus station.

The Argentines seen the Range Rover turn onto Avenida Maria Luisa, and tried to pull away from the kerb and back into the traffic, but as they had pulled into the kerb the other drivers were not so willing to let them through again, they eventually forced their way through and were speeding back the way they had originally come from. However, they could not see the Range Rover with James, Lawrence and John in.

James kept his foot on the accelerator when he could, he could not see the VW Polo in his rear-view mirror and was not helped by the sun, which was reflecting off all the cars so he couldn't really tell what type of car they were.

The Argentinians had spotted them however.

James Shaw pulled up at the Hotel Ayre and his brother John jumped out and ran inside to collect his things and check out. James tapped the top of the steering wheel whilst waiting for John to come back out. Three hundred yards back the VW Polo that had caught up with them pulled over behind another parked car and the soldiers waited for James's next move.

The hotel doors opened and outstepped Lyndon Powell, Chris Hampshire, Mike Williams and Jack Reuben, each wheeling their luggage behind them. Lawrence Sharif lay with his head back and eyes closed until he was brought to by James beeping the horn.

'What's going on?' he said.

'Look who it is.'

Lyndon Powell walked over to James's window and motioned for him to wind it down which he did.

'I jumped out of my skin then, are you here for us?' he asked.

'No, just waiting for my brother then we are off, what about you, are you heading back home?' James asked.

'Yes, we are going to get the train to Madrid then fly out in the morning, back home to Liverpool.'

'Listen, be careful there are people that work for Ramos dressed in some kind of mock uniform, grey jackets, grey pants, they are dangerous and I am sure Ramos has said to keep an eye out for you.'

'Thank you, I thought you said that you didn't want to see us again, anyway we best be going.'

'I didn't think I would that's why, be careful and have a safe trip, if you ever see me in Liverpool buy me a pint won't you.'

'You got it.' Lyndon said as he held his hand out, which James shook and Lawrence reached over and shook with Lyndon.

'Be careful,' James said.

The other three waved at James and Lawrence who waved back, and they set off for Santa Justa station on the opposite side of the road, as they crossed over and walked up the hill John emerged from the hotel and opened the boot; he threw his bag on top of James and Lawrence's luggage.

'Right, are we ready?' John asked.

'Yes, let's get on the motorway,' Lawrence said.

James pulled the car back into traffic and followed the signs for the A92 which they would follow until coming off onto the A45, which would take them the rest of the way to Malaga, as they pulled off in to the traffic the Argentines followed suit, keeping their distance.

Javier Ramos had been sent back to his cell after being formally charged with the murder of Vicente Garcia, he would appear in court the next morning to enter his plea. Ramos protested this, as he had only been arrested an hour ago and had yet to speak to his lawyer. He was told you can have your say when your solicitor arrives. Ramos knew that once his Lawyer got there, he would be bailed and he would be granted further bail after his hearing with the judge tomorrow. He had been arrested before and a bribe to the officers usually had him released pretty quickly, but these officers could not be persuaded, and he had been told if he offered one again that it would go on his charge sheet. Ramos decided he would now sit quietly in his cell until his lawyer arrived, as he did not want to give the officers any reason to add bribery to his charge sheet if he wanted to be released as soon as he had been interviewed.

James Shaw kept the Range Rover at a steady seventy miles per hour. As they passed a town called Osuna, Lawrence Sharif called the British consulate in Malaga to inform them that they would be stopping by in a few hours with some items that needed to be sent back to the UK in diplomatic bags, the person he spoke to said only the Consul could arrange that and Sharif would have to speak to him in person, Lawrence agreed and said to the others that they will go before dropping John at the airport.

James noticed about eight car lengths back a blue VW Polo, with what he could make out in the mirror, contained two people. They still had about fifty miles before they reached the turn off for the A45 which would then take them to Malaga. James kept checking his mirror and there was no change, the VW stayed at a steady five lengths behind. James checked his nearside mirror and could only see a large goods vehicle which he guessed to be about six hundred yards behind him. James made a sharp turn with the wheel to the right and slowed the car down to forty miles per hour, which allowed the two cars behind him to speed past, followed by the VW Polo whose driver could not react quick enough to James Shaw's sudden turn.

'What are you doing Jim?' Lawrence asked.

'Trying to avoid our friends there,' James answered whilst pointing out the Polo up the road which had pulled into the outside lane about three hundred yards in front of the Range Rover, which in turn was three hundred yards ahead of the truck.

'They aren't giving this up, are they?' John said.

'No, what are you going to do James, we don't want to draw too much attention to ourselves, pull in at the next services,' Sharif said.

'I have a plan, wait and see,' James said.

James carried on driving until they were within five kilometres of the junction with the A45, this was where

James sped up to eighty miles per hour, which closed the gap on the Argentines, who in turn sped up but James kept increasing the speed and at ninety he could see the Polo struggling to stay ahead of the big V8 engine in the Range Rover, two kilometres to go, James increased to one hundred miles per hour, the VW increased slowly which brought the front of the big Range Rover to within five yards of the VW Polo.

James maintained that speed and distance; he could see the soldier in the passenger seat looking behind every few seconds. The turn off was now two hundred yards away, James Shaw held his speed and distance.

The turn off was now fifty yards in front of them. Thirty, twenty, ten. The Argentines carried on along the A92 but James pulled the wheel to the right at the very last second causing him to go over the rumble strips and some grass which kicked up a cloud of dust as he straightened the car up and powered along the slip road and joined the A45. The driver of the VW Polo slammed his brakes on and cut across to the other side of the road heading back to Seville to try and join the A45, but by the time he did, the Range Rover was long out of sight.

'I told you I had a plan,' James said.

'It worked; I can't see them,' John said as he looked out of the rear window.

'How did they not see that coming?' Lawrence asked.

'They never expected the unexpected did they, did they think we were going to Granada to see the Alhambra or something?' James said laughing, and the other two laughed along with him.

'Time for some music,' James said as he turned the

radio on and tuned a station in. It was an English expat station playing *The Rhythm of the night* by Corona, the three of them were singing along, and James tapped his hands on the wheel, he sped up to the music. A huge sense of relief passed over the three them, as they could now drive the rest of the way to Malaga without having to worry about being followed.

As Malaga was now less than ten kilometres away, Lawrence began looking for the British Consulate on his phone navigation system so that he could direct James there. As he did that, James's phone rang in his pocket, he could see on his watch that it was Delinda calling. 'Can you get that, it's in my front right pocket,' he said to Lawrence.
Lawrence reached into James's pocket and pulled the phone out.
  'Hello,' he said.
  'It is Delinda, she is asking what you wanted her to call for?' Lawrence asked.
  'Tell her and Ally to get their stuff together and we will pick them up in about half an hour.'
Which he did.
  'OK, see you soon bye now,' Lawrence said as he ended the call.
  'They said OK, nothing else.'
  'We are going away today, we will get tickets in the airport if we have to, see if you can book something now on your phone. I need to call Nadine too before we go,' James said.
  'OK mate, I have found flights, changing in Lisbon

then on to New York, leaving at ten tonight, are you sure you don't want to wait until Thursday, we have hotels booked as well you know.'

'Call them, ask to change the dates, book those flights, we are leaving Spain today!'

'Are you OK mate?' John asked James.

'Yeah fine, just that it is hitting home now about Will, I just need a break to recharge before going back to Britain.'

'OK mate, as long as you are sure.'

They arrived at the British Consulate, and Lawrence told James and John to stay in the car whilst he went inside. James opened his door and stepped out of the car and lit a cigarette, he opened his phone and dialled the number that had tried to call him two nights ago, as he now realised who it was that was trying to contact him. The call was picked up after five rings and a female voice said 'Hello.'

James paused a second then said 'Nadine, it is James Shaw, I am so sorry, Will told me your news a couple of days ago, I am so sorry, if you need anything just ask.'

'You can't bring him back, can you? This is your fault you bastard, if he wasn't helping you, with whatever it was you were doing, he would still be here now, he would have done anything for you, and now it has cost him his life.'

James dropped his head as he did not know what to say, he took another drag of his cigarette and said.

'I am so sorry, call me for anything you need.' he ended the call and put his phone back in his pocket.

He finished his smoke, then he got back in to the car, just as Lawrence was coming back out of the Consulate. Lawrence told them that the consul had agreed to send the confiscated weapons back to the UK in diplomatic bags, he noticed the look on James's face and asked.

'Did you speak to Nadine?'

'Yes, she blames me for Wills death and she is right, it is my fault, he should have been taking it easy, not putting his life on the line with us.'

'Will would have helped no matter what, he would have done anything for you and you for him and he knew that.'

John put a hand on James's shoulder and said.

'Don't blame yourself, we were dealing with some nasty fuckers up there, they will get what's coming to them, enjoy your time away and come back fresh. Get in the back I will drive.'

James climbed out of the driver's seat and jumped in to the back of the car. John drove off to pick Delinda and Ally up from their accommodation. Lawrence was guiding him using his phone, not one of them had bothered to try and work out how the Sat-Nav in the car worked, even though they had had it for a few days now.

John pulled up at a backpacker's hostel, and waiting outside of the main entrance stood with their bags at their feet was Delinda and Ally.

James got out of the car to help them, he put the bags in the boot and the three of them got into the back of the car. Both Delinda and Ally were wearing matching Denim jackets with a white t-shirt underneath and denim shorts, the only difference being Delinda had converse trainers on whilst Ally had flip flops on.

'What is going on?' they asked in unison.

'Why hang around, let's get stateside, we leave here at ten p.m., with a change in Lisbon, then straight to New York JFK,' James said.

'What about the hotel?' Delinda asked.

'All taken care off, me and you will still be staying at the Plaza as planned.'

'I can't wait, I will have a sleep on the flight that's for sure,' Delinda said.

Ten minutes later; John was parking up in a space in the rental lot at Malaga airport, the five of them got out of the car and grabbed their bags from the boot, and headed for the covered walk way that would take them inside the terminal, the sun was slowly setting as the time approached 1830. James took the keys back to the rental desk and completed some forms, he had to pay extra to drop it at a different location. They headed upstairs to the departures entrance. All sorts of things were going on, cars and taxis' dropping people off, families waving off loved ones and coachloads of holiday makers ready to go home to Northern Europe.

They had spotted them pulling in to the car park, but did not want to attract attention by giving chase in such a public place, the two Argentines, who had given chase earlier decided that the airport was as good a choice as any to wait for them and it had proved to be a wise choice. Except for the fact that they had no idea where they were headed, they watched the five of them walk through the entrance of the big glass terminal, they followed on foot hoping to see them checking in, and they would then book tickets to follow them.

James had to check his bag, as he had packed for four months in the Falklands and the bag had various bits of RAF uniform inside putting it well overweight for carry-on luggage. Delinda and Ally would have to check their backpacks too as they were too big to go on the aircraft.

Javier Ramos was taken back to his cell after his interview with the police, this time he had his lawyer present. The lawyer had been unable to get him released, as the police were adamant that they would not let him get away with murder. Ramos had been told his bail hearing was with the judge the next morning, Ramos smiled to himself as he knew the judge would grant him bail, as his lawyer had told him who it was and that he could be paid off. Ramos hoped that once he had been bailed that would be the end of it, and there would be no need for a trial. He hoped anyway as he lay down on the stone bed and tried to get some sleep.

The Argentine soldiers spotted James, Delinda and Ally at the check in desk for the next TAP airlines flight to Lisbon, so they went to the TAP ticket office and asked for two tickets to Lisbon. They were told the flight was sold out. Iberia was the same.

They decided that they would drive; it would take about eight hours. However, they had three in hand to begin with as the flight did not leave until 2200. Once in Lisbon they would find Shaw and Sharif easy enough, just as they had in Seville, once they checked in to a hotel, they would be able to trace their passports. They left the terminal and set off for their car in the car park outside.

James, Lawrence, John, Ally and Delinda walked through to the security checkpoint and after a few minutes were airside, and they went to get a drink in the bar before leaving on their respective flights.

The call for John's flight to begin boarding went up on the screens and he said his good byes to everybody. James said to him 'Thanks again for helping out, tell mum and dad I will see them soon, thanks again brother.'

He shook John's hand and John walked towards the departure gate for his flight to Liverpool. The others would not be boarding for another hour so they ordered another round of drinks.

FORTY-FOUR

The one-and-a-half-hour flight to Lisbon passed without incident. James did not have a chance to ask Delinda what he wanted to, as they were not seated together due to the late booking. However, for their onward flight to New York they would be sat together in the middle row of four seats on an Airbus A340. James and Lawrence decided they would each take an aisle seat with Delinda and Ally seated in the middle.

The Airbus A340 to New York JFK got airborne and levelled out at thirty-seven thousand feet, when the seatbelt sign went out, James reached into his pocket and pulled his phone out, and unlocked the screen, he showed a picture of Javier Ramos to Delinda.

'Have you ever seen this man before?' he asked. Lawrence leant his head forward and looked across at the two of them. Delinda looked at the picture for a few seconds and said 'No, I don't think I have, who is he?'

'Just someone who has caused us a bit of bother whilst we were in Seville, nothing to worry about,' James answered with a smile.

He could see from the expression and genuine puzzlement on Delinda's face that she had never seen

289

him before, she was trying to think if she had and could not recall anything, if she was lying, she would have said no straight away.

Shaw was relieved that Delinda was not involved with Ramos, even though deep down he knew that she was not, he had to make sure. The seats in front had screens in the headrests, on them was a rolling map showing the aircrafts current location, it was showing they were currently over the Atlantic heading North on a great circle route.

'Wake me up when we reach Canada,' James said to Delinda before kissing her.

He tilted his head back, closed his eyes and fell asleep, along with most other people on the flight. They were due to land in New York around 0300hrs local time due to the five-hour time difference, so James did not want to miss out on any sleep. Sleep when you can, was one of his rules, along with eat when you can.

The two Argentine special forces soldiers who had been tailing Shaw and Sharif had decided to bunk down for the night at a motel off the A2 motorway, around two hours outside of Lisbon. They had decided not long after leaving Malaga that they would be best getting a full night's sleep and starting afresh in the morning.

They would pay a visit to a police station and pay an officer to give them the name of the hotel that Shaw and Sharif were staying in, by using the passport registration system all hotels and hostels used. Better to ask the day staff, as the night watch would be busy with drunks fighting and other night time criminals. What they did not know as they slept, was that Shaw and Sharif were not in Lisbon but were an hour into a flight crossing the Atlantic to New York, and their paths would not cross again.

The Falkland Islands are four hours behind Greenwich Mean Time (GMT) and it was currently 2200hrs. The E-3D which had left Ascension Island eight hours ago had just made contact with Air Traffic Control at Mount Pleasant Airfield, after a short surveillance trip over the marked locations on the map that they had been given. The crew in the rear of the aircraft had been instructed to send all footage back to RAF High Wycombe as soon as they landed. They had also been tasked with another reconnaissance flight departing at 0730hrs local time the next morning.

The E-3D touched down and taxied over to the dispersal, where the crew disembarked. They were taken to their accommodation, where they would rest for the night, they still had no idea why they had been sent down here except to fly over the marked areas, as it was dark, they had to use infrared cameras, all that the operators could see on the screens were what looked like oil platforms. They would have better images tomorrow, after which they were to return to the UK via Ascension Island and Gibraltar, where the days footage that had been taken was to be uploaded and sent to RAF High Wycombe as per instructions. The crew discussed that it was odd that they had been asked manually to upload footage, as all footage and images could be sent securely from the Aircraft whilst airborne.

The cabin lights had been dimmed by the crew so that the passengers could sleep, the only two passengers awake were James Shaw and Lawrence Sharif, who were stood in one of the galley areas talking to each other.

'Delinda checks out, I showed her a picture of Ramos, and she had no idea who he was. I could see it in her eyes that she was trying to remember if she had ever seen him before, it was clear she had never seen him.' James said.

'I told you this when you mentioned it, but you were convinced that she had set us up, they were only alerted to us because they have somebody in the police who informed them that two British men had arrived in the city, one who works for the Royal Air Force and the other the Foreign Office, they were curious and foolishly we proved them right. I wonder if they ever found that fella we put in the boot in the car park?' Lawrence replied.

'No, I wouldn't think so, surely we would have seen or heard something if they had, the car has probably got a load of parking tickets on the windscreen and the police are probably too busy to go and check on an abandoned car.'

'Yeah, your right, lets relax for a couple of days, gather our thoughts, enjoy ourselves and have fun, we deserve it.'

'I agree, I will try and speak to Nadine again in a few days as well, see how she is, try and explain what happened to Will. It won't help but it may give her some closure.'

'I would leave it for about a week, to let her process

what has happened, she will still be associating you with his death and you don't want to upset her even more than she already is,' Lawrence said.

'I suppose so.'

'Let's go get some sleep, we have got a few hours left before we land.'

'Good idea,' James said.

They walked away from each other down their respective sides of the aircraft and back to their seats. James sat down and slouched into the chair to try and get comfortable, Delinda woke up and lifted the armrest and cuddled up to James who put his arm around her and they both fell asleep.

FORTY-FIVE

James Shaw woke up as the Airbus A340 was on its final approach to New York's JFK airport, the jerking around had stirred him and he fastened his seatbelt and sat up ready for landing.

'Hey, sleepyhead, I was going to wake you but you looked so peaceful so I left you, are you OK?' Delinda asked him.

'Yes, thank you, how about you, have you been awake long?'

'Only about a half hour,' Delinda answered.

The cabin lights went out fully for landing and it was

pitch black outside, except for the faint orange glow of the sprawling city below, the lights became brighter as the aircraft descended, and the main undercarriage touched down on the asphalt. After shaking and jerking around the aircraft taxied off the runway towards terminal five at JFK airport.

After disembarking and getting through a lengthy immigration queue, James and Lawrence re-joined Ally and Delinda and they headed off to get a taxi to the Plaza Hotel.

'I need cash, I have just remembered I don't have any dollars,' James said.

'This is on me; you can buy breakfast in the morning,' Delinda said to him with a smile.

They arrived at the Plaza Hotel thirty minutes after leaving the airport and Delinda paid the driver fifty dollars, which included a tip.

After getting inside the hotel, the night clerk got them booked in to their rooms and they left the lobby in search of their rooms, having declined the clerks offer of going to find a porter. The rooms were on the tenth floor so they took the lift up. They stepped on to the corridor and looked for their rooms.

'Set your alarm for ten, we can go get some breakfast before we go and do whatever we want,' Lawrence said.

'Ok, see you in the morning, goodnight, Ally,' James said.

'Good night,' Ally said following Lawrence in to the room. James and Delinda walked a few doors down the corridor and let themselves into the room, James dumped his bag next to the door and put Delinda's next to it.

'What do you want to do when we wake up then James?' Delinda asked.

'I don't know, I am going for a shower then some rest,' he said getting undressed and walking to the bathroom. He turned the shower on before stepping in to the stall, he used the hotel shower gel and was out in about two minutes. Delinda stepped in after him whilst he brushed his teeth. Delinda finished up in the shower and cleaned her teeth before they both climbed in to bed. Delinda rested her head on James's shoulder and asked him.

'Are you nervous about meeting my parents?'

'A little yes, it must be a surprise for them meeting me after we have only known each other a short time.'

'We can postpone, if it's a problem.'

'Of course not, I look forward to meeting them,' James said.

'They will love you for sure.'

They fell asleep in each other's arms just as the sun was beginning to rise over the big apple.

Javier Ramos walked out of the Seville court house a free man, his lawyer managed to convince the judge that the prosecution only had circumstantial evidence and nothing concrete to prosecute his client. The judge told the prosecution that unless they could come up with any solid evidence within the next forty-eight hours all charges would be dropped and the case would not be heard in this court. Ramos had been released on bail, but once the forty-eight hours were up, he would be a free man. Free to continue planning his assault on the

Falkland Islands, he did not yet know that he no longer had possession of the drilling permits.

At 0800hrs local the crew of the RAF E-3D sentry were at their consoles onboard the aircraft, as they flew over the target area in the south Atlantic. They could see small arms fire coming from the platforms, not towards the aircraft as they were at forty thousand feet. It was target practice, one of the operators zoomed in on his screen and he could see small targets had been placed in the ocean about one hundred yards from each platform. The operator informed his commanding officer what he and the others had seen, the Flight Lieutenant came over to look for himself, after a minute he went back to his own console and dialled a number on the secure phone. He informed Air Command about what they had seen, and he was instructed to send all footage immediately to High Wycombe and to inform his crew of a job well done, and inform the flight crew to head for home.

In the UK, Air Command informed the Defence Secretary, who in turn informed the Prime Minister what it was that the E-3D crew had seen, he also informed him that there was a Royal Navy type 45 destroyer HMS Dauntless on routine patrol within seventy miles of the platforms. The Prime Minister thought for a moment and said to the Defence Secretary.

'Bring her to within twenty miles, and to be on standby for further orders.'

'Yes Sir, I will inform the admiralty right away,' the Defence Secretary replied.

He went off to M.O.D (Ministry of Defence)

headquarters opposite Downing Street to inform the admiralty of the situation in person.

Having been in the job for only a year, this was the PM's first real challenge, the economy had begun to stabilise and people were beginning to have faith again but he could undo all of that by making one wrong move with this situation. A war would be a disaster, he would lose support quickly as a lot of the electorate had no appetite for war. The best solution was swift action and to stop anything before it starts.

FORTY-SIX

James Shaw and Delinda Saint Germain walked through Central Park together hand in hand having left the Plaza Hotel. Lawrence and Ally had left in a taxi to go to the Guggenheim Museum.

'Just think in a few months' time, you could be calling this place home.'

'Maybe, if I get a job with a firm, I have had no offers yet,' Delinda said.

'Somebody will get back to you, you went to Harvard, it is early days yet, you will get something don't worry.' Dressed casually, James in Blue jeans and a polo shirt with his Clarks desert boots, Delinda in a white vest top with blue jeans and white converse pumps, they strolled through the park talking and laughing. Delinda's phone pinged, it was an email, she stopped to read it and after about thirty seconds shouted 'OH MY GOD, OH MY GOD.'

'What is it?' Shaw asked.

'Goldstein Sullivan have just offered me an interview a week today, I can't believe it, they are one of the biggest Law firms in New York City.'

'Congratulations, well done,' James replied.

He hugged Delinda and picked her up and spun her around, she kissed him and they held the embrace for a few minutes.

They left the park near to Fifth Avenue, and walked down the busy shopping street. The city was bustling with people, and the traffic got busier as they approached Tiffany & Co. They stopped outside the store and looked around before walking inside, it was crowded, mostly with people just looking not buying, but James Shaw was buying.

'Wait here,' he said before going to speak to one of the assistants.

'OK, what are you doing?'

James Shaw did not hear Delinda's reply as he was out of earshot.

A few minutes later he fought his way back through the crowd to where Delinda was stood looking at a display case.

Delinda was giddy with happiness, as James presented a box to her, inside the box was a white gold necklace with a diamond pendant.

'Thank you it is so beautiful, what is it for?' Delinda said deliriously.

'Just a present from me to you, to say well done for getting an interview with a big firm.'

'Thank you, you didn't have to do that.'

'I know but I wanted to.'

'You're the best.'

'What kind of law do this firm specialise in?' James asked changing the subject.

'Corporate law, so finance and that kind of business,'

Delinda answered.

'Big money to be made there then, shall we go to Nashville in the morning, then we can fly back here before your interview?'

'Sure, I will book a flight with Delta, my parents aren't expecting me for another couple of days, a surprise will be nice, I cannot wait for you to meet them.'

'Yes, I look forward to it, what is it your parents do? You never mentioned it,' James asked.

'My father is a corporate lawyer, he is a partner in a firm down there, which is sort of why I am going down that path, and Mom is an Opthalmic surgeon.'

'Very skilled work, did you not want to follow in your mum's footsteps?'

'Oh no, I think what she does is wonderful but it is not for me.'

'Why don't you work at your dads' firm?'

'He asked me, but I want to make it on my own, make my own name here in NYC, all the major firms are here because all of the major banks and companies are based in the city. What do your parents do?' Delinda said.

'Well, I hope it all works out which I am sure it will. Mum is a nurse and Dad is retired now, he was in the Navy, and then he worked for a shipping company in Liverpool. Please excuse me whilst I make a call.'

'I will call the airline and book those flights.'

'OK,' James said.

He pulled his phone out of his pocket, he dialled a number from memory and waited for it to be answered.

'This is Wing Commander Shaw, informing you that I will be returning to the UK next week ready to take up my new post at RAF Waddington.'

He listened and waited for the other person to finish.

'Yes, a week Monday is fine, goodbye,' he ended the call and dialled Lawrence Sharif's number, he picked up after only two rings.

'That was fast. Listen in, I begin my handover at Waddington a week Monday so I am flying to Nashville tomorrow then going back to Liverpool for a few days.'

'Good luck, I am flying back the day after tomorrow myself, enjoy Nashville. Hopefully your car will be waiting for you when you get to Waddington,' Lawrence said at the other end of the line.

'It better be or somebody will have some questions to answer, we will catch up when I am settled, see you back at the hotel later anyway,' Shaw ended the call just as Delinda had finished on the phone to Delta.

'Any joy?' James asked.

'Eight ten tomorrow morning form LaGuardia, we will have an early start. You can stay at my parents' house.'

'OK, well I would have liked to have seen more of New York but it is what it is, shall we go and get some lunch, are you sure your parents won't mind me coming to stay?'

'Of course not, I have told them all about you.'

'I see, nothing bad I hope.'

'Of course not, I spoke to them before you got us in Malaga.'

They walked back towards Central Park down Fifth avenue amongst the crowds of people, a mixture of shoppers and tourists who were getting in the shopper's way by stopping and taking pictures in the middle of the pavement.

'Shall we lunch in the hotel?' James asked.

'No, why don't we try a proper American place, get you schooled up for all that Southern food and hospitality.'

'It's your country, why not,' James said.

They got back to the hotel and packed their bags for their flight in the morning. Delinda carefully placed the box containing her new necklace from James on top of her clothes before zipping up her bag. They asked the concierge to arrange a car to take them to a steakhouse. The driver said that he knew just the place.

The driver pulled up at a stand-alone diner, a rarity in Manhattan. They ordered a big steak each, with all of the sides, James was surprised at how much Delinda ate as he himself felt as though he could explode at any moment. Once they had finished, they arranged for the car to pick them up to take them back to the hotel.

As they had an early start the next day, they said their goodbyes to Lawrence and Ally in the evening. James and Delinda ordered room service and they spent the evening watching the television. James was amazed at the adverts on American TV. They watched Hell's Kitchen, after watching Gordon Ramsay throw food at aspiring chefs and shouting at them, they decided to have an early night, to be raring to go in the morning.

James's alarm woke them both up at five A.M. After getting showered and dressed, they hustled down the corridor and in to the lift. They checked out at the desk and the clerk arranged for a car to take them to the La Guardia airport.

FORTY-SEVEN

After disembarking the aircraft at Nashville airport; James and Delinda picked their bags off the carousel and headed outside of the terminal to get a taxi to take them to Delinda's parents' house. It was a few degrees hotter than New York outside, and a lot more humid.

They were greeted by a driver who got out and put their bags in the boot of the cab, Delinda told him the destination, the driver said sure no problem. Twenty minutes later they arrived at a big set of gates, which led to a drive way running up to some kind of mansion house.

'What's this place, Southfork?' James asked rhetorically.

James and Delinda got out of the cab and grabbed their bags. James paid the driver forty dollars and told him to keep the change, the driver was very grateful as it was only a twenty-five-dollar journey. James and Delinda walked through the gates and up the drive towards the big house, manicured lawns flanked each side of the drive, the plot was surrounded by hedgerows, total privacy from the outside world. There was a silver

Mercedes convertible on the drive along with a white Chevrolet Suburban. James made a mental note to buy a Suburban at some point, it was a car that he liked and could see himself driving. If things got serious with Delinda the Dodge would have to go. James shook that horrible thought from his mind, and gazed around the grounds of the huge house.

Delinda knocked on the front door, as she did not have keys. The door was bigger than a normal size door, and James said to himself *A door that a sofa can fit through, all houses should have these.*

The door was answered by a woman who was clearly Delinda's mother; she stepped out of the house and said to Delinda. 'My baby, we were not expecting you so soon, what a surprise.'

She hugged her daughter.

'Hi Mom, this is,' before she could finish her mum cut in.

'James, so nice to meet you I am Pam, please come in,' she said before kissing both his cheeks.

'How do you do, thank you,' he said returning the double kiss.

They stepped in and James looked around the hall, and was in awe at the sheer size of the place, his parents' house was big compared to most in England but this place was off the scale.

I am in the wrong job he said to himself.

'Leave your bags here, your father is out back by the pool working, he will be so happy to see you,' Pam said. James had his new suit on that he had bought in Seville, he took his jacket off before stepping back outside in to the searing sun.

James had expected Delinda's father to be a J.R Ewing type character, and this was reinforced by the house. However, sat at the outside table was a man who was about twenty years older than James Shaw, he looked in shape but his hair was greying slightly. He was dressed in a white golf shirt and trousers.

He looked up from his MacBook, and stood up from his chair and walked over to Delinda, he gave her a hug.

'Welcome home baby girl. And this here must be James Shaw,' he said holding his hand out.

'How do you do?' James said, as he shook the outstretched hand.

'Very well. Jerry Saint Germain. Please take a seat, I want to hear all about your trip.'

Jerry walked over to an outside fridge and pulled out four cans of Mountain Dew and handed one each to Pam, Delinda and James before they took a seat.

Eleven must be too early for a beer here James said to himself.

Delinda told her parents about her trip, and Jerry had been getting to know James, he was asking him about the upcoming season for Liverpool Football Club. They were getting along well and Jerry was particularly impressed with James's position in the military. A bottle of champagne was brought out to celebrate Delinda getting an Interview with Goldstein Sullivan.

'These things are just a formality, to get to know you and see what type of lawyer you will be,' Jerry told his daughter.

'Well I will find out next week Dad.'

'You will be fine,' James said.

'See, this guy knows what he is talking about,' Jerry said.

They sat and chatted for the afternoon and well in to the evening. Jerry fired up the barbeque and had James help him with the cooking. Any nerves that Shaw had about meeting Delinda's parents had disappeared five minutes after meeting them.

They ate hotdogs, burgers and steaks from the barbeque, James was not used to eating so much food. He decided to put himself on a diet when he got back to the UK.

James and Delinda retired to her room for the evening, her room was huge and had an En-suite bathroom. They sat on her sofa listening to music.

'My parents love you; this has been a perfect day,' she said.

'I love them too, they are very nice people, now I know where you get it from and I love you.'

'I love you too James.'

James woke up to a series of text messages and missed calls from Lawrence Sharif. He called him without reading the messages.

'What's up?' he said.

'I have just landed at Heathrow. I turned my phone on, and I had a text from Peter at DGSE, two of Ramos's special forces troops are on their way to Nashville, they must have a trace on your passport. They are due to land in forty-five minutes, good thing is they won't be armed.

Try and get them as soon as you can. Call me when you spot them.'

'Shit, shit, shit. I will see if I can get them at arrivals. Thanks for the heads up,' Shaw ended the call, and threw on a polo top and jeans.

'I have to pop out, our friends from Spain are on their way. Do you think I could borrow your dad's car?' He asked Delinda.

'Oh no, are they the same two who were following us in Seville? Yes of course he will be up anyway.'

'Thank you, yes, they are Argentine special forces, no problem. I will be back soon.'

'Special forces?'

'Yeah, I will explain when I get back.'

'Be careful.' Delinda didn't know what else to say, she was aware what James's job was, but did not expect it to follow them to Nashville.

James ran down stairs to look for Jerry Saint Germain. He found him in the kitchen eating breakfast.

'Good morning, Jerry.'

'Good morning, did you sleep well?'

'Good thanks, I need to ask a really big favour.'

'Shoot.'

'Can I borrow your car please?'

'Sure, can I ask what for?'

'To get a sim card for my phone, the roaming charges are extortionate.'

'Yeah sure, the mall is a few miles up the road.'

Jerry tossed the keys to James, who felt terrible for lying to Delinda's father. But not as bad as he would feel if the Argentines made their way to the house.

James walked quickly out of the house, once outside he ran to the car, unlocked it and climbed in. He put the key in and started the engine. He looked down for the selector but could see one. He touched the centre console thinking it may have been like the Range Rover one, where you press it in and it pops up ready to turn. After having no joy, he suddenly remembered it was an American car. He put the selector into drive, it was located on the steering column.

At the end of the drive James turned right and gunned the 5.3 litre V8, it made sure the big car accelerated quickly. He followed the signs for the airport, keeping an eye on the clock as he sped down I40 at 90mph.
He looked at the clock and he noted that the flight would have landed around seven minutes ago as he reached the turn off for the airport. Traffic was heavier around the airport, and his speed was cut to 30mph. He got in the right lane for the arrivals, he could see the terminal up ahead. The lane he was in was a pick-up lane, which allowed short stay parking whilst they went inside to wait for their pick up. Shaw put the Suburban in a space and ran across to the terminal. He stopped in his tracks as he could see the Argentinians getting into a Chrysler Voyager taxi. He made a mental note of the cab number and sprinted back to the Suburban.

Shaw joined the outgoing traffic with two cabs between him and the Argentinians. He followed the cab around the parking lot and on the road that would take them westbound on the I40. They were heading for the city. Shaw hoped they weren't heading for the Saint Germain house; he did not want to put Delinda or her family in danger.

Shaw sped up and overtook the taxis in front, he got ahead and kept going. He slammed the brakes on and slewed the Suburban across both lanes, he put the hazards on and got out of the car. He waved his arms in the air at the taxi he had been following. The driver stopped the vehicle and got out to ask what was going on. Shaw ignored him and ran to the passenger doors of the taxi, one of the soldiers was stepping out of the cab and Shaw kicked the door on him, sending him back into the vehicle. He ran around to the other side, opened the door and punched the other in the face, once, twice, three times. He kicked him in his gentleman's area, and ran round to the first guy, who he had hit with the door.

'Get back to the airport and get out of here. If Ramos wants me tell him to come himself. If I see you here again, I will bury you. Do you understand?'

'Si,Si,Si.' The first soldier said, the other was holding his nose from being punched.

'Take these two back to departures, sorry for the trouble,' Shaw said to the driver, handing him a hundred-dollar bill.

'Yes sir, thank you.'

The driver got back into his cab, he drove across the grass verge and headed back to the airport. Shaw climbed back into the Suburban. He copied the taxi driver by driving across the verge and followed the cab to departures. He parked the Suburban in the drop off with the hazards on and followed the Argentinians into the terminal. They went to the Delta desk and booked two one-way tickets to Madrid via New York JFK. Shaw watched them as they went through security. Satisfied they were on their way; he went outside back to the Suburban.

Shaw called Sharif to inform him that the soldiers were now on their way back to Spain.

Relaxed, James head back towards Green Hills and to the mall Jerry had told him about.

He rushed around the mall, he bought a new sim card, some clothes for himself and a present for Jerry and Pam. He got Jerry a Liverpool FC polo shirt and Pam a pair of gold earrings. He spotted a sign in a travel agents window advertising cabins at Lake Radnor, which was outside of the city limits. He went in and booked a night for him and Delinda, they would head up there in the morning.

He returned to the house, Pam's Mercedes was gone, Shaw assumed she had gone to work. He knocked on the door and Jerry answered.

'Let me help you with those,' he offered, relieving James of some of his shopping bags.

'Thank you.'

Jerry took the bags to the kitchen and James followed. Delinda came in to the kitchen.

'Do you want to see downtown?' she asked.

'Absolutely. I have some presents first,' Shaw said as he sorted through the bags.

He handed a bag to Jerry, who opened it pulling out his gift from James.

'Thank you so much, you didn't have to get me this.'

'My pleasure, just a little something to say thank you for letting me stay.'

Shaw pulled a small gift bag from one of his clothes bags.

'This is for Pam,' he said to Jerry.

'Very kind of you, she is in work and won't be in until later, I have to go to the office myself shortly, do you guys want a ride anywhere?'

'Can you drop us on Broadway?' Delinda asked.

'Sure.'

'Do I have time for a shower?' James asked.

'Yeah, I will leave in a half hour.'

James and Delinda headed upstairs to get changed.

'I have booked us a lakeside cabin for tomorrow at Lake Radnor, I hope you don't mind.'

'Wow, really. Why would I mind, it will be amazing. Thank you.'

'It will, I am looking forward to seeing Nashville.'

'You will love it.'

They got showered and dressed.

James put on one of his new shirts and jeans. He had bought himself a new pair of desert boots too at the Clarks in the mall.

Delinda had gone full country style, she had on a white t-shirt, denim skirt and cowgirl boots. She reached into the top of her wardrobe and pulled down a Stetson hat.

'Nice hat,' James said.

'Thank you. I will be back in a minute,' Delinda said as she left the room.

She reappeared a minute later with a black Stetson.

'This is my dad's, put it on.'

James put the hat on and looked at himself in the mirror.

'Not too bad actually,' he said.

'Let's go, dad will be waiting.'

They went downstairs and Jerry was waiting for them by the front door.

'That hat looks great on you; you will blend in now.'

'I will look after it for you.'

'Let's go, James you sit up front with me.'

'OK.'

They hustled out to the Suburban, and Jerry set off for downtown Nashville.

Jerry turned onto Broadway, the main road for bars and restaurants. James looked out at all the neon signs in amazement.

'Stop here dad,' Delinda said.

Jerry pulled up outside a three-tiered bar called Honky Tonk Central. James and Delinda said goodbye to Jerry and got out of the car.

It was early afternoon, but the bar was busy as was Broadway. Delinda ordered four bottles of Miller, two each for her and James. There was a live band performing and people were dancing to the music. James and Delinda joined in.

They ordered food and ate on one of the upper floors. As afternoon changed to evening, they left the bar and walked up Broadway, to a lilac painted bar called Tootsie's, which according to the sign was the oldest Honky Tonk in Nashville. They headed for the rooftop, so they could have a smoke. James ordered six bottles of Budweiser which came in an ice bucket. He and Delinda sat at a table and decided it would be a better idea to head to the lake in the afternoon, as they would be too hungover in the morning.

The next morning, they got their things packed for the night at the lake. Pam had already left for work; Jerry was sat outside with his computer. He said Delinda and James could take the Suburban, as he would be working from home for the next few days. They said goodbye to Jerry and loaded the car, they needed to stop at a supermarket to get food and drink for the trip.
Delinda got in the driver's seat and set the GPS up for the lake. James thought she looked tiny behind the wheel of the big car. She was not the best driver and made James nervous. At the supermarket, he offered to drive the rest of the way.

They arrived at the cabin and unloaded the shopping and their luggage; James had bought an ice box and bags of ice for the beer.

James left Delinda to sort the shopping out. He headed out to the boat hire place. He hired a speed boat for the day. He pulled up at jetty to the cabin he and Delinda where staying in. He tooted the horn, and Delinda came out.

'Wow, I haven't been on a boat for years.'

'Tie this to that post, please' James said as he tossed the rope to her.

When the boat was tied up, James went in to the cabin and returned with the ice box, he had filled it with ice and beer. Delinda followed James onto the boat, and they sped off into the middle of the lake. They spent the day sunbathing and drinking beer. Not wanting to be anywhere else at that moment.

There was no doubt in both of their minds that they were deeply in love with each other. That night they sat outside watching the sunset over the water. That was when they realised that leaving each other was going to be difficult when James had to fly back to the UK in a few days.

FORTY-EIGHT

Lying unconscious in her own blood was the long-suffering wife of Javier Ramos. Upon returning home from his second court appearance, Javier Ramos had accused his long-suffering wife of betraying him to the police, in a fit of rage he punched her square in the mouth, knocking two of her teeth out, before she could react, he struck again, this time breaking her nose causing blood to spray across the sitting room, she dropped to the floor in a heap. Ramos walked away and left her where she lay.

HMS Dauntless was cutting through the waves of the South Atlantic at thirty knots, following her new orders to pick up all persons on the oil platforms and take them to Port Stanley for processing. If fired upon, the crew were ordered to return fire. As the destroyer approached the first platform, a message was shouted from the P.A system, which said *Prepare to be boarded and do not attempt to fire, or we will fire upon you.*
A squad of eight Royal Marine Commandos were lowered into the ocean on a dingy, and then they sped towards one of the platforms, they could make out about fifty people coming out of the various cabins that had been lifted on to the platform. Shots were fired towards the dingy, the Commandos did not return fire, but HMS

Dauntless fired a shell from its main gun two meters to the left of the platform, which was enough of a warning for the Argentines to surrender.

Another two squads of Royal Marines followed the first crew out to speed up the process of getting the Argentines aboard HMS Dauntless, as they had other platforms to pick up from. Two hours later, and with no resistance, all of the oil platforms had been cleared of Argentine Forces and HMS Dauntless set a course for Port Stanley with its new prisoners aboard.

Flying at seven-hundred miles per hour and five-hundred feet above sea level, were two RAF Typhoons out of Mount Pleasant airfield. Eight minutes after departure they arrived at their target and fired guided Paveway bombs at each of the platforms, before performing a vertical loop and returning back to Mount Pleasant.

The Prime Minister had been informed of the situation, he was a relieved man as a major crisis had been averted, he was not at all happy with the under-hand tactics of the Argentines, but he would not take any more action against them, a warning had been sent to Argentina that Britain will always be ready and the PM hoped that they would take notice of that.

After a tearful goodbye at terminal 2 departures, James Shaw was now sitting in the departure lounge at New York's JFK terminal 8 waiting to board his American Airlines flight to Manchester.

Delinda was flying back to Nashville after her interview, which she had passed, she had been asked to start in two weeks. James had promised her that he would come over to visit in a few weeks, once he had completed the handover at RAF Waddington.

James Shaw and Delinda Saint Germain assured each other that they would make a long-distance relationship work.

Shaw scrolled through his phone as he waited, and he went on to BBC news to check the headlines.

Head of Espoil arrested in a case of mistaken Identity.

James clicked on the headline and read through the article, which said *Javier Ramos had mistakenly been arrested just over a week ago but had been released without charge after the police admitted they had arrested the wrong man.*

Why do we bother he said to himself, angry that Ramos had been allowed to get away with murder again, two weeks ago he had never heard of his name, now he could not stand to hear it and would be glad if he never heard it again.

On a positive note, he read that RAF Typhoons had destroyed illegally built oil platforms in the South Atlantic.

It wasn't all for nothing then he said to himself.

His flight was now boarding, he stayed seated as everybody else jumped to their feet, eager to board the aircraft, he was in no rush to leave the USA, he was missing Delinda already.

FORTY-NINE

Six weeks later, Group Captain James Shaw sat at his desk in the station commander's office at RAF Waddington in Lincolnshire, he had often sat in these offices before but not as the man behind the desk. It had been two weeks since he was officially unveiled as the station commander for RAF Waddington, after completing the handover process.

Shaw put his cap on his head, as he had to deal with a charge for a young SAC (Senior Aircraftsman) who was being charged with assaulting his corporal.

Why is this shit coming to me? he said as there was a knock on his door.

'Come in,' Shaw said.

And in marched the young SAC he saluted Shaw, who saluted him back, he was followed in by the corporal that he had assaulted, he was also the one bringing the charges.

Shaw smiled inside as he saw the blackeye and cut lip on the corporal. As Shaw read out the charges, his computer pinged with the sound of an incoming email. The SAC accepted the charges and punishment, he was polite and respectful throughout the hearing. Shaw sent the corporal on his way and invited the SAC to sit down in the visitor's chair. Shaw sat down too; he noted the notification on his screen to inform him of a new e-mail.

'Look son, people like him go about their day winding people up, thinking that they are the big man, striking fear in to the juniors like yourself, well not anymore because you taught him a lesson. If you do it again make sure nobody sees you do it. That is how you ended up here because of witnesses, do you understand?'

'Yes, Sir,' he replied.

'Good, now off with you, get back to work and don't worry about this, the paperwork won't be getting filed,' Sames said as he ripped the charge sheets in two and threw them in to the bin. The SAC stood up, saluted and left the room.

Group Captain Shaw opened his computer after it had locked itself out, the e-mail was from Lawrence Sharif, using the SIS (Secret Intelligence Service) encryption system. He unlocked the attachment with a password the two of them had agreed on a number of years ago.

The attachment was a video, as it downloaded, he got up and walked over to the side unit and poured himself a cup of coffee from the percolator. When he sat back down, the video had downloaded, he clicked play and a four-way split screen appeared of a car park and some slip roads, it was closed circuit television footage.

'What's this he has sent me?' he said out loud as he watched and nothing happened, after a minute and a half, Will Ramsey's Volvo come onto the screen after leaving the motorway. A few minutes passed, and then on the small screen in the bottom left he watched as Will got boxed in and tried to Ram his way through, he could see the shots being fired by the muzzle flashes on the screen, he felt sick at what he was watching and closed the video down, he could not watch anymore.

Shaw picked his mobile up and dialled Lawrence Sharif's number. He picked up after about twenty seconds, he answered Shaw's question before he even asked it.

'I am at Stansted already, see you in a few hours.'

'OK, I will fly down from here, see you soon,' Shaw replied.

Group Captain Shaw asked his driver to take him to the operations room of 51 squadron, who operated the Rivet Joint reconnaissance aircraft. As he walked in to the operations room everybody stood to attention, Shaw waved at them to remain seated, he had been uncomfortable with this ceremony ever since he had become a Squadron Leader, but he accepted it was part of the way things are in the military. Shaw found the officer commanding the squadron, and followed him in to his office which was away from the main room.

'How fast can you have an aircraft ready to fly to Seville?'

'Thirty minutes Sir, can I ask what for?' the Wing Commander asked in return.

'Good, make it happen, navigation checks, test flight, put down whatever you wish.'

'Understood Sir, I will speak to my staff and arrange fuel and flight plans, I will fly myself, I need the hours, with the young Flight Lieutenant you seen on the way in, go and get ready sir and meet you back here in half an hour.'

'Thanks Steve,' Shaw said.

He left the operations room, and was driven back to his office on the other side of the station. Shaw got changed out of his blue uniform and into the green flying suit in his office, one of the perks of being station commander was having your own flying suit, even though he was not a pilot. He asked his driver to take him to his house so that he could pack a bag.

In the station commanders house, James Shaw packed a pair of jeans and a polo shirt that was already ironed, he had a new pair of Clarks desert boots already on his feet after getting changed in to his flying suit, he went in to his bedside drawer and pulled out something heavy and metal, which he put on top of his clothes. It was two Glock 17 pistols, one for him and one for Lawrence Sharif, all packed and ready, he got back in to the car and was taken back to 51 Squadron, where he met Wing Commander Steve Jones and Flight Lieutenant Dave Smythe.

They walked across the aircraft servicing platform to the Rivet Joint aircraft, which still had the fuel tanker underneath it, the operator was winding up the hose after fuelling the aircraft. The three men boarded the aircraft and took their seats. James Shaw sat in the engineer's seat behind the two pilots. Ten minutes later they were airborne and on a southerly heading, towards Andalucia.

After landing at Seville airport, the Rivet Joint taxied over to the cargo side of the aerodrome and came to a stop. The Spanish Air Force had been informed of the flight and they were happy to allow the aircraft to land at Seville. Group Captain Shaw climbed down the small ladder first, followed by the pilots.

'Thanks Steve, Dave, do you mind waiting here for a few hours, I will give you a call when I am on my way back,' Shaw said.

'No problem, Sir, we will go and get something to eat, we have got jackets to cover our insignia,' Wing Commander Jones replied.

'Very well, thanks again, see you soon.'

The afternoon sun hit James as soon as he stepped out of the shadow of the aircraft, he had only just gotten used to the cool of the UK. He walked over to the entrance to the cargo area and could see that Lawrence Sharif was stood waiting next to a white Ford Transit, that was obviously hired because it was clean and not covered in grime and dirt like most vans.

'When did you get here?' James asked.

'About an hour ago, did you bring the goods?'

'I did, they are in the bag with my flying suit, I got changed just before we landed, how did you know I would be coming this way?'

'How else would you get here, being the station commander has its perks, that is why I sent you the email from my phone, so that I would have a head start on you, getting here.'

James threw his bag onto the centre seat and climbed in to the van.

Lawrence drove off towards the eastern suburbs of the city. James reached in to his bag and pulled out a packet of cigarettes, he put one in Lawrence's mouth and lit it for him, as he was focused on the traffic which was getting busier as they drove through the new town, past Hotel Ayre, where they had been a few weeks earlier and past the Ramon Sanchez Pizjuan stadium, the home of Sevilla Football Club. Ten minutes later they arrived at Javier Ramos's Street, Lawrence stopped the van about a hundred yards short of Ramos's house. He was not home as there was no activity or any cars on the drive. They waited in silence for Ramos to return.

An hour later, James spotted a Ferrari coming towards them, it stopped a hundred yards away and turned in to Javier Ramos's drive. Shaw and Sharif grabbed their Glock pistols, jumped out of the van and ran towards the house, nobody seen them as the houses were set to far back from the road for anybody to be a nosey neighbour.
   'Let him get to the front door,' James said.
They ran up the drive past the Ferrari California, and Ramos was insight, just about to open his front door.
   'Excuse me, is that your car?' Shaw asked Ramos.
   'Shit, it is you, what do you want?'
'Open the door and go inside,' Shaw replied, pointing the Glock at him.
Ramos opened the door with his key and stepped over the threshold, followed by Shaw and Sharif who closed the door behind him.
   'What do you want, I have done nothing to you?' Ramos pleaded.
   'Your men killed my friend in cold blood, on your orders,' Shaw answered.

'They were acting alone; I did not order them to. What about the men you have killed, you are.'

James Shaw punched Ramos in the mouth before he could finish his sentence and sent him to the floor in a heap, Ramos looked up at Shaw, who then kicked him under the chin, sending him flying across the hallway like a football, followed by three of his teeth and a spray of blood. Ramos was struggling for breath, as he turned to look at Shaw with his eyes begging for Mercy, Sharif left the house to go and get the van, leaving Shaw and Ramos alone.

Ramos got on to his knees, and he launched a spear attack at Shaw and sent him charging in to the wall, Shaw hit him in the kidneys causing him to flinch and turn away in pain. Shaw followed through with a kick to the stomach then an upper cut as Ramos crouched over in pain from the kick to the stomach.

'Please, don't kill me, please,' Ramos begged.

James punched him again, this time square in the face knocking Ramos out cold.

'I may be a killer but I am not a murderer, hopefully that will teach you a lesson,' he said to his unconscious body.

Shaw picked the keys up for the Ferrari that had fell from Ramos's hand when he first hit him, and left the house. Shaw jogged over to the van and said through the window to Lawrence.

'Drop the van at the rental place, then I will drive us to the plane, you can stay with me tonight before heading back to London.'

'OK, thanks, let's go then.'

Shaw called Wing Commander Jones and informed him that he was on his way back to the airport and to start the engines for an immediate departure. James got in to the Ferrari and admired the luxury inside before he sent a text which read.

I cannot wait to see you it has been too long, love you.

The journey back to the airport took twenty minutes, after handing the van back to the rental company. Sharif got into the passenger seat of the Ferrari and commented.

'Nice car, shame we can't take it home, are you just going to leave it here.'

'Yes, why not.'

James drove through the gates of the cargo area, after showing the security guard his RAF I.D card, she waved him through and he parked fifty metres from the aircraft. They climbed aboard and Flight Lieutenant Smythe closed the door behind them. Wing Commander Jones immediately taxied the aircraft, before the others had taken their seats. After clearance from Air traffic control, the Rivet Joint was airborne and En-route back to RAF Waddington.

FIFTY

Lyndon John Powell, Mike Williams, Chris Hampshire and Jack Reuben were sat at a table in a Liverpool restaurant, discussing plans for Christmas which was only two weeks away. The men were laughing and having a good time, the R&A jewellery shops Lyndon had taken over from his parents were doing better than ever, after investing some of the funds they had received from Javier Ramos, and from legitimately selling South Atlantic Oil and Gas to Royal Dutch Shell. They had opened a shop on the Ponte Vecchio in Florence, and it was doing better than they had expected amongst its rivals who had stores on the bridge for years. The company was also buoyed by the Christmas period. The four of them felt relieved to be involved with a legitimate business as they could now relax and enjoy their money.

Javier Ramos was forced to resign from ESPoil, after further information had come to light about his behaviour and wrong doings. His long-suffering wife had finally built up the courage to leave him, and she fled to the United States to start a new life in Florida away from the man who had made her life a living hell for the last seven years.

Group Captain James Shaw sat at home planning Christmas dinner, he had already made the decision not long after taking over as station commander that he would not require any stewards or chefs for Christmas dinner, and that they were to have the day off with their families, they had thanked him profusely.

'I am so nervous about my folks meeting your parents' for the first time,' Delinda Saint Germain said to James. She never took the job in New York, instead taking one in London after passing the UK law exam, she commuted back to Lincolnshire on Friday afternoons and back to London on Sunday nights, where she had an apartment paid for by her Law firm. She was involved in corporate financial law and was making a name for herself as an associate in the firm. She was a rising star and had brokered many deals between companies in her short time, as the partners had faith in her abilities.

'Don't worry it will be fine, my brother will be there as well as Lawrence and his new partner, who I haven't met yet, I have also invited Nadine and the baby,' James said.

'It is going to be such an awesome day; I am nervous and excited.'

'I hope everybody likes my cooking.'

'It will be great, I will lend a hand, my first Christmas in England, I hope it snows.'

'Not much chance of that happening, maybe in New York but not here.'

'Well, it would be nice.'
'I love you,' James said.
'I love you too' Delinda replied.
They could not be happier, as they sat discussing the festive period, they were in love and James was going to ask her to marry him on Christmas day.

THE END

A preview of the upcoming Always One Last Time, due for release late 2022.

ALWAYS

ONE

LAST

TIME

BY JAMES HAMPSON

ONE

Five months after getting engaged on Christmas day, James Shaw and Delinda Saint Germain were at opposite ends of Europe. Delinda was in Malaga waiting for her parents and other family members to arrive, along with her best friend Ally Simmons. She looked up at the arrivals board and it showed that the Delta Airlines flight from New York had just landed.

James Shaw was drinking a beer in the departure lounge at Manchester Airport Terminal 3, he was with Lawrence Sharif, his brother John and his parents' Tim and Debbie. He and Delinda were due to be married in two days. The rest of his family and friends were flying to Seville the day before the wedding. The gate appeared on the screen and the five of them drank up, picked up their hand luggage and set off towards the gate.
James slowed his pace as he had spotted somebody up ahead who he had not seen in some years. Walking towards them through the crowd was Claire Jones and her mother, along with three other women, he did not recognise them. James turned his head away but it was too late.
'Oh my god, James. Long-time no see,' Claire said.
'Hello Claire, how are you?'
The others in James's party carried on to the gate, as did the ones in Claire's, except her mother, who remained in earshot.
'Where are you off?' Claire asked.
'Seville, how about you?'
'Marbella, it's my mum's hen do.'
James looked at Helen 'Congratulations,' he said.
'What are you going to Seville for, a holiday or to go museums and stuff?'
'Jim let's go,' Sharif shouted.
'Must go, was nice to see you, have fun in Marbella.'
'You too, enjoy Seville. Do you still have the same

number?' Claire asked.

'Yes,' James said regrettably, he made a mental note to change his number when he got back home from his honeymoon with Delinda.

'I will text you, see ya.'

'Bye,' James said, he hurried to catch up with Sharif. His parents' and brother were already in the queue to board.

'A blast from the past Jim,' Sharif said.

'You can say that again. Please don't call me Jim in your speech.'

'No problem, you know I only say it to wind you up. How are you anyway, nervous about the big day?'

'Yes, but in a good way. I can't wait to be honest with you. Could have done without seeing Claire then, why does something always happen to piss on your chips when you are happy?'

'You still don't have feelings for her, do you?'

'No, course not, I just would rather not be reminded of my relationship with her two days before my wedding to the most wonderful person I have ever met.'

'Good, now let's go and get on that plane.'

They boarded, and found their seats, James, Lawrence and John sat together and Tim and Debbie sat together and had a spare seat next to them, the flight was only three quarters full.

Two and a half hours later, they landed in Seville, they collected their hand luggage and stepped out into the searing Andalusian sun. After collecting their hold luggage from the carousel, they headed outside and jumped into two taxis to the Alfonso XIII hotel. Thirty minutes later the taxis pulled up outside the main entrance to the hotel.

'Back to the scene of the crime,' James said.

'I know, hard to believe that this time last year, we were fighting Argentinian special forces on these streets,' Sharif said.

'Time to reflect on that later, let's get checked in.' James and John helped their mum and dad unload their luggage from the taxi, Sharif paid both drivers. Debbie Shaw was carrying Delinda's dress in a carrier. They got checked in at the desk and headed up to their rooms. The night before the wedding, as was tradition James and Delinda would be spending it apart. James and Lawrence were booked to stay at the EME Fusion Hotel, half a mile away from the Alfonso XIII. Delinda would stay in the suite where she and James would be staying that night, and it would be their honeymoon suite for the night of the wedding.

TWO

Delinda Saint Germain sent a text to her fiancé to let him know that herself, her parents and Ally would be in Seville in around three hours.

James Shaw called down to the reception and made a reservation for dinner that night at the hotel's San Fernando restaurant. After speaking to the reception desk, he knocked on everyone's doors to inform them of the evenings plan. He, Lawrence and John decided to go and have a beer before Delinda and her parents arrived. They headed to a bar on the riverfront. As they waited to cross the road at the lights, a red Ferrari California sped past them.

'Isn't that Ramos's car?' Shaw asked.

'It certainly looks like it. We won't be seeing him this time,' Sharif said.

'You should have finished him off when you came back,' John said.

'Shoulda, woulda, coulda,' James replied.

They crossed the road and took their seats at an outside table at a bar next to the Torre del Oro. The waitress came over and they ordered three beers. James lit a cigarette, and his phone beeped. It was a text message from an unknown UK number. He ignored it as his beer was placed on the table.

'Gracias,' he said to the waitress.

After a few sips, he opened his phone and read the message from the unknown number.

Was good to see you before, hope you are OK. How long are you in Seville for? Claire.

He looked at his phone blankly, he started typing, then deleted it. He typed A few days; *I am here for a wedding* and pressed send.

'That was Claire, asking how long I am going to be in Seville for. I am not happy, first seeing her in the airport, and Ramos's car just now.'

'Don't read too far into it, it's just one of those things,' John said.

'One yes, but not two. Excuse me.'

James left the table and called Delinda, to see how long she would be. She said that they were on the train and hopefully would be at the station in around and hour and a half. James said that he would meet them there. His phone beeped again with another message from Claire.

Who is getting married?

He decided to call her instead of texting back and forth.

'Hi Claire, I am getting married.'

'Who to?'

'Delinda.'

'Weird name, where is she from?'

'America, how is Marbella?'

'It's sound yano.'

'Good, have a good time and take it easy.'

'It could have been us, getting married if you hadn't left me that day.'

'Could have been. Goodbye Claire,' he hung up and returned to the table with Lawrence and John.

'Everything OK?' John asked.

'Yeah fine, I am going to meet Delinda and her parents at the station. Ally is with them too.'

Sharif smiled.

'What was Claire saying?' Sharif asked.

'I told her I was getting married, she went on about how it could have been me and her, I said goodbye and put the phone down.'

'Best thing to do, you don't need that shit mate,' John said.

Sharif nodded in agreement and asked to borrow James's phone. He handed it over and Sharif pressed a few buttons and handed it back. He then did something with his own phone before setting it down on the table. They ordered another beer before James went to Santa Justa station to meet Delinda.

James Shaw boarded a metro train at Puerta Jerez, he left the metro at San Bernardo and made his way to the mainline station which was opposite the metro station. He boarded a train to Sevilla Santa Justa, the journey took five minutes. He only had to wait ten minutes before Delinda's train was due to arrive from Malaga. He bought a packet of chewing gum from the shop, then moved to the area at the top of the moving ramps. Below him and right on time, the white train entered the station and came to a halt at the platform. He watched as the passengers stepped out of the train. He spotted Delinda, her parents, and Ally. They had the most luggage of anyone getting off the train, they got themselves sorted and Delinda and Ally led the way to the moving ramp. Delinda waved at James with her free hand, he waved back. They had not seen each other for almost two weeks, as Delinda was busy working on some kind of merger and James decided that it would be best if he stayed in Lincolnshire on the weekends to allow Delinda to rest.

Delinda dropped her bags at the top and ran into James's arms, they held each other for well over a minute.

'Finally?' Delinda said.

'I know. Is everything OK?'

'Yeah, shall we go?'

'Yes, let's get a taxi outside.'

'Good to see you Ally.'

'You too.'

'Pam, Jerry. Welcome to Seville. How was your flight?' Pam hugged James and Jerry shook his hand.

'Long, we are beat,' Pam said.

'Yeah, I could use a beer,' Jerry said.

'Come on then let's go, no good hanging around here all day,' James said.

The five of them left the station and stepped out into the heat. They sorted two taxis and they left the station and headed south towards the Alfonso XIII Hotel. Once they arrived and got checked in, they headed up to their rooms. Debbie and Tim Shaw were sat by the hotel pool. Lawrence and John were still drinking by the river. James and Delinda lay next to each other on the bed, holding hands.

'I have missed you, are you excited for the day after tomorrow?'

'Missed you too. You could have just said the wedding,' he laughed. 'Yes of course, can't wait to be honest with you. Then two weeks together on honeymoon.'

'I am so excited, Florence and Venice are awesome, but being with you will be extra awesome. Then Greece, relaxing on the beach. It is perfect.'

'Yeah, it is, I have booked us in for dinner tonight at eight, in the San Fernando restaurant. By us, I mean everyone.'

'Great idea.'

They kissed and rolled around on the bed before getting down to business.

Afterwards they showered and met the others in the bar of the hotel's San Fernando restaurant. Tim Shaw handed out the drinks from the bar. Jerry Saint Germain moved over towards James and Delinda.

'Mind if I borrow your future husband, sweetie?' Jerry asked his daughter.

'Sure dad.'

James and Jerry walked into the courtyard of the hotel, where a year ago James had sat with Sharif and his brother as they took down Javier Ramos.

James Shaw lit a cigarette and offered one to Jerry, who kindly accepted.

'You OK Jerry, you're shaking like a shitting dog?'

'I have never heard that before, is it an English thing?' Jerry laughed.

'Yeah, what's up? You can't be about to give me the menacing father speech. Sit down.'

Jerry sat down and James took an ashtray off the next table.

'It's work. I want to offer Delinda a job, she would be the senior associate, but it would be in Nashville.'

James took a long drag on his cigarette.

'Good, I think she should take it. I would be able to work something out with the RAF, some kind of force liaison gig. What is really up? This isn't about offering Delinda a job it is more serious than that.'

Jerry stubbed out his cigarette.

'Do you mind? Mine are in Pam's purse.'

'No, help yourself,' James put the pack on the table and lit another for himself.

'I know that you work in intelligence for the Air Force. Maybe you will be able to help.'

'What is it?'

'A bank that my firm represents is laundering money for drug cartels from Central America and it looks like money is coming in from Europe too. And the cartels are taking that money out and moving it around.'

'I thought most drug dealers did stuff like that?'

'They do, but the sums being received from Europe are billions of dollars. I don't want the firm I am a partner in being caught up in this type of stuff. I also think that the managing partner is aware of this and is doing nothing about it as he is being paid off.'

'Not ideal, wait here will you.'

James left Jerry sitting in the courtyard and went back to the bar, he pulled Sharif aside and told him what Jerry had just told him.

'We will take it on, I will call London now, get it set up. Most likely Islamist groups putting the money in from Europe, but why would they be paying the cartels, we will figure that out. Tell Delinda to take the job and move to Nashville, ask for a job too.'

'Will do.'

Sharif dialled his office in London. He was on the phone for around three minutes in total.

'After your honeymoon, send Delinda to Nashville, you get back to Waddington and sort your stuff out then meet me in Istanbul.'

'That was quick.'

'Yeah, well we need to find out what is going on. Go back to Jerry, then our table will be ready.'

James Shaw went out to the courtyard and found Jerry where he had left him.

'Can you offer me a job?' James asked.

'Sure, what would you like to do?'

'Paralegal would be best, can't pretend to be a lawyer, I would get found out too easily. As a paralegal I can go through all the files and not even be questioned by anybody. We will sort this out Jerry. Now let's go and enjoy our meal.'

They walked back into the restaurant, the others were being seated at the table, James and Jerry joined them. Sitting opposite Delinda and Pam respectively.

The two families and best man and Maid of honour, chatted, shared jokes and seemed in good spirits, with just one more day to go until the wedding.

The meal had finished and James and Delinda were in their suite getting ready for the next day. James was due to play golf with his brother, Sharif, his dad and Jerry. Delinda, Pam, Debbie and Ally were going to a spa for a pamper day.

'What were you and dad talking about earlier?' Delinda asked.

'About him offering you a job at his firm.'

'Oh that, I wanted to talk with you first.'

'Go for it, it is a big step up so early in your career, you can't afford not to take it.'

'What about you and your career?' Delinda asked.

'My career is coming to an end, yours is only just beginning. I will be able to sort something out with the RAF. Your dad said I could work at the firm if need be.'

'So, I can tell my dad, that my answer is, yes?'

'Of course, tell him now.'

Delinda got on the phone to her dad to let him know the good news. James mouthed to her that he was nipping out. He left the room and went down a floor, he walked along the corridor and knocked on Sharif's door. Sharif answered the door and James walked into the room.

'Jerry has sorted a job for me. What is the plan in Istanbul?'

'It is known as a hub between east and west, most likely any money will be held there. On second thoughts if you go to Nashville start work and try and find out where the funds have come from. Could be the same bank, the money is deposited at a branch in Istanbul into an account in the states that is run by the cartels, then they do whatever they do with it.'

'Will the law firm have those records?'

'That's for you to find out, if not they can get them. Find out what you can as fast as you can then we will go to Istanbul.'

'Fine, I am only doing this as a favour for Jerry, otherwise I would have said no.'

'There is always one last time,' Sharif said.

'This better be, I am going to ask for an exchange to a USAF base so I can be near Delinda, let her career blossom. Who knows, I might even like this paralegal stuff, and stick with that.'

'Don't talk like that, remember who the deputy director of MI6 is?'

'Yes, you,' James said.

'Exactly, if you leave the RAF, I will get you fast tracked and stationed in Nashville.'

'Let's discuss it another time, I am supposed to be getting married and here we are back on another job.'

'No rest for the wicked. Go and get some sleep, golf tomorrow.'

'Good night, see you in the morning,' James said.

'Good night, James.'

James Shaw left Sharif's room and headed back to his and Delinda's. He walked in and Delinda was sat in front of the mirror straightening her hair, James kissed her on the left cheek and went outside onto the balcony. He sat on one of the chairs and lit a cigarette. He was hoping this would just be a routine investigative job, no shooting or fighting, he wanted to come home to his wife unscathed. He finished his cigarette and went back inside to Delinda. James went to the bathroom and cleaned his teeth, and climbed into bed and Delinda followed after she had finished straightening her hair.

Early the next morning the men from the wedding party were at Real Club Sevilla Golf course, being measured up for their hire clubs. After fussing around in the club shop, they eventually had all their clubs sorted and they had hired two buggies, to help them stay out of the heat.

'Are you nervous son?' Tim shaw asked James.

'Yeah, I haven't played since last summer.'

'Not the golf you tit, the wedding.'

'Oh yeah, a little bit.'

'Do you want some advice?'

'Nope. Now let's play some golf.'

They made their way to the first tee and Tim went first, driving around two hundred and fifty yards down the middle of the fairway. Followed by Jerry, whose ball landed an inch or so to the right of Tim's. John went next and went beyond his father's shot but into the rough. Sharif played it safe with a 3 iron and laid up short but straight. James took his driver out of the bag and hit his shot straight down the fairway, it looked as though it would bounce onto the green but it fell short and landed in a bunker.

'Let's start as we mean to go on,' James said with a chuckle. As the day went on the play got worse, even saving energy with the buggy's their energy levels were low.

On the last hole, all five of them put the ball in the water.

'I am done, time for a beer,' James said.

'Yes, a well-earned drink,' Lawrence said.

'You should have had the wedding here, it is great,' Tim said.

'Yeah, you should, instead of that rooftop,' John said.

'Don't come then,' James said.

The ladies were at the AIRE ancient baths for their spa day. They had each had a wine bath and were making the most of the various treatments, before meeting the rest of the wedding guests later that day.

'I hope Tim isn't too drunk when he meets the rest of your family,' Debbie said.

'They will be fine, I am sure; Jerry will be the sensible one, keeping them in line,' Pam said.

'Mom, you don't know James, and all four of them are military men, they will be leading dad astray.'

'Don't be silly Delinda, he is getting married tomorrow he will want a clear head.'

A seven-seat taxi pulled up outside of a bar on Plaza de la Alameda Hercules. James, Lawrence, John, Tim and Jerry walked into the bar. James ordered five grande cerveza.

'Shouldn't we take it easy, big day tomorrow,' Jerry said.

'We will only have a few then head back, it will be fine,' James said.

It was not fine; Jerry had been trying to keep up with the Englishmen and it had not gone well for him.

'Look at the state of him, we need to sober him up and fast otherwise Pam will have kittens,' Tim said.

Jerry was sat in a chair asleep; John had come back from the bar with two large glasses of water. He threw one in

Jerry's face, who immediately stirred.

'Jesus Christ,' James said.

'What the,' Jerry slurred.

'Drink this,' John said handing him the other glass of water.

'We only had four beers, what is wrong with you?' Tim asked.

'They were large ones.'

'Whatever, have a few more of these then we will walk back to the hotel along the river, try and sober you up a little bit,' James said.

Lawrence helped Jerry up and the five of them threaded their way through the maze-like streets to the river front. Jerry seemed to gather himself together as they strolled along the river bank.

'You need to watch that champagne tomorrow Jerry, or you will end up in bed before we even have something to eat,' James said.

'I will be fine, I think a combination of lack of sleep, strong beer and heat got the better of me.'

'Get a shower when we get back, try and pull yourself together before everyone else gets here.'

'You're the boss.'

Delinda's Grandparent's and cousins were flying into Madrid that evening, they would travel to Seville by train and were due in around eight thirty. James's family were flying into Malaga from Liverpool and would get the train from there, they were due to arrive around eight. James and Delinda had arranged a reception in Liverpool after their honeymoon and another in

347

Nashville so that the rest of their family and friends could celebrate their wedding.

They arrived back at the hotel; the ladies were still at the spa. James went to his suite to change into his swimwear, as he wanted to spend the afternoon at the pool. He knocked on Lawrence's door on his way.

'Going to the pool want to come down. Dad and John are at the bar.'

'I will meet you down there, I just have to nip out.'

'Where are you going?'

'To get some cigars for the big day.'

'Good idea, want me to come with you?'

'No, it's fine, you go and have a swim.'

'OK see you soon.'

James headed down to the pool area and Lawrence followed him down. he then turned the opposite way as he left the hotel, he was checking his phone every few seconds. He stepped onto the tram at Puerto de Jerez station. He left the tram at San Bernardo which is the end of the line. He checked his phone again and weighed up whether to get the train or the bus. He opted for the bus as it was already at the stop, and he didn't want to lose time by going down the escalators and potentially missing the train.

Fifteen minutes later, Sharif left the C2 bus outside of Santa Justa station. He ran through the car park and across the taxi rank. He entered the station through the main doors and looked at the arrivals board. He had made it, the train from Malaga had arrived. He hustled into the platform area. The train on platform 10 opened its doors and a stream of people exited from each one. Sharif had spotted his target. He let the target walk past him, he fell in behind and followed.

THREE

Sharif's target got into a taxi at the rank, it pulled away as Sharif got into the one behind.

'Sigue ese taxi por favor,' (Follow that taxi please) Sharif said to the driver.

The driver pulled away and followed the taxi in front. The taxi pulled up outside of a hotel on the periphery of the old town. Sharif didn't catch its name. He gave the driver twenty euros for a five euro journey. The driver was extremely pleased.

Sharif followed his target inside and let them check in before making his move, he overheard the receptionist give the target their room number. After checking in, the target walked over to the lift. Sharif headed for the stairs, he swung back the door and stepped onto the third-floor corridor, he looked at the room directory and went left. He heard the motor from the lift stop and the doors pinged. His target stepped out, looked at the room directory signs and went left. Sharif let the target get the door open before making his move.

Sharif jammed his foot in the door to stop it closing, he had his Sig-Sauer P226 drawn.

'Sit on the bed and don't move,' he said calmly.
The target sat on the bed and looked at Sharif in fear.

'I seen you in Manchester airport with James,' Claire Jones said.

'Indeed, you did see me. Now what you are going to do, is get your arse back on the train to Malaga and stay away from James Shaw and Delinda Saint Germain.'

'Is that her name?' Claire chuckled. 'I have already paid for my room; he should have been marrying me.'

'If you are not gone tomorrow morning, I will have you arrested on terror charges. It will take months to clear yourself, so think about it.'

'You can't do that, who are you?' Claire asked.

'Never mind that, my threat is real as is this gun. You and James finished a long time ago and he is all the better for it.'

'How is he better for it? I love him more than anyone

else ever could.'

'Tomorrow morning, I want you gone. Here, this to reimburse you for the hotel and train,' Sharif said throwing 300 euros on the bed. He left the room and ran down the stairs back on to the street. He found a Tabac shop and bought ten large cigars. He put the Alfonso XIII onto his phones maps and allowed his watch to guide him back to the hotel.

A part of the Alfonso XIII restaurant had been closed off as the staff were preparing it for the wedding the next day, so the wedding party decided to eat out at a riverside restaurant. Both families got along with each other, not much alcohol was consumed as everybody wanted a clear head for the wedding in the morning. James and Delinda held each other as the others walked along the riverbank back to Alfonso XIII, Sharif was smoking a cigarette as he waited for James.

'Love you, see you in the morning. Don't be late,' James said.

'Love you too. It's the rules for the bride to be late. I can't wait.'

'Me neither, have a good sleep.'
They kissed and Delinda hurried to catch up with the others.

James sat with Lawrence and lit a cigarette of his own.

'Last night as a single man Jim. What do you want to do?'

'Go for a few beers, suits are hung up, shirts ironed, shoes polished and rings stored away safely. Only a few though, don't want to end up like Jerry earlier,' James said.

'That made me laugh. He was OK at the meal. That was the place that Ally and I went to last year, remember.'

'Of course, it was my first date with Delinda, we met you there. I called the Whitehall operator from a payphone to get John over here.'

'Crazy how time flies, now here you are getting married to Delinda. And me and you back working together.'

'What I don't get is, how you were so quick to take this on, especially as it is a personal thing,' Shaw said.

'Think about it, big time money laundering from terror groups, cartels involved. This is big, and me and you can be at the front of it. We can take down cartels and terror groups at the same time. What we need to find out is what their game is.'

'You mean why are they working together?'

'Yes exactly. Not to worry for now, nothing is going to happen yet, otherwise GCHQ the CIA and everyone would be aware of it. You just focus on your big day tomorrow.'

'Yes, shall we go and have a drink in Chile's?'

'Sounds good to me. Are you happy about getting married to Delinda?' Sharif asked.

'Couldn't be happier, really that woman is amazing, the best thing to have happened to me.'

'Good, now let us go and celebrate.'

They walked in the direction of bar Chile, when they got there they ordered bottles of Cruzcampo and took a seat on the street, watching the traffic go by as the sun was setting.

It was the morning of the wedding; Sharif had taken his and James's things back to the Alfonso XIII, leaving them with just their suits, watches and phones. At the Alfonso XIII, Delinda was getting her hair and make-up done, as were the other ladies. John and Tim Shaw were sat with Jerry having breakfast next to the pool.
Shaw and Sharif were sat on the balcony in their hotel dressing gowns eating room service breakfast.
'This is it then, the first day of the rest of my life,' Shaw said.
'What a day for it too. Nervous?'
The heat was already intense, and Shaw noticed a tense expression on Sharif's face.
'A little, you seem more nervous than I do.'
'Yeah, just want to make sure everything goes right for you two. And the speech.'
'It will be fine. Here have one of these,' James said, tossing his pack of cigarettes onto the table. They both lit one and sat back and relaxed.
'We have an hour before we need to get ready, fancy a little something to calm those nerves?' Shaw asked.
'Yeah, why not.'
James Shaw called room service and asked for two large glasses of scotch to be brought up to the room. The waitress brought the glasses up along with an envelope, she took the cart away with the remains of their breakfast. Shaw handed her a twenty euro tip for the trouble.
Sharif looked at the handwritten envelope and

panicked, he thought it must be a letter from Claire.

'Let's see what this is,' he said.

He tore the envelope open and unfolded the letter, he glanced at it and breathed a sigh of relief, before reading it aloud. It read.

Dear James and Delinda

Congratulations on your wedding day. We were once enemies. You spared my life, like a man of honour. For this I am eternally grateful. It has also given me a new perspective on life. Please accept this gift as a token of my appreciation.
I wish you and Delinda much happiness in married life.

Forever in your debt

Javier Ramos

Enclosed, was a cheque written out for the sum of €500,000. Sharif handed it over to James, who read the letter twice and turned the cheque over in his hands.

'Cheers, Ramos la. Fuck me, I can't believe this. We will be able to get a house in Nashville, maybe I will semi retire, work as a paralegal at Jerry and Delinda's firm part time. I can become a man of leisure. First let's get married.'

'Pretty big that isn't it. See it pays not to always kill the enemy.'

'Literally, I will go and see him tomorrow and thank him personally.'

'I will go with you, just in case he has something up his

sleeve. Come on let's get ready, you shower first, you need to get rid of that stubble.'

Shaw got into the shower and shaved, got washed and repeated the sequence, he towelled himself down and air dried whilst Sharif was in the shower. He did not want to put his shirt on until the last minute.

Dressed in blue linen suits, white shirts, pink ties, brown belt and shoes and with pink button hole flowers, James Shaw and Lawrence Sharif left the hotel to walk to the wedding venue which was adjacent to the Real Alcazar. They were shown to the terrace by one of the wedding planners that James and Delinda had been dealing with. James and Lawrence shook hands and hugged the guests before taking up their spot at the front of the terrace with the priest. Due to the bureaucracy involved with getting married in Spain, they decided on a catholic ceremony not in a church, as Delinda had been christened a catholic it was a straightforward process.

The wedding march came out of the small speakers on the terrace.

'Here we go Jim.'

James and Lawrence took their positions as Ally led the way in front of Delinda and Jerry. James smiled as he looked at Delinda, she was in a white dress that fanned out at the bottom and a silver tiara in her hair. Everyone took their positions and the priest began the ceremony. The rings had been exchanged and "I Do" had been said. James and Delinda were followed outside by their guests. Delinda threw her bouquet over her head, which was caught by Ally. James and Delinda climbed into a horse drawn carriage, smiled for photographs and waved as the coachmen led the horses off.

At the hotel speeches had been given and the meal had been eaten. The master of ceremonies asked for Delinda and James to take to the dance floor for the first dance.

As they danced to *Heartbeat* by Carrie Underwood, James whispered into Delinda's ear

'I love you Delinda Saint Germain.'

'You mean Delinda Shaw?'

'Of course, I love you Delinda Shaw.'

'I love you too James Shaw.'

One Last Time – Available Now

Rock And A Hard Place – Available summer 2022

Valley Of Death – Available winter 2022

Always One Last Time – Available December 2022

Printed in Great Britain
by Amazon

43053657R00209